a novel

Valerie Gately

JEL-EEE

This book is a work of fiction. Names, characters, businesses,
organizations, places, events and incidents either are the prod-
uct of the author's imagination or are used fictitiously. Any
resemblance to actual persons, living or dead, events, or locales
is entirely coincidental.

Edited by Cara Lockwood

ISBN 978-1-7320578-0-7

Library of Congress Control Number: 2018902977

First Edition

Valerie Gately Books
PO Box 81
Linwood, MA 01525

• CHAPTER 1 •

"Is this a vanity plate?" I asked the woman at the DMV.

"No," she answered, evidently not appreciating my concern as I stared at the plate that read, "JEL-EEE."

I looked up at her. "You're kidding, right? Did you see it?" I tried again, holding the plate for her inspection, but she didn't budge, keeping her eyes firmly on the screen in front of her.

"Don't plates have letters *and* numbers?"

"It's not a vanity, it's *your* plate," she said, not remotely interested in my dilemma.

"Hmmm," I said, thinking somehow this must be a vanity reject that got lost in the mix. "I couldn't maybe get the next one in the pile there? Would that be possible?"

Not even a smile.

"Take your plate," she said, waving me on to go, "I've already filled out all your forms. Have a nice day."

"But..."

"Have a *nice day. Next.*" She looked past me like I was invisible. We were done.

JEL-EEE. They couldn't do that, could they?

It was a used car. New to me, but used. I'd had such anxiety just getting it, such a big investment, and when you got it wrong, well... It was a dark blue Hyundai, the radio sounded amazing. Not a dent, no scratches, (okay, no *big ugly* scratches), seriously good condition for an older car. Four door sedan, automatic, no frills, and it drove fine. And now it was to be, from this day forth, the "JEL-EEE" car. Crap. I could already hear the comments from everyone I knew. I would no longer be able to go to the grocery store and not be self-conscious, fearing someone would comment on my need to buy jelly that very day. And peanut butter. There had to be a peanut butter comment in there somewhere. Oh, of course, "I suppose your other car is..."

Think positive, I told myself. At least this was just for the life of this car. No sense thinking that one little plate could end up turning my life upside down.

* * *

"Do you work for a jelly company?" I had stopped at the gas station. Clearly, the question was not: Do I *own* a company that makes jelly? The older car itself answered that. Now I was too far into my sulk to laugh it off.

"No." I shook my head and nodded at my plate. "Just the luck of the draw."

"'Cause I know someone who used to work at one. They'd love to have a plate like that." Someone, please stop her.

"Well, I'm sure you can pay for something similar," I said, wondering if I should just pull the nozzle out now. Was a gallon in there yet?

"Oh, of course." She smiled.

I went home and got myself ready for work. Glancing in the mirror I saw I was now sporting the look of defeat. Excellent. I'd promised myself by my 35th birthday I would have accomplished a couple of biggies in my life: first, change my relationship with my mother by somehow letting go of the friction I always felt with her (it was always such an effort with her) and second, somehow find my own direction in life. I felt totally at a loss as to what I wanted to be when I grew up and ummm... 35! Yeah... And then as a backup — if all else failed, as it usually did — just treat myself to a vacation, a real vacation. And even though that one sounded easy to do, I didn't enjoy the thought of going anywhere alone, so... no travel plans yet.

While my new license plate had nothing to do with my mother, I could already hear her reaction to my absurd little plate and thus my mood took a hit once again. I still had a few months left to achieve these long-term goals but as of this moment, I didn't see it happening.

* * *

I got to work just before three, just as Ginny was leaving her shift for the day. "Hey, Lainey, how's the new car?" she shouted as she saw me get out and I shut the door.

"Okay, come here, but don't say a thing," I told her, deciding I'd try and turn this around somehow. She hadn't seen the plate from her angle.

"Oh, Lainey!" She laughed. "Oh, Lainey no!" She was laughing too hard to actually say anything else.

"Yeah, I know, and they wouldn't let me exchange it, the woman brushed me off like I'd insulted *her*! Seriously, I didn't know what hit me!"

"Well, just be glad we don't work at some kind of pancake house."

"Thanks, Ginny! That really helps!" She was referring to the fact that we worked at Milly's Diner. Not exactly a breakfast house, more of a lunch and dinner type spot, but we did serve breakfast. Just the fact that jelly of any sort was in the building didn't comfort me.

The restaurant was your typical New England style diner. It had a silver and turquoise dining car front, but also had sides that made it larger than the standard one car diner. Inside, there was a long turquoise counter that had brown vinyl stools, as well as brown vinyl booths with turquoise table tops nested under the front windows. Naturally, those were the most popular spots. My section. The side sections had dark brown tables with turquoise and peach tablecloths. Somehow, it came off as more colorful and fresh and less retro.

"Meg's gonna love that!" Ginny said. Meg was the owner of Milly's Diner. Milly, if there ever was one, was long gone and Meg had owned the place forever. "Well, I gotta get home. Dennis will be wondering what's for dinner." She shook her head and added, "Find someone that likes to eat what you do. I think being food compatible should be some kind of requirement."

I believe that was about the millionth time she'd mentioned that to me, and then she pointed to my license plate and had yet another good laugh for herself.

Ginny was older than me, in her mid-forties, and had light brown hair, stood about medium height, and was a bit of a force to reckon with in the diner. Sometimes, she'd throw pearls of wisdom at me, but usually she was just Ginny: good sense of humor and easy to talk to, my closest friend in there. She'd been with Dennis since high school.

"Goodbye, Ginny," I said and had to smile. Okay, maybe there was some humor to the plate. Then I looked back at it and my smile faded. No. Scratch that. Nothing funny about it.

My shift was generally from three till closing, which was around 11:30, or midnight, after everyone had finally gone. I really loved my schedule.

In the daytime, I usually went to some kind of class at the community college. The adult education classes, not the college courses. They had a good selection of classes in the daytime, although the bulk of them were available at night for the after work crowd. I just took what looked interesting on any given day, not really pursuing anything specific. My trouble was I would be very interested in one of them, take the class, and then not want to pursue it any further. I truly had no direction.

So, I'd taken things like basic accounting. Who knew? Maybe it would come in handy if I remembered it correctly. I'd also taken a few different types of art classes, which were fun. But they had to give me a project, rather than have me work on my own. I'd taken a few computer classes, always good to know, (then obsolete once I'd walked out the door,) and a chemistry class. Okay, that was a mistake, but again it was just for entertainment really.

My job at the diner was, however, nothing short of a blessing. I'd been there close to nine years now. I worked so many other jobs before this one, mostly retail jobs. I never liked those. I'd also worked at a lot of other restaurants, but there was always something off with most of those places – the pace was different, the atmosphere dreary or they were overly managed or poorly managed. But somehow Milly's seemed to have just the right balance. Even in my worst moments here, it was better than anything else I'd ever found!

"Lainey, I'm afraid you'll have to cover Paula's section tonight, too," Meg said the moment I got in. "Her kid's got some kind of bug so I told her to take a couple days off." She shook her wet hands over the sink, then dried them on a hand towel.

"Besides, I don't want her here if the kids are contagious. Because then maybe she's contagious. One out, then everyone's out. Anyway, no one else was available, and really it shouldn't be so bad tonight. I'll still be here." She looked down at her watch, a fun multicolor watch, with hands that looked like crayons, something her grandchildren must have given her. She was probably calculating exactly how many minutes until we left.

"Oh, sure, Meg," I said, walking out to the front and thinking, *great, it's going to be exhausting tonight.* Okay, yes, I did have *some* miserable moments there — but overall... No sooner had I thought that, than a party of six walked in, and Meg had already disappeared back in the kitchen.

Somewhere in the mix, I seated two men, one looking very familiar, but I didn't think he'd come to the diner before, so I couldn't place him. Then it hit me, he'd been in one of my classes. Was it the accounting class? I couldn't remember.

"Lainey? Is that you?" Oh, wow, he remembered my name! I was stunned.

"Oh, hi... I remember you... weren't we in a class together?" I was vague, but it worked.

"Yeah, we took the *Excel* class together. How are you?"

"Fine, I, uh, yeah I'm fine and yourself?" *Excel*, of course!

"Good," he said and then looking at the other fellow said, "We took a class together, a couple months ago. Lainey was pretty good. She could give you some pointers!" They laughed briefly and I didn't know to what extent that was sarcastic, so I smiled too, and took out my pad and asked if they wanted anything to drink. How on earth would he know if I was any good at *Excel*?

"So is this where you work?" he asked me instead, and I nodded with the, *okay, totally wrong thing to say to me*, look. "I mean, are you still in school too?"

"Yeah, I'm still taking classes," I said, hoping to avoid the *what is my vocation* question. "How about yourself?"

"No, that was just a quickie for work. We all needed to get some training, and I missed the classes they had at the office so I had to make it up. I thought they were pretty good, though. I think I got more out of it than they did at work, a much more extensive class!" he continued a little bit too enthusiastic for the scope of the class.

"Ah, yes, well I'm glad I took it," I said, knowing I had nowhere to go next. "Anyway, I'll let you two look over the menu, and oh, what did you say you wanted to drink?"

The other one ordered a coffee and "my guy" said he'd have the same. I wished I'd asked his name but my moment seemed to have passed me by. Another couple had come in and I was feeling pressure to get over to them. With Paula being out, I knew I had to move it. I could see even Meg, now back out on the floor, was getting her fair share of activity.

I came back in a few moments with the coffee, ready to take their orders. They seemed to be deep in conversation, much to my relief. They ordered without much more banter and I was able to regroup. I was trying to remember anything at all about him from the class but I couldn't think of much. I saw so many people between work and the classes, it was the exception when I remembered someone. I think the only reason I did was his long ponytail, and as I would have suspected, he was there for work. So many of the computer class people were. I was usually the oddball in those classes.

I looked over as they were leaving and he gave me a quick wave, leaving me to wonder once again what that was all about. I waved back, my smile feeling a little too forced.

To my delight, the steady stream of customers eased up, and we were able to leave at 11:30 that night.

* * *

Meg really wasn't all that strict with us. I think as a group we all had good work ethics, and she appreciated that, so she didn't have to grill us for every single thing. She'd given us all the standard food handling rules; the no nail polish was one she really enforced, but then there was this whole bit about perfume. It started out as "just don't wear it." But was later updated to — "well, keep it to an absolute minimum." Then somewhere along the line it morphed into, "if you *must* wear something then wear something food oriented, like a spice type scent: vanilla, cinnamon, or citrus, maybe something like lemon." I think she'd been to some kind of marketing seminar since "if you must wear something" sounded more like "I *would like* you to wear something food-oriented."

While I liked the vanilla scent, it made me want cookies all day long and that just got on my nerves. Then I tried lemon and felt like a room cleaner. Then, strangely, I found I really liked grapefruit.

It had a fresh scent to it, and was a little bit energizing when I was lagging towards the end of my shift, so that's pretty much what I wore. I had it in a little spritzer bottle and was good to go. Ginny thought I was insane.

"Soap. That's good enough for me." I believe was her comment. Though I noticed she mostly used a *lemon* soap.

I got home and immediately went to bed. Work, sleep, get up in the late morning and have my "day" or school, and then back to work. That was the routine. I liked that things were open in the day; I could get a lot done. Unlike Ginny, lamenting her cooking woes, eating was never really a problem since I often had something at the diner, and, hey, their food was pretty good. It was your basic diner fare of burgers and fries, different soups, meatloaf, the turkey dinner, etc. etc. All things comfort food. They made a mean baked mac and cheese.

Well, everyone loved the comfort food factor there. Probably what brought the computer class guy in. He didn't know I worked there did he? No, of course not. But now I felt there was more to it, but I couldn't say exactly why. I just couldn't put my finger on it.

• Chapter 2 •

I woke to the chirping of my smoke detector — the low battery chirp. I was a little fuzzy thinking it was my alarm clock at first, then I realized no, this was now a project for me. Fortunately, I kept a good supply of batteries on hand. After replacing them, I sat there a little unsure if it would go off again, but hoped that would be the end of that.

Next on my agenda, I knew I was supposed to take a drive out to see my sister with my new car. I felt a smidge of reluctance and humiliation, as I thought of my license plate. She wasn't exactly good in the sense of humor department, and I wasn't in the mood for disapproval. I figured maybe I could steer her away from the back of the car and just have her sit inside or something. After all, the car itself was nice enough. I'd been so proud of it before the killjoy plate.

It was a half hour drive to her house, and I hadn't been there in a month or so. I loved my sister, but I wasn't so keen on her infuriating husband. He'd be at work now so I was fine. I wouldn't be staying until he got home, having to get back for work myself so that was all good.

Jill was waiting outside when I got there, her dog, Memphis, barking away by her side. Memphis was a Dalmatian that her daughter just had to have, absolutely adorable as a puppy, but more than just a bit on the surly side now. I think he took after the husband.

"Jill, hey, good to see you! You look great!" She had on a navy and white print outfit that looked like she'd just bought it. Jill was the blonde and I was the brunette, but we both shared the same grey-blue eyes that everyone noticed. Smokey eyes, go figure. She came running to me and the car. Memphis checked it out as well.

"Not so bad," she said, nodding at the car. "Looks solid, no rust."

"Yeah, no rust." Rust? Is that the best she could come up with? Is that all she thought of my choice? It might be old but it beat my last car in every way possible. Oh, okay, now that one did have rust...

"Well, it looks great. Gonna give me a spin around the block."

"Sure, hop in," I said going back to the car and before I could ask about the dog, she let him in the back seat. Great.

We drove around just a little bit, and I knew she had no interest in the car at all, but was being polite. Memphis, I wasn't so sure about.

We got back to the house and went inside without incident. (Meaning, thankfully, she didn't notice the plate.) She had started making lunch before I got there and went right back to it without missing a beat. Cheddar cheese, apple slices, and real turkey on a baguette with some wild kind of orange-flavored mayo. Even working in the diner I was a little bit food challenged, so this was great.

Her daughter was now in middle school, and I really did want to say hello to Janie, so I figured I would stay for a moment or two after Janie got home before I headed back. Today I was in at 3:30 so I should just make it.

"Between you and me," Jill said, as we settled into the kitchen, "something strange is going on with Seth. I'm not sure what the deal is, but there's something he's holding back on." Her somewhat hushed tone surprised me more than her question.

"You think he's cheating on you?" I asked going straight for the jugular. I couldn't help myself.

"NO, absolutely *nothing* like that!" she said, insulted. "But there is something going on, I just can't figure it out. It's just that he's been acting different, like he wants to tell me something but can't. I know he probably won't say anything to you either, but if you notice anything, have any kind of inkling, let me know."

"Notice anything, well, yeah sure, of course, Jill," I said, completely unsure I could do any such thing, not without jumping to all kinds of conclusions myself.

She no sooner got the sandwiches on the table when I heard "JELLLEEEE" booming in the door.

"I told Seth to check out your car if he had time to run home at lunchtime. What's he saying *jelly* for?" Jill tilted her head with a curious look. Just my luck.

"What's up with the vanity plate? What on earth possessed you? Out there looking for peanut butter?" He asked, pointing his thumb outside to the car.

Oh, crap.

"Hi Seth," I grumbled. "No, it's not a vanity plate."

"What are you talking about?" Jill asked still looking perplexed.

"What vanity plate? I didn't see that, and what do you mean peanut butter?" she asked, but was out the door before I could explain.

"Jill, I…" Then, I turned to Seth. "No, I just got it at the DMV, just lucky."

"You should return it. Why didn't you give it back? You don't have to put up with that kind of crap. You should go back, and have them give you a normal plate! Why didn't you give it back?"

Jill reemerged. "Lainey, why did you get that plate? What's the significance there?"

"There *is no* significance! It's *not* a vanity plate, they just gave me that plate," I said, exasperated.

"You should return it. Why didn't you return it?" Seth was still insisting.

"I tried, but she wouldn't take it back."

"Didn't try hard enough, Lainey. You should have made them take it back."

"Seth, it's fine, I…" I searched for words that would get him to drop it without flat-out telling him to shut up.

"It's not fine, that's b.s. You should take that back. Who wants to be known as jelly all the time? Sounds like you're weak, sounds like you're some kind of wishy-washy…"

"Seth, it's fine."

"Seth's right. You really should take it back."

"I told you, I *tried*. Anyway, it's no big deal." Total lie. I knew that would just launch round two, but I had no other defense, it was too late to try the, *isn't it funny* approach with them.

"Anyway, let me take a look under the hood there. See if you did any better with the car than the plate," he said, lacing his fingers together, and then stretching his arms and turning his palms out, like he was about to do some serious damage.

"No, it's okay, Seth, you don't have to..." I winced a little.

"Go on, give him the keys, Lainey. He really does have a way with cars. And then you'll know for sure. I tell you there's nothing like someone who knows cars. Someday, we'll have to find a nice mechanic for you, Lainey." I never commented when they said something like that. What was the point?

I fished out my keys, just slightly wanting to do a number on Seth's car with them, but I handed them over nicely, regretting it as I did so. Jill smiled like her prince charming was going to save the day by looking under the hood.

I choked down some of my lunch while Seth was out violating my car. All the while counting the minutes until Janie got home, and I could bolt.

"So, how's work?" Jill asked me, back to pleasant conversation.

"Good, good. One gal's out sick—well, her daughter is sick—so I've been busy. But, it's pretty much the same there. I'm taking a poetry class that's been pretty interesting though."

"Reading or writing it?"

"A little of both, you know." No, she didn't know. Jill didn't take classes. Jill worked part time at an upscale clothes store, a couple of hours a week. She bought the finest threads for her family with a little discount and life was good. I am pretty sure she saw my classes as a waste of time but she would never actually say that to me. I felt this sense that she believed everything she did was important in the grand scheme of life, and what I did, well, not so much.

We finished our sandwiches and Seth came back in, pronouncing my car to be safe and sound. *Oh, sigh of relief.* I smiled, but he was telling me like he was my hero or something and it was such a good thing that he'd come home or I would never have been sure. I'd never sleep safely if he hadn't told me. I'd be a wreck every moment of my pathetic sad little — what was it? — wishy-washy life if not for him. I obviously owed him so much.

"That's great, Seth. Good to know."

He had some lunch and then had to get back to work, still informing me that I really needed to get that plate changed.

Would it never end?

I thought again about what Jill had said about Seth, but I saw no difference whatsoever with him. I had a feeling I wasn't going to be much help there, but I would probably now be hyper-vigilant around him — as if I wasn't already. Excellent.

Janie came bounding in from school not two minutes later, laughing about the plate. "Oh, Aunt Lainey, that's so funny, that's the best *ever*, I have to tell my friends!" I felt more normal, but then had to head back to work.

I was so drained by the time I got back home, I put on extra of my energizing grapefruit spray, then threw on my uniform and went off to work.

Ginny was still inside when I got there and waved me over.

"Some guy was in asking when you'd be on tonight. I didn't know who he was so I was vague. Is there something I should know about, or did I do the right thing?" she asked as we huddled in the doorway, not wanting customers to overhear us.

"Some guy?" My mind went blank, then right to the computer class guy. "No, I... did he have very straight sandy brown hair in a long ponytail, little goatee, medium build... shirt and tie...?"

"The executive wanna be rock star type? Yeah, that's him. Who is he?" she asked.

"Wow, he was in last night, he recognized me from a computer class we took... Why would he be in again?"

"Guess he likes you." She grinned, now feeling better about him.

"I don't think that's the reason, but I don't know..."

"What's wrong with him? Wrong vibe? I didn't get a creepy vibe, is something amiss or what?"

"I don't know. It was just weird that he knew my name. I can't remember his."

"Um, Lainey, you do know you're wearing a name tag, right?" she laughed but then said, "He must have just liked you and noticed you. Doesn't really mean anything," she assured me.

"But he came back so soon."

"Maybe he wants to ask you out, or just get to know you. *Or*, maybe, he just liked his sandwich!"

"Maybe, just... well we'll see if he comes back again."

"Trouble gals?" Meg came over. I must have been looking very serious.

"No, no trouble, just confusion, but no, we're fine." I waved my hand, indicating it was nothing.

"Ginny tells me you got a great license plate yesterday."

"This plate is going to do me in, I swear. My brother-in-law insisted I need to take it back, not to be treated like that..."

"You never liked him, did you?" Ginny got a laugh with that, and moved out of the doorway to let Dillon, one of the cooks, pass through.

I looked at her and said ever so sarcastically, "Thanks, big help."

"Well, it sounds like a great one to have people seeing near the diner, you'll have to park it out front," Meg insisted.

"Oh, Meg no, that's customer parking." She couldn't argue with that logic.

"No, they'll get a kick out of it," she insisted again.

I didn't want to have it *known* was the problem. Cute one time around, maybe, but every day? No, no, no. I decided a smile was the answer for now. I'd have to figure out a better one for later.

* * *

Computer class man didn't show up on my shift and I felt a little disappointed, although I had no idea what I would say to him if he did. I'd had no vibe whatsoever from him in class, I guess he wasn't all that unattractive, I just failed to really notice one way or the other.

Most of my classes were like that though. Some people went there to meet other people, but I met so many people at the diner I felt like classes were my time to focus in on whatever I went there for, no distractions.

Okay, that was the thinking, although I suppose if there had been a little more chemistry, I would have paid attention. I decided it was best to dismiss the whole thing.

I got home and an orange cat was sitting on my front step. The porch light was on and it sat there as if it was waiting for me to come home. As I got closer, I could see it was a rather vibrant orange, and looked very well cared for. No one I knew in the area had a cat. I said hello and it jumped down to the walkway and then slid behind the shrubs. Okay, my new friend was shy. But who did it belong to?

• CHAPTER 3 •

With no sign of the cat in the morning, I figured it must have found its way home again. On my way back from my poetry class, I stopped off at the grocery store. I pulled through a parking spot to be able to pull out facing forward. I had hoped there would be a spot to parallel park in where no one could see the plates, but no such luck. (I was still fuming about it.) Ahead of me, I saw a light blue SUV driving out of the lot with the vanity plate "I HEARD." I HEARD, what kind of plate was that? What did that mean? *I heard* you got a strange plate yourself. Thanks.

I ran into the store to do my shopping. The clap of thunder nearly shook the store while I was still mulling over "I HEARD" in the produce section. I looked up at the ceiling. Really?

I finished my shopping and saw the pavement was wet but somehow I had missed the brief downpour itself. That delighted me to no end, until I got back to my car and I saw someone had put a note under the windshield wiper. I pulled out the note, but whoever had written it, did so with a felt tip pen. Whatever they had to say was now all running together from the rain. I pulled a tissue out of my pocketbook to wipe off the purplish ink on my windshield. I could barely make out a few letters on the note, but not much else. Was I parked funny? Did someone hit my car? I looked around but didn't see any damage. Was it someone I knew? Or — oh, no — was it some comment on my plate? I winced at the thought.

My machine was blinking when I got home, with a lovely message from Jill. "Did you take it back?" she started without even saying hello. "Seth is insisting you don't have to put up with that, and I have to agree. Of course, Janie's told all her friends who think it's 'so cool!' Anyway, I told Mom you'd be by as soon as you could to show off the new car, so I hope you get the new plate by then because you know how humiliated she'll be. See ya."

I deleted that one.

My mother. My mother would now be waiting for me to call her, and would not call me until I got back to her. There was something wrong with all of them, I thought. The dynamics were just wrong... but then that must include me. I'd call her later, I would be good, but now I had to fix a quick bite to eat and get to work.

The phone rang, startling me. It was Ginny, talking fast into my machine. "Lainey, I'm in the parking lot at the Home Depot and there's a car here that says 'PNT-BTR' I can't get over it! It's a silver car, BMW I think. It's an older one but I just can't believe what I'm seeing."

I picked up quickly and said, "What? Have you seen them? Who is it?"

"I don't know, and I've been waiting for about ten minutes. I can't really wait any longer since I'm on at three today, but I was so excited I had to call."

"That's so weird, Ginny. I just got some odd note on my car too, but I couldn't read it. I wonder… no you're on the other side of town. Of course, now I'll be wondering for the rest of my life who drives that car! I don't know if that's a 'thanks' or a 'what did you do to me?'!"

"BMW, Lainey, your soulmate."

"Yeah, probably the wife of my soulmate, mother of his four children is more like it!"

"No, she's driving the minivan. Okay, gotta go. See you in a bit."

I did not have a soulmate out there driving a car with PNT-BTR on it. That was beyond disturbing. License plates were running, no — make that ruining — my life. Since I'd gotten that plate I realized I'd been tensing up with each and every single plate that said anything interesting and immediately wondered what it meant, and then rejected the idea just as fast. As if they all had a message for me, that I refused to acknowledge.

See, these signs, all that… No. Part of me said I absolutely wasn't doing it. On the surface, it might be funny, but it didn't *mean* anything. If "I HEARD" hadn't done a job on me then here my "soulmate" with the PNT-BTR plate certainly would. And I wasn't about to let that happen. Better to figure out how did one go about returning a plate? Maybe that woman at the DMV was just having a bad day herself.

When I got to work, I parked in the front of the parking lot to appease Meg. Now that I knew I had a mate out there, I already wanted the mystery over with, find out the guy's a winner, (meaning loser) and be on my way.

Who did show up, however, was Mr. Computer class man. This time he was alone. Ginny got him first and put him in her section.

She had the side sections. I think she was trying to let me get a grip before I had to talk to him. All I had to do was say no if I didn't want to go out with him, so what was the big deal? It must have been all the hoopla of him showing up when I wasn't there that spooked me. And even at that, he might be a really nice guy. But I knew I just wasn't interested in him.

I walked by. "Oh, hello, nice to see you again. You must have liked the meal the other night." I said, just being courteous.

"Lainey, hi, yeah, actually I was wondering if I could talk to you for a minute? Do you have a minute, or do you have a break coming up soon or anything like that?"

"Oh, I, well…" I looked over at my section, which was pretty calm at the moment. Meg frowned on us chatting at length with customers, well, beyond the regulars, they were okay. I said, "In about twenty minutes I have a break, do you mind waiting?"

"No, that's good," he said, but I noticed he was fidgeting.

So, glancing around, I sat down, not waiting for my break, and he said, "Thanks for talking to me now, it's just that well, I was wondering, do you have a sister, Jill?"

"What?" I asked, caught totally off guard.

"Jill, I know that's weird, but when I met you in the class and heard your name, well I couldn't help but think you looked a little like the Jill I knew from high school." I felt myself pull backwards as he said that.

"Why didn't you just ask me then?" I said, still slowly backing up in my seat, but relieved this wasn't about me.

"I wasn't sure, but just kept thinking about her and when I saw you here I knew it couldn't be a coincidence again, I mean could it, do you have a sister, Jill?" He looked eager for my answer as he leaned closer to me.

"Well, yes, I do."

"YOU DO? It is her? Jill, with grey-blue eyes like yours, but with blonde hair?" His hand nearly knocked over his cup of coffee.

"Well, sounds like Jill to me, so how do you know her again?" I asked cautiously. "And why couldn't you just contact her your-self...? Does she even know you?"

"Oh, of course, she knows me, or at least she did. We went to high school together that's all. I'm just curious how she is." My impatience — and mistrust — finally slid down a few notches.

"She's fine. Married, daughter, busy. I tell you what, give me your card, name, number, whatever, and I'll pass it along to her, tell her you wanted to know how she was." Seriously? This could have waited until my break. Why was he so fidgety?

He took out his wallet and gave me his business card. "I'm in sales, but I'm guessing you don't actually need a video adapter or a graphics adapter...graphics card maybe?" I laughed for the first time finally feeling comfortable.

"No, I'm good, but Jill, you never know! So, you were in her class?"

"I moved after two years in her class. Mid-year. Not far, but in school another town might as well be another country. We weren't in the same circles at school but she was always nice to me."

I knew someone that moved away, mid-year too. I thought it was so unusual, but maybe it happened more than I knew.

I got up from Mr. Computer class, a.k.a. - Steve, and Ginny gave me an inquisitive look. I shook my head with a tight smile to let her know there was no date involved.

Harold Burns was next to come into the diner. Harold could be found at the diner three times a week at least. He was an older gentleman, widowed; I believe he had a couple of adult children who were married. I also think he had a bit of a crush on Meg, but she was either not catching on or just wasn't interested. Harold wore a black derby hat that he always placed on the seat next to him when he sat down. It always looked like he was saving the seat for someone.

Burns was also the local celebrity. He hosted a small radio program in the wee hours of the night on AM radio. Old time: *how's the car running? good sale at the hardware store, how'd you meet your wife?* kind of talk radio. But he was known more for being the person who went to every store opening, every parade, every civic event, every charity event, you name it, Burns was there.

Ginny seated him and then I heard them laughing. He could be quite entertaining, so I didn't think much of it until Ginny waved me over.

"Hi, Harold. How are you today?"

"Hi, Lainey. Ginny tells me she's found you a soulmate but wanted to know if I knew who it was."

"Ginny, you didn't!" I gasped and she grinned ear to ear.

"Oh, that's alright, I didn't know who it was but I'll have to be on the lookout, not often you get a stroke of luck like that dropped in your lap. Don't let that one go!"

"At this point, I think I want to let the car go!"

"No, you don't. This is a marvelous opportunity. I'll ask on my show tonight."

"*NO*, please. *NO*, Harold. I really don't want that kind of attention on it."

"Oh, don't worry. No one listens to my show but lonely old folks. At best, someone's kid has that plate. But, who knows what will turn up. I've done 'find the license plate' shows before, lots of interesting things have turned up. Mostly, if it says something, that's what they do for a living, or it's their name, but sometimes it's just for fun, and some you can't figure out what they mean."

"I know some are really great, but those are vanity plates, mine, so help me, I just got assigned this thing! It was some kind of vanity reject mess up. I would never have gotten a vanity plate intentionally. I do not want the attention it brings."

"Well, I'll use a little finesse. Really it's just fun. And I won't mention your plate."

"Oh, okay, then. Now I'm going to have to listen to your show! Ooh, but I haven't got time to record it, I'm not always home before it starts."

"Yeah, I'm not either," Ginny interjected, clearly delighted now by the stir she'd created.

"I'll bring you in a copy, and let you know what happens. That's no problem. This could be fun. Thanks for the inspiration!"

"Well, okay, I guess you have Ginny to thank, I'm just stuck with some crazy plate that makes me feel like a moron."

"You have to think of it as an unusual opportunity. You never know where things lead. Be open to the possibilities." He gave me a big smile, and I shook my head to say *I don't know*, and then had to get back to a couple that just came in the door.

I did meet all kinds of people here, I'd give him that, but too often it was on the strange side of town and not necessarily a good thing!

The next day I called Jill and told her about Steve in the diner and said I had his card for her. I told her I was just going to drop it in the mail if she wanted it, and that I still had to call Mom to figure out when I could get over there. She was stunned about this Steve guy but said she remembered him pretty well. He moved away in the middle of their junior year. He was there one day, and gone the next. She had thought about him a few times, where he had gone, but never once thought he would remember her.

"You told him I was married, right?"

"Yes, Jill, I told him, married with a daughter, but no more than that, I didn't give him your married name or anything."

"You know what, hold onto his card until I see you next, just give me the number, but don't mail it, just hold onto it. I don't want Seth to be curious about *what's this from Lainey in the mail?* It's no big deal, and I don't want it to become one, just by looking like it's something important." I had a hint of, now who's not telling who information, but decided to let that one go.

"Sure, no problem. Well, I should call Mom, get that done, I'll talk to you later." I hung up with the next assignment in hand. When to visit Mom?

* * *

Everything in my family changed when Jill and I were just barely teenagers. To be exact, Jill was 13 and I was 10. My father died unexpectedly in a car accident. Most of that time became a blur for us. Whatever normal had been, was lost.

First, we had the trauma of losing him to deal with. But then it was the change in my mother.

"Well, I've taken a job at the grocery store, just till I figure something better out," she told us, rather proud of herself for getting the job there. She still works there. That was all good.

But then the weirdness was when she started whispering to others maybe she had an inkling that the accident was going to happen. Maybe she had a gift and didn't know it, maybe instead of thinking she was just worrying she could have done something, but she had ignored the signs. The "signs" and the "gift" were all news to us. Some gift!

She told this to her friends in the strictest confidence, which naturally we overheard in bits and pieces, putting the story together ourselves. Since we'd always been told not to draw unnecessary attention to ourselves, we said nothing to anyone about it. But we also never talked to *her* about it. Like it was forbidden.

But her friends must have encouraged her to use these gifts, because then, one by one she started giving them little readings. Of course, *the strictest confidence* was a bona fide way to get more and more people to know about this gift without advertising it.

So, yeah, Mom secretly became a fortune teller on the side, without ever really being one...

Every neighbor, every friend, loved getting readings from her, but it was always "just between you and me," hush hush, and into the kitchen with the door closed. Jill and I were sure she was just telling them the common sense things everyone felt about them anyway, but wouldn't say to their faces. Otherwise, she must have just been making stuff up. She never said she was a psychic or anything else. She just did the readings. She just let them believe she had a "gift." Mom had it down.

She never spoke to us about the readings either. Although once she caught me trying to listen and I got a look that said above and beyond the *get out of here*, to *NOT SAY ANYTHING, do not repeat a word of this.*

There were no signs otherwise. She didn't know things ahead of time, we did not benefit from all this new-found talent. No insight. It was all a taboo subject and I really hated thinking she was a fraud. But I just didn't know.

* * *

I picked up the phone and called, expecting to get her machine but she answered. The grocery store where she worked was just down the street from her apartment and she worked days, so our schedules weren't usually in sync.

"Hey, Mom, how are you?" I asked and then started right in with, "I was wondering if you wanted to see my new car, I thought I could come by sometime maybe early next week." After some schedule rehashing, we set up a time for the following Tuesday, which was my day off, and I felt good I'd finally taken care of that.

On my way out to work, the calico cat made a reappearance sitting poised on the porch. "Well, hello again," I said as it just sat there watching me. It didn't move as walked past it and shut the door behind me.

* * *

"You should have parked in front again," Meg was saying when I got into work.

"Habit, Meg, just a habit you know," I'd done the front once, and thought wasn't that enough?

A couple walked in and I jumped to seat them so the conversation would go no further. She wouldn't make me move it once I got underway with customers, but I could see my resistance and her insistence becoming a problem, so I would probably park in front once or twice more, make sure she saw it there, and then she could just forget about it.

I had some teenagers come in and they seemed to want to stir things up. Just loud amongst themselves at first, but then taking several of the salt and pepper shakers and sliding them all around the table like a game of air hockey. I tried to quiet them down a few times by distracting them, telling them about the specials and the like, and then Ginny came by and gave them the, "Boys, do your best not to get thrown out" with a big smile. Then, she said to me, "Ah, yes, just like my own!" with an even bigger grin. She casually scooped the extra salt and pepper shakers off the table. Ginny didn't have any kids. Did the trick though.

A few minutes later Meg called me into the back. I was getting ready to tell her yet another reason why I couldn't park in front. *Make something up, Lainey,* was my first thought, but she had called Ginny back as well. She closed her eyes for a moment then said to us, "Do you remember a few weeks ago when I asked you gals what would you think if I were to sell the diner?"

I hadn't thought twice about it, because it seemed to be asked in a moment of frustration, just to relieve some stress.

I nodded, and Ginny smiled and said, "Yes, and it was a little bit traumatizing when I thought about it later!"

Meg didn't smile back, "Well," she looked at the floor first, then looking back at us said, "I was offered a very generous deal on the diner, and I'm seriously considering it. Nothing has been decided, nothing is final, but I thought I should let you know there is the potential. And if you don't mind, please don't mention it to our regular customers, not till something is decided."

"Oh," we both said, stunned.

CHAPTER 4

Meg's news was still weighing heavily on my mind the next day as I went into the student lounge area to pick up the latest course catalog. I hadn't slept very well thinking about it all night. Was I about to be out of a job? That couldn't be true. I could not look for another job. I loved this one! Was there something in the catalog I should be looking at in earnest? I settled into one of the many waiting room style chairs there to look through the catalog yet again.

If Meg really did sell the diner, maybe I could still be a waitress there. This was the only job I'd ever really liked. Ginny was there, and all the regulars, and they felt like family. I would definitely stay if the new owners let me, but what if they didn't keep us, or only some of us... Oh no. And what was the time frame on all of this. Even if nothing had been decided yet, this might take place soon...

She hadn't said anything else, and I think we were too shocked to ask. Could I really be out of a job? I'd been there for almost nine years now. I loved the diner. What was I going to do? I seriously did not want to think about it.

"Lainey?"

I looked up to see Steve the computer guy.

"Oh, hi, how are you? I didn't expect to see you here," I said.

"I'm signed up for the *PowerPoint* class now. They suggested it at work. You never know when you'll have to make a presentation, you know, put all the *Excel* work to use." He shifted a few folders from one hand to the other.

"Oh." The *Excel* class was several months ago, quite the gap.

"So, did you talk to Jill yet?"

"Uh, yeah, she remembered you." I said, but I wasn't sure where to go next. I hadn't given her the card yet, but she did have the number. I had no idea if she was going to contact him and felt like my part was essentially done in the whole deal.

"She did? What did she say?"

"She said she remembered you." Then I smiled to make nice, my eyebrows might have hit my hairline but I had no way of knowing for sure.

"Oh, that's all?" he said as he plunked down across from me, dropping his folders on the empty chair next to him. I couldn't tell if he was crestfallen or just mildly disappointed or what. But then he sat up a bit and leaned over towards me.

"Was I supposed to tell her something else?" Now I was feeling irritated — what was the deal here?

"No," he said, pulling back again, but still looking at me. "You know, just curious what someone remembers about you. That's all. Anyway, are you back for another computer class too?" he asked changing the subject and making me feel a little more at ease.

"Not computer this time, just checking out my options." I didn't want to mention that I was here more often than in my own apartment, or that I might be here with a more pressing assignment this time.

"Oh, a real student then?"

"Something like that." I must have frowned at the thought, my award-winning social skills out the door today.

He decided to call it quits with me, much to my relief, and said, "Well, I'm off then."

* * *

I parked in the front at work, as Meg suggested, thinking it was just for a day or two. Paula saw me pull up and wanted to know what the deal was, why I parked in front, and I told her about the whacked license plate I got, and she immediately had to go out and check it out. "That's perfect," she said as she returned.

"I'm sorry I don't get 'perfect' at all. What it is, is a freakish event never to repeat in my life, and okay, it's amusing to all that do not have to drive it, but perfect?"

"Sorry, wrong choice of words," she said, stifling a giggle.

"Understood." I nodded but felt a little sulky and walked away.

Ginny told me Paula had returned to work and immediately wanted to know what was new. She felt like she'd been in exile for the few days she was gone.

Paula thrived on the diner's gossip. Ginny told her she'd best go and see Meg, as there was a change in the air. We hadn't gotten much more information from Meg about the particulars. Meg had only said she was considering it, although that was more than enough.

"What do you think will happen if she does take the offer?" Paula asked me as I walked into the kitchen a few minutes later, my arms filled with a tray of dirty plates.

"I really don't know. Best case scenario, they keep us all, and they keep things as they are, that's what I want to believe, but who knows!" I answered, really not wanting to acknowledge it at all.

"Who made the offer?" Paula asked now wiping down one of the counters.

"You know, she didn't say," I said moving out of the way along with the tray of plates, still trying to get to the sink.

"Should we ask?"

"We could... we probably won't know who it is anyway."

Ginny came in and said she was off in a few minutes. Filling her in quick, we all decided we'd wait to ask. Meg hadn't offered any details and somehow it seemed as if our not knowing made it less real.

Ginny really liked changing her shifts back and forth, days to nights, filling in whenever she was needed. I think she only slept like five hours a night and had so much energy. If I missed my eight and a half hours, I was a zombie. Fortunately, I had no trouble falling asleep, or staying asleep. But, it was pretty critical that I got to sleep immediately after my shift.

"Hey, who has the jelly plate?" asked one of the regular diners when I walked out again, and I knew I would not be able to tolerate more than a day or so of that. Unfortunately, Meg was within earshot and piped in, "I know isn't that funny! We're on the lookout for peanut butter." She didn't give me away but ugh. It was already more than I could take.

Harold Burns came in a little later and I was anxious to hear what his efforts had resulted in. "Well, Lainey, we've gotten some interesting feedback but I haven't found the mysterious peanut butter yet. But I plan to keep at it. I even had a drawing at an opening the other day, some clever stuff but not our plate! Again, a lot of them were just the person's name."

"I've only had the plate what — a week now — and I'm officially losing it!" I shook my head. "Well, thanks... I think!"

"Don't give up," Harold said.

I smiled and nodded thinking Harold's not giving up, but as for me — I realized I didn't actually want to meet this person. Just know who they were, curiosity, that was fine, but I had no intention of really connecting with them.

* * *

Tuesday, I was on my way out the door to go to my mother's and the phone rang. Let it ring, I thought, what couldn't wait? Unless it was my mother cancelling. That might be a good thing, since I now had the added bonus of having to tell her about the diner. I waited the one more minute and heard Steve the computer guy's voice. I was already running a little bit late so I scooted out while he was still talking. That could wait.

I got there just before lunchtime. She'd moved to this small apartment, not too far from the grocery store she worked at, a couple years ago. Small, yes, but it was a very nice apartment. She was waiting outside when I got there.

"Let me see that stupid plate Jill was telling me about, or did you go back and get it changed?" she said, before I was fully out of the car.

"Oh, she told you, did she?" I said, trying to laugh it off. Leave it to Jill, anything to sound smug about something that happened to me. "Yeah, I still have it. Even Harold Burns, you know the local talk show host, is trying to find equally absurd plates just to make me feel better about it." I went around to the back of the car where my mother was already ahead of me.

"You wouldn't have to if you changed it," she said. "Why would you call into a show about your plate? Why would you want all that attention on yourself? Do you like being absurd?"

"I didn't call in. He's just someone that eats at the diner," I answered. "Anyway, the snippy, bitter woman whose sole purpose in life is to make you feel bad about yourself, wouldn't let me change it." I said, maybe a little too harshly.

"You should have gone back and changed it anyway. That must be causing such a commotion," my mother said, pointing at the plate and crinkling her face like it also had some kind of foul smell.

"Well, forget the plate. Do you like the car? I thought we could go for a spin and then out to lunch what do you think?"

"Oh, well, if you insist."

"I insist," I said, knowing she didn't care about the car, but lunch she might enjoy.

We got to a nice restaurant and when I got out of the car some kids snickered. "Hey, I guess you've just gotten out of a jam, eh?"

I smiled my *yeah, I get it* smile, but my mother shouted back.

"She refused to take it back, can you believe her? She'd rather have punks making fun of her than stand up for herself and take it back."

"Mom, it's not a big deal," I said in my nicest, *please shut up* voice.

"It is a big deal, they're making fun of you and you just stand there and take it, I don't understand that."

"It's just a joke, Mom. Really, it's no big deal." I wasn't going to point out they weren't punks, in case they *were* punks, but they seemed to be less interested in us now, not more, so I just said, "Why don't we go inside?"

I feared it was going to get more uncomfortable by the minute. Appetites were a little off by the time we landed at the table. Not looking at each other, we both sat down and immediately picked up our menu's.

Feeling somewhat defeated already I decided I'd go for broke and tell her about the diner.

"So, Meg just told us she's thinking about selling the diner."

"Lorraine! What on earth will you do?" My mother asked with more force than I was prepared for. And real name. Ouch.

"I'm hoping I'll still be able to work there, she might sell, but it's still a diner, they'll need help," I said, putting the menu down and trying to downplay my actual anxiety about the situation. Then I flashed on my birthday goal —releasing the friction with my mother? Okay, so that was out of the question for today. And finding my direction, yeah, not today either.

"Lainey, there aren't *that* many good restaurants in the area. You don't know what will happen." *Nor do you*, bubbled up inside me, but she was actually right. If we all lost our jobs, it was possible only a few of us might find something right away.

I looked around the room, they didn't seem short on staff. Then I felt a little foolish as the waitress caught my wandering eye and came right over to take our lunch orders.

"One step at a time," I said once again downplaying it. "She may not even sell, she's considering it."

Then, changing the subject I asked, "So what else is new with Jill?"

I had just seen her, and now I hoped that wasn't going to be an issue as well — that I'd gotten over there before getting to see my very own mother.

"Well, you saw her, she's good. Janie is doing well in school, and Seth is the same." My mother actually liked Seth. She didn't see his arrogance; she didn't see his over-inflated sense of self-importance. She just saw that he took care of Jill and Janie and I guess that was all that mattered to her. I think it was that he did what he had to do, much like my mother, and that was important to her. So, Jill was married, Jill was stable, and I, apparently, was not. I tended to irritate her.

* * *

Somehow, I made it through the lunch. Then, as we were about to leave, I asked her if she forgot her sunglasses. She pretty much always wore them when we were out, and I didn't see them on her. She looked lost in thought for a moment and then said almost to herself, "Oh, they're over at the house."

"House? What house? Do you mean the apartment?"

Looking very surprised she said, "Oh, no, well, I've bought this house."

"Wait, what? You *bought* a house?" I asked, both confused and shocked. "I thought you loved your place, and you're right near the store."

"It's just a small house." She said somewhat defensively, then added, "Well, you know, things at the store have been good and somehow, somehow, I'd put away a little bit to buy this small house."

Things at the store had been good? She hadn't mentioned any

raises or bonuses or anything "good" like that, at least not lately. She was probably doing more and more of her readings. What on earth was she telling these people that they kept coming back?

Now I was feeling a little bit slighted. Here I was with my new old car and thought that was a big deal — and of course the news on the diner. But buying a house? That was huge! Why hadn't she told me she was even in the market for one?

"I was just looking... but then I found this little place... it's not too far away," she said, sounding like she still wasn't telling me the whole truth.

"Can we go look at it? Now? Today?"

"No, it's not ready yet. I don't want to jinx it. Not that you're a jinx. Just not yet dear."

"Does Jill know about it?" I asked.

"Yes, well... honey, she helped me find it."

"What? How come she didn't mention it to me? What's going on here?"

"Oh, don't be like that. Really, you don't want to see it now."

"But, I do."

"No, not now." She was done.

* * *

Rain began just as I left my mother's and I tried out the wipers for the first time. Ah, nice. It wasn't five minutes of driving and the full force of the storm was kicking in. I noticed another car's plate that read, SNAP2. What did that mean? SNAP 2 in general? SNAP 2 it? SNAP 2 with my mother. It was a sign all right. Sign beyond my understanding!

I got home and saw my answering machine was blinking away.

Steve, the computer guy, had left a message. Steve the — *he had to look up my number to get me* — computer guy. Any word from Jill?

I called Jill immediately and told her we might just have a situation on our hands. I had no idea what his obsession with her was but he'd just left this message. And, by the way, what was up with Mom and the new house she'd never mentioned thank you very much.

"Oh, Lainey, we were just looking at places, just looking. We thought it would be a fun way to spend some time. But that was months ago. I thought it was a step in the right direction but then she never brought it up again. I thought it had fallen through."

"Oh, so, I wonder why the secrecy?"

"You know Mom."

"You know, sometimes, I don't."

"No, Lainey, she's probably just being cautious."

"Cautious of my knowing?"

"No, just superstitious cautious."

"The logic you can't argue with." That would define my mother actually.

"Exactly."

"Anyway was there more to the Steve thing than you care to mention as well? Any superstitions there too?"

"Don't be silly!" she said, hanging up.

I realized I hadn't told her the diner news, but she'd hung up on me. Fine, now we were even.

I paced a little, feeling seriously agitated, and then decided I had had enough. I grabbed a raincoat and went back out and looked at my car. My family was frustrating me to no end. They would never stop harassing me about that license plate, and I was not going to let Seth, or Jill, or my mother get the better of me. I would stand my ground, I would not be walked all over, I would speak up for myself and the thousand other things they would accuse me of not doing. I would get this done. I would just go out and return that horrible plate!

All the way to the DMV I was rehearsing what I was going to say. This was a terrible mistake and I was humiliated by this, I'm sure they could understand why I wouldn't want such a plate, the ridicule, and for what?

As I walked into the DMV I was immediately struck with the terrifying thought that I would get the same woman. I hadn't even considered that. But I didn't see her so I felt a little calmer.

I sat there with my numbered ticket kind of restlessly bouncing my knee up and down, staring at the floor. Then I looked up and over to another window and to my horror, I saw her there. My body froze. NO. NO. NO. Under no circumstances would I go back to that woman!

The ticket numbers flashed on screens above the window I was supposed to go to. I looked down at my ticket and decided I just wouldn't go if she got my number. I'd pretend it wasn't me. Who knew, maybe the person with that number was in the restroom, maybe I could casually leave like I'd never even been there, maybe I was just here waiting for someone else, they didn't know.

But my number flashed on the screen above a young girl a few windows down, and I nearly jumped over to see her. She smiled at me and asked what she could do for me. I hadn't brought the plate in because of all the rain, but I had all my paperwork, and told her my situation. I was so proud of myself. I was going to be rid of the plate and this whole thing would be over with!

She smiled at me numerous times, nodded in all the right places, and then at the end said, "Well, hmm, what a situation." Then, she leaned in to me and said in the nicest voice, "you know I'm fairly new here, and I haven't had to deal with something like this before. My supervisor is on vacation this week, but I'm going to get someone who can assist us. I'll be right back."

"Oh," is all I got out, before she hopped off her chair and ran over to, NO, NO, NO — Madame Dread herself.

I heard just enough in muffled tones to know this wasn't going well. "This isn't a department store... does she know how many cases of vehicle fraud we deal with...?" she demanded, her hands flailing, "We have strict regulations..." And then came the definitive, "I don't think so!"

She returned with the sweetest smile, but eyes that said *RUN!* and said to me, "I can't really do anything for you right now, but if you would like to come back when my supervisor is here..."

I couldn't get out of there fast enough.

Completely defeated, fuming, and humiliated, I returned home. And there, waiting for me on the doorstep, was one rain soaked calico cat. I felt so sorry for the poor thing that I let it in when I walked in the door. It looked the way I felt. And like an obedient child, it followed me into my apartment and sat happily on the throw rug immediately trying to lick off the rain.

I found myself looking in my closet area for a very old, half-empty bag of kitty litter. I used it for ice storms on the front porch and walkway. Nice traction. No salt. I emptied out a cardboard box that could double for a tray, that I must have lugged in from the Wholesale Club. I poured in a bit of kitty litter and put it down for my new friend to inspect. Then, I moved it into the bathroom.

Just an overnight guest. I figured at least while it was raining this one was going to stay put. Next question, what do cats eat? Tuna or eggs?

I let the cat take over my thoughts rather than face my realization that I was not only stuck with that plate forever, but there was the growing possibility I was out of a job and had absolutely no idea what to do about that as well.

CHAPTER 5

"Mind picking me up for work today?" Ginny asked me on the phone.

"Sure, what's up?" I said, letting the cat back out and feeling a little sad to see it go.

"Oh, Dennis took his car in for a full tune-up. Usually, we do this on my day off, but he forgot I was working and made an appointment. We both go, leave his car, I take him to work, go back home, pick him up, we both go back, he gets his car, etc. Anyway, he'll come and get me tonight."

"Sure, that's no problem."

I arrived at Ginny's a little early but she was already waiting outside on the stairs. Ginny's whole house was not much bigger than my own apartment, with the exception of her very large basement. The problem with the basement, though, was there was no entrance to it from inside the house. They had a bulkhead in the back of the house, charming cement stairs, another door inside that, and *then*, voila, enormous finished basement! They had, of course, talked about building a staircase up into the house, but space was so limited inside that the only real solution would be to put an extension onto the back of the house and that just hadn't been an option so far. Ginny loved her basement, but it was good to remember to never ever, ever mention it after a snowfall.

Ginny got in and looked at me with a bit of desperation in her eyes and asked, "What are we going to do? I can't believe she's going to sell the diner. That's our home! The idea of getting another job at another restaurant, oh, it pains me."

"I know!" I said. "I'm hoping it will just be a smooth transition — if she even does it." I added with all the hope I could muster. "I keep thinking she won't, really, but if she does, maybe we'll just be the new employees for whoever buys it. Sometimes deals go that way, with the stipulation that the employees stay. Meg seems like she'd be one to do that for us."

Ginny bobbed her head, mulling that one over, and seemed to agree with me. "Still, we have to find out what the real deal is. When it's going to be sold, all of that, otherwise we're just in limbo, and I am *not* looking for another job until I know for sure."

About halfway to the diner, a car passed us with the license plate "WLD1." I pointed it out and said, "I swear, Ginny, the plates are out to get me! I keep seeing them all the time now and it's driving me crazy." She looked at the plate and laughed. We needed the laugh!

"But *world one*?" She said, "What on earth is that all about?"

"*World*? I thought it meant *wild one*!"

Wild one reminded me of the cat, and I told her about how it had been sitting on my doorstep, and that I'd let it in and needed to grab some cat food on my way home tonight. She gave me a look. "You took in a stray cat? What's the matter with you? Who knows whose cat it is, where it's been? What it's got for heaven's sake!"

She motioned her hand in front of her as if to shoo away germs.

"Not a cat person, Ginny?"

"No, can you tell?"

"Let's see, my sister has some surly cretin posing as a Dalmatian, so I say, why not take in a good-natured stray? But, I don't think it's a stray, stray. It's too well-kept, and I'm telling you it has good manners and a nice personality. It's either from the neighborhood or newly displaced. I can't tell, and, of course, it can't tell me."

"You need one of those pet psychics." Ginny laughed.

"Pet psychics? Yeah, right." Pet psychic, if my mother wasn't enough reason not to *ever* believe anything like that I didn't know what was. "No, what I need is a real psychic," I continued, being completely sarcastic, "to tell me who has my supposed soulmate's car first, and get that over with, then, and only *then* I can find out what the cat knows!"

"We should do that!" Ginny said, now looking at me with a gleam in her eye.

"Ginny, I'm joking."

"Actually, Lainey, we should go," she said, her tone turning more serious. "Maybe they could tell us what's going to happen with the diner. Maybe we'd know if we were going to be out of a job soon. Or what we should do! No, really, it would be fun."

"No, I don't think so," I said, not wanting to pursue it.

"It would be great," she insisted, clearly not hearing me at all.

"Then, you go, tell me what you get. Really, it's just not for me."

"I know we'd have a lot of fun." She was still determined.

"Until they tell you about the axe murderer," I said just to make it sound even more absurd.

"I don't think they do that," she said, seemingly serious.

"*No?* Then, why go? If all they're gonna tell you is good stuff... don't you want to know the real stuff?" I had never discussed my mother, the psychic fraud, to Ginny. It all felt too tangled to even go there. And I was pretty sure all my mother did was profess good things were going to happen and people just wanted to have that hope. But why was I always angry about the whole deal? I pushed the thought aside. Nope, this was not happening.

"Who says good isn't real?"

"Okay, I'll think about it," I said with absolutely no intention of doing any such thing.

"Actually, I'd also like to find out what to make Dennis for dinner. Do you know how hard that gets? I never know what to have. You might find out the very same thing with that cat. I hear they can be fussy." She laughed. "Yeah, definitely a pet psychic for you! What will become of the diner for both of us, and what to make for Dennis' dinner for me.

"Last night it was all about how we never eat anything exotic," she went on, switching back to the food train of thought, much to my relief. "Does he expect me to *cook* exotic? Because that's just not ever going to happen. I wouldn't mind if he was suggesting an exotic restaurant to go to, to um, *take me to*, although truth be known, I don't like eating things when I don't know what I'm eating. I don't know. But he wanted something 'different' without offering any kind of suggestion of what *different* might be. Something exotic. Well what's *exotic*?"

"Hey, I think they have some cooking classes over at the community college, all different kinds. Would you be interested in something like that?" I asked her.

"You mean for him? Take a cooking class for him?" Ginny said, glaring at me.

"Wow, did I hit a nerve?"

"Um, yeah! Why doesn't he cook? Why doesn't he take a... Of course, I know why." She stopped mid-sentence. "I wouldn't eat it. Well, this is a situation, isn't it?"

"You don't like his cooking or his exotic cooking?"

"Like I said, I like to know what I'm eating. So, fancy stuff kinda freaks me out."

"Ginny, you work in a diner for heaven's sake. Food freaks you out?"

"No, fancy food, exotic food, things I'm not used to. Huge difference. Meat and potatoes, I'm fine with. *That* I'm used to! Anything on Meg's menu, perfect."

"Suppose it depends on the cook, huh?" I said, just goofing. "But couldn't he *tell* you what's in it?"

"You're not getting it: if I don't know what it is, I mean, if I've never had it, I'm not about to have it now. I passed the point of trying new foods long ago."

"You can't be serious!"

"I'm afraid so."

"Well, if you're interested in a cooking class, you know where you can see what it is you're putting in the food — or *not* putting in the food, as the case may be. I'll take one with you. If you want, you know. It sounds kinda fun."

"Sure, and then you'll go to the psychic with me."

"Very funny."

Harold Burns made his way back to the diner. He'd already given me the copy of the "plate show" but he was still at it. "I've gotten some more good ones if they're of any interest to you. But you know what, yours wasn't an intentional vanity plate. It's just a fluke, so maybe the other person's is a fluke too."

Harold, oh, Harold, why does there *have* to be another person, another plate? I argued with myself.

"Ginny thinks I should see a psychic. Get to the bottom of this once and for all." I immediately wanted to take it back. Ginny was talking about the cat; *I* had made the leap to the plate. And I never brought up the word psychic on my own!

"Well, depending on the psychic." He laughed.

"I know!" I felt such relief hearing that. I also knew it was *possible* there were real psychics out there, but it was such a stretch, and I'd never really wanted to go there. It was too touchy for me. I could kick myself for opening my mouth.

A group of loud kids came in and took my attention away from my car for about a minute, make that less than a minute when they said, "Well we see JEL-EEE is back but what about the matching one, where did that one go?"

"What?" I said, suddenly aware of the volume of my voice.

"Yeah, we saw the two of them here the other day, and figured it was quite the bizarro couple or something."

"What plate? What did the other car look like?" Was this the Peanut Butter one or a different one? Had they seen my plate? How humiliating. They must have.

"Silver thing, didn't notice what it was."

"Oh my goodness, when was that again?"

"The other day, I guess. I don't know. Whose car is it?"

"I don't know. I didn't even know it was there!"

"Yeah, like *that* was random!" one of them said sarcastically.

They asked for a to go order and bolted out the door just as fast as they'd come in.

Meg wasn't in that night so I couldn't ask her.

"Oh, man, I don't believe this, *GINNY...*"

I walked back over to Harold and asked if he'd heard the whole thing. He did and sat there quietly amazed. "Well, it's not a coincidence. That happened for a reason, Lainey."

"Oh, wait, they didn't say what the plate was." I looked out the window but didn't see a sign of them.

"Well, if that person *parked* near my car maybe they noticed too. Maybe they'll be back wondering the same thing. I don't think anyone in here has been asked about *who* owns my car or they would have told me. But, then they might have thought it was a customer. Anyway, my guess is, they'll be back."

Poor choice of words, I guess, as the next person to walk in was "Steve the stalker" as I now thought of him. We'd had such a nice start — ha — but this was too much. I told Ginny to seat him since I wasn't going to go near him. Unfortunately, she put him next to some of my other customers and made me deal with him anyway. Clearly, tonight she wasn't actually listening to me.

"Lainey, did you get my message?" he asked eagerly.

"Um, yeah, Steve. Jill's been pretty busy, you know, mother, wife, life, kind of thing. Unless there's something urgent, you might want to chill a bit," I said and could hear the stress in my voice.

"No, you have it all wrong. I'm just wondering, that's all."

CHAPTER 6

Ginny came in the next day and announced that yes, she wanted to take a cooking class after all. Dennis was just so unreceptive to dinner and it was getting on her last nerve.

"I don't know, part of me just wants to throttle him and make him figure this out, but another part... anyway, I'll see how it goes." She sounded very resigned but then exploded again with, "Cooking! And I work in a diner. I should just have him meet me here for dinner. That would solve it. Every night!" Her eyes burned with resentment, but then she settled in again with a deep sigh. "I know, I know, I know, I'll take the class."

"Great! I'll bring in the catalog," I said before she could turn on me again. "I think I have a spare in the car, and we can see what's available right now. My poetry class is over so it's perfect timing." Also thinking, while we still have time, before we have to go job hunting.

I brought in the catalog and we settled on a French cuisine class. I told Ginny it might say it's French but that didn't mean the ingredients were! She could probably handle that. I didn't dare suggest the authentic Indian or Thai classes.

Ginny then squealed with delight flipping the pages. I had no idea the class meant that much to her until she said, "AND LOOK, here Lainey, a psychic workshop! That's perfect! We can take both and solve all our problems at once!"

"Let me see that," I said, swiping the catalog from her. Usually those kinds of workshops were held at a whole different facility, not at the community college; this must be a borderline mainstream kind of class.

But it didn't matter. There it was: a psychic awareness class. Okay, it wasn't as if I would be seeing a psychic, this I could do. Not a private reading, just a do-it-yourself class. More of an intuition thing. I could intuitively know what the cat was all about — and the car, and now the job. Not a problem. Maybe I could tell Mom a thing or two. Scratch that, I would never, ever, ever, bring this up.

Meg walked by and we quietly asked her if she could elaborate on the fate of the diner. She took us to the back and said, "Well, the buyer's name is Walt and he was absolutely fascinated with the structure of the building. I took that as a good sign. I hadn't really ever thought about selling the diner before, but once he made the offer, I did start to think about retirement. And I hate to tell you, but that sounded pretty good."

"But, Meg, selling it?" Ginny winced.

"Like I said, he was so interested in the building, it felt right, not everyone appreciates this kind of retro design. Most would just want it for the land, demo it, and start again. I couldn't do that!

"But more importantly my daughter would really appreciate it if I had more time to spend with my grandchildren. It would help her out so much. Her work has gotten the better of her these days. I've been trying to help here and there, but she needs someone more full time.”

Ginny nodded looking unconvinced that we weren’t losing our jobs.

“Well, we haven’t worked out any details yet, but he was so enthusiastic about this place. I’m still thinking it over, but more and more it’s starting to feel right. I just wanted to let you know a change was in the air. I’m sure you’ll like working for him, or whoever he puts in to manage the place. He has such an upbeat way about him.”

Ginny and I looked at each other not so sure, but tried to smile.

* * *

As an introduction to the cooking class, I had Ginny come over for dinner to cook up something “different.” Easy, but different. I suggested Dennis come along but Ginny thought she’d just bring him something back. I think she wanted to vent without him there.

After we made some gravy and cut up some prepackaged chicken strips, she asked me, “What’s going on with that guy from your class. Do you think he’s interested in you?”

“Doesn’t matter, Ginny. I’m not interested in him, and since I think he’s stalking my sister, I don’t think a relationship would work out.”

“Do you really think he’s stalking her, for real? Maybe there’s some really cool reason he’s so interested. Wouldn’t that be a hoot?”

“A *hoot*? Ginny, this century please!”

“No, really, just think: what if he donated blood for the blood drive and then thought your sister was in an accident and he wanted to know if he saved her life. He’s been curious ever since.”

She pointed the vegetable peeler at me having finished shaving a bunch of carrots.

"You can't even be serious! There was no accident."

"I'm just saying, you decided *not a chance,* before you even heard, or found out what the deal was. Is that how you treat every potential date?"

"First of all, he's not a potential date, I'm not interested in him. But also, it still might be a tad safer than assuming every derelict is really a millionaire in disguise! Not that he's a derelict, I'm just saying." I rinsed off the potatoes I had peeled.

"Lainey! I'm just putting out the possibility that you jump to conclusions before you give them a chance, not that you should hook up with an axe murderer — to use your term. But not every-one is one!" She chopped up the carrots, and I watched as she gave them a little extra oomph with the knife.

"Well, okay, but I really haven't met someone who I've been drawn to or thought 'hmmm, maybe.' It just hasn't happened."

"Okay, maybe that psychic can help you in this department as well."

"GINNY! First off, it's a psychic *awareness* class. She's not going to be doing any readings. And she's not going to pick up on my lack-of-a-love-life vibe, and proclaim I'm cured or anything of the sort." I started to wonder if maybe the class had been an incredibly bad idea after all. Knowing Ginny, she'd probably raise her hand and ask about my love life. Oh, man, my love life, our jobs, the car, and the cat! But of course she'd have to find out about Dennis and dinner too! Yes, big mistake.

"Okay," I continued, "we'll just leave that open for the class. I'm not going to make any psychic predictions about the class myself."

"But I think it's going to be good. I can just feel it."

"Enough with the predictions!" I said, exasperated and wanting to change the subject. I didn't know what I really believed about "real psychics," maybe they could tell you something, but I just wasn't ready to find out. I just didn't want to deal with them.

"Anyway, back to the meal here." I put all the vegetables into a pot with water to boil for a little bit before we added them to the gravy and chicken. We were making a chicken pot pie stew. Basic chicken pot pie, just no crust. We'd throw in croutons at the end and call it done. Different, but all the same stuff. "I keep thinking maybe you just *think* you don't like to cook but part of you really doesn't mind it," I said hopefully.

"It isn't the not liking to cook so much as the same old, same old. Now you've managed to make something a little different here, I don't have that imagination it seems." I really didn't either, and had scoped this one out online but I let her finish.

"And it's same old, same old, in Dennis' eyes at any rate. Well, yeah, I get bored too, I guess, or maybe I just anticipate rejection. I don't know what the exact problem is, maybe it's just the effort of having to dream up something different. Half the time I just leave something for him to reheat anyway, when I'm working the later shift... So, then I don't even really know how he reacts, I just imagine it.

"Maybe that's it, or that it *feels* like so much work. If I had a plan, maybe it wouldn't be so much effort."

"Ah-ha, planned meals," I said. "Do you just go into the grocery store and ask yourself what's for dinner tonight, and then go home and work with what you have? Or do you look through a cookbook or two for ideas beforehand?"

"Not so much with cookbooks, again the effort...I don't know what I'm looking for...Okay, I don't even have cookbooks. So yeah, I end up thinking: what do we have? What do I need to pick up? The usual stuff."

"Maybe we could try and go through a few cookbooks and plan a week's worth of stuff."

"Doesn't that kill the spontaneity? I mean, what if I don't feel like what I planned?"

"Spontaneity, Ginny, hello, you're saying you can't think of anything new to eat. Sometimes spontaneity takes work!" Okay, ironic, but I could see what was holding her up! Not that I was any better at it, often just standing in the kitchen shaking my head, but I got it, sometimes one or two new meals thrown into the mix could help. At least, I didn't have the added pressure of considering what someone *else* would want to eat! Ugh.

I took out a few cookbooks, the ones with great pictures to give Ginny a good idea where she was going and she seemed to be taken by one or two pictures.

"They're not ingredients I would have on hand. Okay, I see that, so that's part of the problem."

"So, you make a list. I know, I know, the spontaneity, but how's this, the spontaneous part is when you're dreaming it up, not the day you cook it, does that help?"

"Okay, I gotta admit that makes it feel better! You're brilliant."

"Obviously."

CHAPTER 7

Jill called me in the morning and told me to meet her at my mother's apartment. Apparently, there was a problem with her move. I asked what she was talking about but she wouldn't go into it. Typical Jill to keep me guessing. I wanted to ask if Seth would be there, since I was not in the mood to deal with him telling me what I should do with the plate. Even though I had tried to return it again, it would make no difference to him. I'd still get some flack over it.

On my way over, I spotted another car with the plate 2-B-OR. There was no "not to be." All the way over I kept asking myself, "To be or what? To be or what?" As I pulled into my mother's parking lot I smiled to myself suddenly thinking, "To be or ELSE!" There was no way that was what they intended, but it worked for me. Made no sense, but it worked.

"So, what seems to be the problem?" I asked my mother when I got there.

"What are you talking about? And nice to see you too, Lainey."

"Jill told me to meet her here. She said you were having some kind of problem with the move. Is that...what's going on?"

"I haven't talked to Jill. She isn't coming over to my knowledge."

"Well, that's what she told me. I thought you had a problem, she sounded…" I paused for a moment. "I'll bet Jill's got a problem and didn't want to say in front of Seth or Janie. What do you think?"

"I think we'll have to wait and see if she gets here. Anyway, let me put some coffee on. This sounds like it could take a bit. Let me see what I have to eat."

"Oh, I'm okay. Just the coffee, thanks."

"Fine, but I need something. I wasn't expecting either of you, not that that's a problem." She smiled and opened the cabinet for the coffee. "I just… let me get the coffee." She shook her head, sounding thoroughly bewildered.

We settled into her quaint little kitchen, the tiny table had three chairs around it that you could actually sit on and a fourth wedged between the table and wall. She fixed the coffee and then fixed herself a bowl of instant oatmeal and some toast. It was a quick meal I'd seen her eat all too often, oddly spooning the oatmeal onto the toast, like a cheese spread or something. Or jelly. My face fell the second the word hit me. But my mother thought I was sensing something ominous would be coming from Jill.

"You think it's that bad with Jill?" she asked, leaning forward with intensity.

"No, I'm just… no, just lost in thought," I tried to cover and was spared when we heard the rap at the door.

"JILL," my mother semi-screamed and ran to open the already opening door. "Jill, honey, what's wrong?"

Jill threw up her hands exasperated. "Hi, Mom. Hi Lainey, I know," she said, looking past my mother to me. "I don't know if he was even listening, but I just couldn't talk with Seth there. I just can't stop thinking about that guy from high school. It's driving me crazy but I don't want Seth to know."

"What?" my mother and I said in unison.

"Jill, what happened?" I asked, feeling somehow responsible for the whole situation. "Did he contact you, or did you get in touch with him? I feel like he's been stalking me trying to get information about you and it's been really bugging me. But I haven't really told him much more or anything."

"He has?" she asked, looking stunned. "Wow, no, I haven't talked to him yet, but I just can't stop thinking about what he might want."

"Wait, you haven't talked to him and you're in a tizzy?" I pressed, although I'd been presuming just as much or more.

"What's that all about, Jill?" my mother asked, looking at her very suspiciously. I had no idea if Jill had even mentioned this guy to our mother. They were closer, she probably had.

"Why don't you just see what he wants before you work yourself up like this? What are you doing anyway? You have no idea what he's going to say." Now I was thinking clearly, now that it was her problem.

"*I know*, but I can guess, can't I? That's what has me so flustered. I just know I'm not going to know how to handle whatever he has to say."

"Jill, you're assuming what? That he's interested in you and is going to ask you to leave your husband and run away with him? Is that where you're going with this?" my mother said, now giving her the look only a mother can give, and get away with.

"Oh, I know it sounds crazy."

"So, you *are* thinking that?" my mother demanded.

"Well, I don't know, but what if it is something along those lines. Something far-fetched like that," she said in her most delicate voice.

"Why is that even an issue? You're happily married, *right*?" fragments of anger were starting to show on my mother's face.

"Oh, of course, of course, I just…" she trailed off like she just couldn't pull the thought out, or my mother had scared it from her.

"Jill, I'd just call the guy, get it over with. If he makes a play for you, you're not available, don't encourage him and that's all there is to it." Way to go, Lainey, I congratulated myself. "I told him you're married. Probably six times. Why don't you call him from here? Then, if you don't want him to call you again, he'll have mom's number on the caller ID if he has it. I'm sure he'd love to chat with her and all!" I said while my mother gave me the nod of her head and an "oh, yeah" smile.

"You think?"

"Jill, call and get whatever nonsense is in your head out," my mother told her sternly.

"Okay, okay, I do have the number. This is a work number anyway, right?"

"Yeah, he gave me his business card, so it must be."

"Okay, okay," she said, breathing a little bit deeper, and dialed. She walked all of four feet away from us into the living room.

We heard her exchange all the usual pleasantries and then update him on who did what and when, then she listened for a bit with a few, "oh reallys" and she smiled at us and hung up.

"He just wanted to say 'hi.' That's all, not a problem, I guess I overreacted."

"Wait, that's it? What was all that, 'you did?' and, 'are you sure?’ all about?”

“I’m not sure, since he was talking about work and stuff, his family, when they moved... I don’t know it was all just to say hello again, sorry I dragged you into this. Really. Okay, that’s done. I guess I should head back home, unless... say, how’s it going with the new house, Mom?”

With one fell swoop, she dismissed the entire event.

My mother was even less forthcoming telling us it was going “slowly, it’s going slowly” and that was about that. We asked if there was anything she needed, but “no” was her standard answer for everything from if we could help, to if she’d be moving by the end of the month.

“In news from the diner,” I decided to tell Jill now, and get that over with too, “is that Meg is probably going to sell the place. There’s this guy that really loves our building and he’s looking to buy it. She hasn’t given us much more information than that, but we’re all hoping it’s just a transfer of ownership.”

“But you might lose your job?”

“Well it’s a possibility, but I got the feeling that he just loved the fact that it was a diner, and he’d probably keep it as it is. I don’t know, but that was how it sounded.” I was really trying to stay with this optimistic thing.

“Oh, because what would you do otherwise?” Jill asked, purposely throwing that reality in my face.

“Well, I could get another waitress job, I suppose. If I had to. But really, I don’t think it’s going to come to that,” I said, so very unsure of myself.

“No?”

“No,” I said, shaking my head no, completely unsure.

"Hmm," my mother added in her most skeptical tone.

I looked back and forth to each with my, *oh of course it's going to be fine,* expression, but thinking of how much I did not want to have to find a new job, and refusing to blurt out, "I have absolutely no idea what I'm about to do."

All and all, a great time at Mom's.

• CHAPTER 8 •

My class with Ginny would last for eight weeks on Thursday evenings, which could have made it a little tight juggling our schedules, but Meg was agreeable about switching people around, so we were lucky. I hoped our new owners would be as flexible, if it came to that.

The class was held in what looked like a home economics classroom. I couldn't imagine what the real college had for classes in there. Did they have home economics of some kind?

I think Ginny was expecting someone like Julia Child to be teaching the class because she started looking around the room like *where is she?* when this petite woman, with short curly blonde hair, began speaking to us. In that moment, I suddenly realized if either one of us had thought of it, we could probably watch a few cooking shows a whole lot easier than this! I'd best keep that revelation to myself.

The class looked to be pretty full, and Ginny and I felt right at home with all of our diner expertise. We weren't the cooks at the diner, mind you, but we knew our way around a kitchen gadget or two. Just don't ask us about the food.

Upfront with our French chef, a.k.a. Lori, there were all sorts of spices and oils and miscellaneous ingredients she had assembled telling us what we might be interested in trying and why.

There were a couple of folks there who looked like they never spent a minute in the kitchen. One guy was joking that he'd never actually been in a "real" kitchen before, but that he did know his way around the refrigerator. Meanwhile, another woman was whispering to her neighbor that she too had no idea what half the stuff was for, and was feeling a bit overwhelmed.

Our teacher, who didn't seem much older than me, was quite the powerhouse of information on traditional French cuisine. I was grateful we only wanted to learn a recipe or two and wouldn't actually be graded on the course, since I already felt I was falling behind! Ginny must have been feeling the same way because the minute Lori started talking about the multitude of cheeses consumed and where and when they were typically used, I could see a bit of panic in her eyes.

A woman sitting next to me meanwhile was busily taking notes, trying not to miss one tidbit of information. I mentioned the notes to her at the first break and she said her new boyfriend was French and she wanted to make a good impression on him. Ginny piped in with "Oh, don't worry honey, one good lasagna and he's yours for life!" She looked suddenly confused, but I smiled and told her I was sure he'd appreciate all her efforts. Even Italian food!

Then, Ginny pulled me aside and said, "I'm telling you, you don't understand how serious being food compatible with your mate is. She's got a lot to learn."

"Well, it looks like she's trying."

"Alright, but the bit about the lasagna is also true, so I do know what I'm saying. Maybe we're both on the right track though, I probably should have done this years ago with Dennis."

"I hope he likes French food," I said, knowing this particular class was my idea.

"Anything *different* right now, that's all he's looking for, so I'm sure this will be fine." She sighed.

The woman sitting on the other side of Ginny turned to her during the next mini break. "You feel like you should know this stuff but who has time?"

"I know what your mean." Ginny laughed. "I'm here to basically get dinner ideas, if you can believe it. My husband looks at me as if I've served him stale bread for dinner every night. It's getting on my nerves."

"Oh, you're cooking for *others*, I can't imagine! It's just *me* and I feel overwhelmed. How did my mother do it? I ask myself all the time. I'd never ask her, though. I know I wouldn't like the answer!"

"Gotcha!" Ginny smiled. "Well, my friend, Lainey, here talked me into the class." She pointed to me and gave me an evil eye.

"Oh, an accomplice, I get it! I had to drag my sorry self here alone. But I wanted to get motivated. I'm Anna, by the way," she said. "So, do you think we'll be pros in eight weeks?"

"Well, I figure that's time enough to learn four meals we like, and four we don't," Ginny said, and then introduced herself.

After the round of information from Lori, we began with a dessert, a basic chocolate mousse. Dessert — I hadn't thought about that! We whipped those together with gusto.

Then after putting those in the refrigerator to chill, we went on to make a basic quiche, well in our case here, a couple of mini quiches. They cooked faster. She told us this is where we could have some fun because there were so many variations we could make. It really was just what we felt like, and this was one place we could really experiment. I looked over at Ginny and nodded. Anna was smiling too.

By the time the class was over, we had decided Anna was our new best friend.

"I work as a medical receptionist over at the cancer center, which means I live and breathe insurance forms, so this is a nice change of atmosphere!" Anna told us as we were packing up our stuff to leave.

"Lainey and I work at Milly's Diner," Ginny told her. "You might make the natural cooking association, that we already know oodles about cooking, but it's anything but! We, rather I, needed to learn to make a few new things for my husband! Lainey's just being a good sport!"

We were still talking about what we'd do after we'd learned all eight recipes, and then still didn't know what to make for dinner as we were walking out of the building. Ginny wasn't sure how many other types of cooking classes she was prepared to take, and was saying how our schedules may go haywire in a while with the diner, when Anna suggested we think about taking turns researching a meal and then getting together to all try and make it.

I could see that this could be fun to do. I wondered if it was also something I could really get into, and I started to think about this as a long-term idea. Was this something that could actually work for me? I'd never really thought of it before.

We chatted all the way to the parking lot and were just about to part ways when Anna saw my license plate and pointed to it laughing. "Look at that, isn't that something! You think they were here for the cooking class? I wonder who owns that car?"

Ginny and I stared at each other.

Slowly the words came out of my mouth, "That's actually my car. It was a mistake at the registry and I got stuck with it."

"You're kidding! That's so funny, don't you think? But here's something even weirder — my neighbor's plate is GRAPE!" she said, sounding really excited. "We'll have to get together at my place, Gerry has to see this! You'll have to meet Gerry!"

Something in my stomach lurched. I wasn't sure if it was a massive grip of fear or a bad reaction to the quiche and mousse we'd consumed. Either way, I knew it was time to bolt.

"Well, I really should get going, we'll figure this out next class okay?"

"Sure," she said, probably feeling totally cut off.

I jumped into the car feeling completely nauseated. Ginny continued to talk to Anna waving goodbye to me, slowly walking away from the car.

I should have driven in with Ginny. I should have taken her car, was all I could think. For all the kidding around we had done with PNT-BTR, I felt meeting that person would *never* become a reality. It was one thing to see the oddball plates out on the road, but I had no interest in meeting these folks. PNT-BTR was probably someone just like Harold Burns, an older gent only married, grandkids. Someone I'd never really have to deal with. But to actually come face to face with another person with a related plate, was now causing me such anxiety. I did not want to meet this Gerry. I did not want to see the "grape" car. I did not want to have to deal with this, not now, not *ever*.

GRAPE—what kind of a person drives a car that says GRAPE?

My head was screaming. That had to be intentional. It made the fact that I had this ridiculous plate seem ten times worse.

I got to the next red light and realized my hands were completely clenched on the wheel. I tried to pry them open momentarily and it felt like some sort of supernatural force was working against them.

If I didn't have the JEL EEE plate, GRAPE wouldn't have been a problem. I wouldn't even care. But this felt *way* too freaky. It was the idea that this was some kind of cosmic setup. And never in a million years was I going to be setup based on that plate of mine! It wasn't funny, it wasn't right, and I didn't want to be identified with it. And as bad as my plate was alone, I felt like the combination of plates would make me a total laughingstock.

I got to the next red light, my hands now mechanically opening and closing, and I noticed the car in front of me to the left, had a license plate that read, DRM2BE.

LEAVE ME ALONE. I could hear myself screaming inside, JUST LEAVE ME ALONE!

Chapter 9

"So, I exchanged numbers with Anna and she's going to call this week. So how weird was that with the plate?" Ginny said all swirly the next day at work.

"I know, I know, I know," was all I could say at first but then had to add, "I don't think I want to meet this guy, Ginny, I don't feel very good about this at all."

"Oh, Lainey, he's just a neighbor. It's just a funny coincidence. It's not like you're obligated to marry him or anything!" She was clearly trying to make a joke out of it.

"I KNOW," I said *way* too loud. Feeling this no longer had anything to do with Ginny or Anna. No, Anna hadn't said it like it was some kind of a setup, but somehow and for some reason I still felt like it was. Me, and what was his name... Gerry. Gerry the GRAPE. GRAPE GERRY! Oh, no. Oh, no. It was getting worse and worse.

Meg came in and completely interrupted my train of thought, telling us how excited her daughter was that she would be retiring. Her daughter's job had gotten so much more demanding in the last few years and knowing that she would be around to help out with her kids really put her at ease. Meg seemed so happy with the idea — even a little giddy.

I knew Ginny was as apprehensive as I was that the new folks wouldn't be anything at all like Meg, but we did want the best for her.

"Well at least it looks like it's all going to work out," I said, trying to work up some enthusiasm for her and she smiled.

I turned to the door and in walked Steve the stalker. "I have to get this one," I said to Ginny motioning towards Steve. "Jill made contact with him, and all is fine. I just have to say hello," I told her, before she got all concerned for me.

No longer actually feeling he was a stalker, I went over to seat him. After he was settled, and I took his order, he took out a small box.

"I was wondering if you could give this to Jill for me?" he asked. "I thought I'd be able to do it myself but I'm going to be out of town for a while now on business and I really want her to have it."

"What is it?" I asked a bit confused and suddenly anxious all over again.

"It's a necklace," he said.

"You're giving her a necklace?" I demanded. "What is going on? Why would you be sending my sister jewelry now? What is the deal with you two?"

"Huh? What do you mean with us two?"

"I mean she's acting all weird and now you're giving her jewelry. Why don't you give it to her yourself?"

"No, this is *her* necklace. She lost it in high school. I found it, but didn't have a chance to return it. There's nothing going on here. I was embarrassed I still had it after all this time, and wanted to *return* it. What do you mean she's acting weird?"

"Wait a minute... *Her necklace*?"

"Yeah, it's hers." He proceeded to open the box. I couldn't believe what I was seeing. On many occasions, Jill would borrow jewelry from my mother or myself. This necklace of "Jill's" was none other than my mother's favorite necklace that my father had given to her on their tenth anniversary. It was a delicate gold chain with a filigree drop, mixed with a spiral of tiny sapphires and emeralds. Like an ocean wave, my mother said.

Jill never told my mother or me that she was the one that had lost it, leading my mother to believe she had lost it herself. Some psychic, huh? My mother would be so happy to have it back, but if *I* returned it to Jill, Jill would be forced to confess to my mother that she'd lost it, since she would know I knew. I wondered if she was up to that. No doubt, Jill didn't expect the return route to go through me! That would not sit too well with her. I could tell Steve he had to return it to Jill himself or...

"Thanks," I said, taking the box. "She'll be thrilled to get it back."

* * *

I could hear Ginny talking to Harold about the GRAPE. "Lainey," he called over to me. "Seems we've been barking up the wrong tree, huh?"

"Hi, Harold," I replied. "Well, who knows." Even I could hear the weariness in my voice.

"No, this could be a very good thing. I think I need to give you an attitude adjustment somehow," he said as he stirred his coffee.

"An attitude adjustment! Thanks, Harold, that's all I need!"

"Lainey, you're resisting a good thing!" he said, seeming very excited.

"How do you know this is a good thing?" I asked. "This might be a horrible thing. This might be the worst thing to ever happen to me. How can you just say this is a good thing when you don't know?" I demanded and then immediately felt awful for blasting Harold, who was only trying to help me out.

"Sorry," I said quickly.

"Lainey, all I'm saying is it's a quirk in the fabric. Just have some fun with it. If you think of it as fun, then no matter what, it's a laugh, right? I think you're taking this too seriously. All I'm saying is you got a lemon, make a little lemon meringue pie!"

"Sounds like work," I said wearily again, but trying to smile. "Maybe Ginny would like to try that!"

"Hey, keep me out of this."

"You're right in the middle, and hey, *you* keep bringing *me* in deeper and deeper!"

"When do you meet this person anyway?" Harold wanted to know.

"Oh, we haven't set anything up yet," I started but Ginny interrupted.

"Sometime next week. We'll see Anna on Thursday night and check in then."

"Anyway, nothing's definite yet," I said more to comfort myself than negate Ginny.

"Well, you know I'll be back in to check on things," he said with a big smile, which made me suspect more radio show snooping was in the works but I smiled back.

"Attitude adjustment. I'll see what I can do," I said more under my breath than to Harold, and went back to check on some of my other customers.

* * *

After work, I knew I had to give Jill a call but sat for the longest time wondering exactly what to say to her. "Hey, you'll never believe what I got," or "Jill, something you'd like to tell me about Steve?" No, that would never do. "So, imagine my surprise…"

The phone rang mid-thought.

"Jill, hey, I was just going to call…" As soon as I figured out what I was going to say.

"Have you seen that guy Steve again?" she asked. "He was going to get in touch with me but he's not answering his phone."

"Um, as a matter of fact he came by. He's going out of town on business for a bit, so he left something with me."

"He did?" I could hear the gulp.

"Yes, Jill, he did. Do you care to explain?"

"Explain, what's to explain? If he gave it to you, you get it. I lost it, he had it." Hit that nerve pretty hard. "Don't tell Mom. I'll deal with it."

Then, she hung up.

• Chapter 10 •

Ginny and I had signed up for our psychic awareness classes, which were on Tuesday nights. Paula said she'd cover for Ginny, and I often had Tuesday off, so I was good. And this one was just a couple of classes.

Our first class was just days before we would meet up with Anna again. I was nervous about going, and then remembered it wasn't a reading, so I didn't have to be nervous. It probably wouldn't amount to all that much anyway. I'd be told how to be more intuitive, more aware. I probably would not become more psychic, given my history.

If Ginny had been expecting Julia Child in the French cuisine class, I was expecting the gypsy queen psychic and once again got anything but. Stephanie looked like an English teacher. Short clipped brown hair. Perfect posture. A tan suit jacket and skirt with a brown no frills blouse. Flat brown shoes.

"You were expecting someone more new-agey," she said to all of us, and got a chuckle out of the class. I think we were an easy target.

"Honing your intuitive skills doesn't require an outfit, we've all been doing it for years," she started.

And just like that, I was hit with anxiety 101. I had this feeling she was going to uncover something I really didn't want to know. Something that was lurking under all the layers of frustration I felt about my mother. I started franticly thinking why was I in this class again? I looked over at Ginny who was totally absorbed. I was, without a doubt, on planet *get me out of here.*

"Some of you are here out of curiosity. Some of you were dragged by others." She looked right at me, *right at me,* even Ginny turned to me eyes wide open, unbelievable. "And some of you have been trying with little success to get in touch with your 'psychic' or intuitive side."

I was getting nervous and clearly starting to fidget. The piece about not really knowing if my mother was "for real" started to nag at me. There was something else there, something really bothering me that I just didn't get.

Ginny was hooked. Absolutely spell bound. I was having trouble paying attention, then I heard the words, "but with some people, if they're too closed, they won't get anything." Did that mean she couldn't read me, if I was too closed, or *I* couldn't read me?

* * *

Anna had called Ginny while we were at the psychic awareness class. She said she would see us in class Thursday and she'd been wrong about the plate and that she'd explain when she saw us. I felt like a huge weight was removed and I could breathe again. Grape Gerry was not going to be a problem after all. I could relax.

Then, on Thursday before our class began she said, "Well

you're going to laugh, but I guess his plate doesn't really say *grape* after all.

"Oh," I felt the sigh of relief again.

"His plate says *great PE* spelt 'GR8 PE' after the plastic industry he works in. But people think it's grape all the time. I think he likes that.

"Then I told him all about your plate. He laughed and said he'd still like to meet you."

"Why, it's a mistake right? That should be the end of that!" I said, trying to sound lighthearted at the same time.

"Well, you don't have to, he just wanted to meet you because he said he'd actually seen your car before at a diner and took a picture of it. He wasn't sure if it was a customer or someone who worked there."

"Wait, at the diner... Does he have a silver car?" I asked remembering the kids who'd seen the cars together. Was it this grape car and not the PNT BTR one?

"Yes, it is silver. Why?"

"Some kids mentioned they saw the two of them together."

Why was I being subjected to this? How much humiliation could I take from that thing. I was parking in the back from now on. That was it: enough was enough.

"Oh how fun. Anyway," Anna continued, clueless to my ordeal, "I was looking through some recipes this week and I have one I think might be fun to try, want to come over anyway and just do our own cooking class? Nothing too elaborate."

I didn't want to answer just yet, still uncomfortable with the plate, but Ginny said, "Well, you know I did try our first dish on Dennis, and he was fine with it, just a little different. Not overwhelmed, but I've made quiche before. I used canned asparagus this time so it was a little different. Fresh might have been better but there's still the whole time factor." She looked from me to Anna and then a guilt-ridden confession poured out of her, "Okay, so I didn't make the crust either. My version is quiche in a muffin tin. Perfect little size, but I skip the crust. They're small so he'll eat a bunch of them, I just don't call it quiche." We both nodded like that made perfect sense to us.

"Anyway, I'll be trying tonight's out on him tomorrow as well. More than one in a week, wow, I don't know if we can handle that." Then, she laughed. "What's a good time?"

It was like pulling teeth at that moment. The cooking, yes, but Gerry, no. I just...oooh...and we settled on late Saturday morning.

* * *

Ginny stopped by my apartment so we could go together to Anna's. With the directions in hand, I said to her, "Do you want to drive?" Completely forgetting my car was one reason for the meeting, also having complete amnesia that I was somehow involved in all this. But only momentarily.

"No, you're driving, Lainey. You're driving the jelly-mobile, remember?"

"Oh, right, yeah of course," I said, coming back to reality and all my fears.

"I can drive it for you..." Miss helpful said.

"NO, no, I just forgot, okay? I'm...I just don't want to do this is all."

We arrived at Anna's, and her apartment building had a small "L" shaped parking lot. I slowly drove past each and every car and to my surprise the silver GR8 PE was nowhere to be found.

"Guess he's a no show!" I said to Ginny as we circled back and found an empty spot to park in.

"Or he's coming later," she said reviving my dread. "I don't know if Anna set an exact time with him, just a vague drop over."

"Yeah, whatever." We got out and buzzed Anna's doorbell. She buzzed us in and had her door already opened as we approached.

"This is going to be such fun!" she squealed as my stomach lurched once again. "I've got a great recipe for us to try. I hope we all like it. I realized I don't really know which way your tastes run, I guess I'm assuming since you work in a diner they're pretty traditional, but I'll bet each of us has a different take on what traditional is, depending on what we grew up with." She stopped and took a breath. "I'm rambling. I guess I'm nervous you really won't like it." She grinned, a little too wild eyed. I finally had to laugh. I thought I was the only nervous one in the group.

"Anyway, I thought we'd go simple but different. I'm going to assume none of us want anything that takes too long to cook, or is too involved! I for one don't own a food processor, so why don't we say no recipes that use one."

Ginny and I nodded at the same time, while she exclaimed, "Awesome!"

"Okay, then I've got a cheeseburger pie recipe and salt and vinegar potatoes, are you with me?"

"This is gonna be good!" Ginny said, looking pretty excited.

* * *

Anna's apartment was small but really nice, tidy and sparse actually. When we walked in, we were in the living room with the dining room to the right. There was a galley kitchen just off the dining room. The bedroom and bath were just beyond the living room. Beige carpet, white walls. She had a bright red and violet carpet laid on the diagonal in the living room to add a big punch of color, and then I noticed all her accessories —pillows and knick-knacks — were all in reds and violet too. On the dining room table, a small round four-seater, she had a stack of blue-violet ceramic plates and bowls with four red placemats. After all the red and violet, wicker baskets were her next accessory. Any clutter seemingly filling baskets all around the place.

Her kitchen had white laminate cabinets and counters, peppered with red utensils and small appliances, violet tea towels and pot holders balanced the room. Wicker baskets sat along the countertop.

"Wow! Your place has a lot of energy to it!" Ginny said, taking it all in. Her own house being a blend of hand me downs from both her parents and Dennis'. All of it was very solid, well worn, and completely mismatched. Not unlike my apartment.

"Really, lot of energy," I repeated. "Wow."

"Oh, I know," Anna said, looking a little embarrassed. "I work in offices of cream and beige, with hints of mint green and peach all day long. Soothing, calming, designed for the patients, and by the time I get out of there, I need color, something bold. I know I went crazy but... it actually does serve the purpose for me."

"No, don't apologize. It's nice! It really does have a lot of energy," Ginny said.

I was still on the fence, so I said, "Truly, a lot of energy!" Part of me felt all that color would wear on me after a fashion but at the moment it looked great.

"Well, thanks! Let's get started with the dinner! Well, early afternoon dinner! I want to show you all the stuff I got."

She had printed out recipes for each of us, clearly an office gal. I wouldn't have thought to do that, and now, well now she'd set the bar a little higher for us. I was hoping I could keep up.

We got started on our meal and did start to have a little fun, tasting, complaining, and oohing and ahhing as we went. I had completely forgotten about our soon to be guest as we were polishing off the meal, all our leftovers still on the table, when there was a knock at the door. "Hi Anna, it's Gerry."

Again with the stomach lurch only this time it was personal. "I need your bathroom," I said to Anna with a sense of urgency.

"Yeah, right there." She pointed as she went over to open the door.

I made it to the bathroom just in time, and could hear the conversation in bits and pieces through my distress. "Oh, what looks so good?" Lots of laughter. Normally a good sign. Today... not quite so much. I steadied myself, splashed just a bit of cold water on my face and then knew that was a mistake, as it washed away most of my make-up and I could see and feel my face growing redder and redder.

Composure, composure, composure.

I opened the door and could see Gerry's back, who didn't know I was there yet, and proceeded to walk back through the living room only to trip on the protruding corner of Anna's red and violet rug.

"Lainey!" both Ginny and Anna rushed at me as I hit both the couch and the small coffee table in my decent.

"Oh, oh, I'm... I'm humiliated," I said, making my way upright again and put on my most convincing smile.

"Are you okay?" Gerry said now in front of me as well, and extended his hand, at which point I wasn't sure if it was to help me or just to shake as an introduction.

"I'm—I'm—I'm..." was the best I could do, looking down and brushing myself off, and then finally said, "So you're the grape. I'm Lainey." I extended my hand to shake.

"Well, not exactly. I'm Gerry," he said, smiling and shaking my hand. "Didn't Anna tell you? It's not really grape." He gave my hand a slight squeeze at the end. "It's great PE."

"Yeah, oh, of course, that's right," I said absolutely dizzy with embarrassment. It must have been Anna's apartment, screaming with the color purple. GRAPE, GRAPE, GRAPE.

I sat on the couch before my legs gave out. Gerry sitting quickly as if afraid to be left standing.

"But, it's true a lot of people make that mistake," he continued, smiling as if he wanted them to make that mistake, but I could only stare at him because I'd lost the beginning of the sentence in my head. So, I smiled and nodded.

"But isn't it a hoot?" Ginny said, eyes aglow. "Lainey's plate was a mistake at the registry. You saw it outside, right? I just think it's such a hoot. So, Gerry, what is it you do? Lainey and I work over at Milly's Diner."

"Oh I've been there," he said. "I even saw your plate there when I was there, but I thought it was a customers'. Good meatloaf."

"Yeah, well, that's Meg's recipe," Ginny piped in. "She owns the place. Pretty standard fare, but that's what you want in a diner! Anyway, that's why we were taking a cooking class: to get a little more variety and then we met Anna. Funny how that all worked out," she rambled on.

"So, Meg must love your plate, at a diner," he said to me.

"Oh, she does!" Ginny was just having a grand time answering for me, and I was having a grander time not speaking.

"I'm in plastic parts actually," Gerry said, now answering the first part of Ginny's question. "Or I was. I seem to be moving more into general plastics at this point, but it's all related. Not the most interesting if you're not in the business, but, anyway, I see you ladies are still having dinner here, so I'll…"

"No," Anna said, "we're just about finished here, and I thought I invited you for coffee and dessert. Why don't you stay for that! I promise I won't tell Karen," she said, teasing him and went into the kitchen.

"Karen's your wife?" Ginny asked.

"No, Karen's my sister. I've been staying with her while I find a new job. The company I worked for had layoffs recently and I was part of the casualties. But see, Karen only eats organic food, and I might just be something of a disgrace to her working in plastics and all!" He added a little reluctantly.

"And no, I'm not married," he continued, looking back at Ginny who smiled.

"Well, I am," she said, and then added, "and that's another reason I'm taking the cooking class, I needed ideas for my husband, I just dragged Lainey into it."

I could not have forced a syllable out of my mouth, so I smiled. Emphasis on Lainey again. We didn't need to do that.

"Chocolate oatmeal cookies and ice cream," Anna announced. "Almost good for you!" She brought out the cookies we'd assembled before Gerry's arrival, and little dishes of vanilla ice cream. The cookies were "no bake," but you still had to cook them on the stove, then drop them on a sheet of waxed paper, and they were done. The ice cream blended perfectly with them. "Coffee, anyone?"

We all had the cookies and ice cream, then coffee with a few more cookies, and proclaimed the meal a success.

"We could have done ice cream sandwiches!" Anna said when we were all done, and we all laughed, but I could tell she was very proud she had thought of something else we could have done with them!

I then announced I had to go in to work soon. I had intentionally left my usual schedule intact, much to Ginny's annoyance, but I knew I wouldn't be able to get through the whole day if I didn't have an out. I'd barely made it as it was!

"Sure, you go to work," Ginny said, getting up to leave with me. "And I must slave away making dinner for Dennis!" she said, shaking the doggie bag she'd made for him.

Aside from the whole Gerry thing, the dinner had been fun, and I wondered if despite Ginny's sarcasm, she'd take to the whole cooking thing too.

• Chapter 11 •

I had a message on my machine from Jill when I got home. She wanted to know if I would go with her to return the necklace to my mother. Very brave, I thought at first, then I thought, what a chicken calling me. But what were sisters for, if not moral support? Of course, she'd have left me in the dirt, but why be petty? I called her back and we decided to go early the next day before my shift.

My mother looked absolutely stunned when the two of us appeared at her door. Jill was afraid she'd chicken out so we didn't bother to call. Just do it, get it over with, let the chips fall where they may.

"Umm, the strangest thing happened," Jill began and then she took out the necklace. My mother just stared at her and asked her to repeat where she got it. "That guy, Steve, that's actually why he called, he's had this since high school. I must have lost it, and he found it." Jill took a deep breath but my mother's eyes were already welling. She took the necklace and stared at it for a long moment of silence. "It's like a piece of me has come home," she said very quietly as the tears fell down her face.

I felt like I was looking at a whole different version of my mother. The one before my dad died.

Jill and I had shared a room in a house that was probably no bigger than my mother's apartment now. She sold the house after we moved out. But growing up it was just home. And it was a happy home. The house was essentially a box with four rooms and a bath. We had two bedrooms on one side, and a kitchen and living room on the other, with the bathroom wedged between the bedrooms. But, we also had a screened in porch that ran along the whole front of the house, which doubled as a playroom for Jill and me. We had a couple of old-fashioned school chairs with the attached writing board that could fold down. We used them for all of our projects, puzzles, toys, games. All of which were stacked on a bookcase at the end of the porch. There was also a glider out there, and our parents would sit there talking late into the night.

They had been such a happy couple, my folks. I never really spent any time thinking about that anymore.

* * *

"Did you hear that?" I asked as we were midway back to Jill's house. Jill had left her car at home. I had gone to her house and we rode together to my mother's place in my car.

"What? I didn't... Oh, that?" Jill answered as the metallic scraping noise grew ever louder.

"Oh, no, that's not good. I'd better pull over," I said, already doing so.

"Oh, Lainey, what is it?"

"How should I know?" I answered, rather shortly but knowing she was just being concerned.

"Well, you'd better call someone," she was quick to reply. I could probably drive it for a bit but I had one of those "this could get ugly" feelings and knew she was right.

"Yeah, did you happen to bring your cell?" I asked her, since I didn't have mine on me, and again did not want a conversation on how irresponsible it was not to have one with you at all times in this day and age.

"Honestly," she started, which I interpreted as the lecture part, but then she abandoned it. "Yeah, here I have it." She fished it out of her pocketbook.

"Let's see," I said, going through the glove compartment for warranty numbers and whatever else I could find.

I called for a tow and could feel my blood pressure rise as I told him the plate was "J E L-E E E." But I spelled it out, not wanting to say the word once again.

"Wait a minute, is that jelly? Like the food? You must have been hungry when you ordered that one!"

"Yeah, I know, what a riot, eh?" I replied to his all too witty take on my plate.

"I'll call Seth when we get to the garage," Jill informed me. "Maybe he can come and pick us up if it's going to be a while."

I nodded with the heavy shame of having to accept Seth's help.

The tow truck arrived shortly, put my car on the bed, and we squeezed into the cabin. The view was altogether different so high up there in the cabin, which was pretty exciting for the better part of a minute and a half. Then as we took off, we discovered the driver was pretty intent on tailgating the cars in front of us, lurching on the breaks every other second, taking us for quite a ride! Relieved to arrive still intact at the garage. We descended, weak knees and all, into the waiting room.

As I relayed the information about the metallic noise to the mechanic, Jill didn't miss a beat calling Seth to come and save her. I heard her say, "Not now, she's been through enough here," and I knew it was yet another jab about the license plate.

He was probably asking, "Why did I still have that plate? What was wrong with me…?" and on and on, while I was secretly thinking, *hey, didn't you give the car a 'once over?'* So much for his advice!

"You may tell your husband I did try to return the plate." I informed Jill when she hung up. "And again, they would not take it back."

"You did?" She sounded astonished.

"Yes. So, yes — I am stuck with it." I wasn't going into the details. She'd pick up on the fact that I could try yet again, when the supervisor was back. (Which was never going to happen — and I wasn't having that conversation!)

The mechanic returned after a while and all I actually heard was something had knocked something loose, and there was something stuck in the undercarriage and they'd have to take it out, might take a while to remove it, and make sure there wasn't something else going on there. Although, he might have actually used real mechanical terms. I think at one point I had the option of waiting for one item, but I had to get to work later so that really wasn't an option for me.

Jill smiled. "Well, Seth's on his way anyway, so we'll be fine."

"Excellent. Now, Jill, have you figured out what's going on with Seth, or is that still a mystery?" I decided to probe while we waited for him.

"No, nothing more, it was just a feeling," she said, straightening out her shirt a little bit, and brushing off some imaginary lint from her slacks. "I'm sure there's nothing more to it."

"Oh, sure." I nodded my head, deciding she meant that she'd wished she'd never mentioned it to me. Now I actually wanted to get to the bottom of it. Perhaps, I'd even ask my mother's take on it.

Seth arrived shortly after that, and then dropped me off at home. I settled in, arranged a little bit of carpooling with Ginny, and then it occurred to me that not a single item in my mother's apartment had been moved. Nothing was in the process of being moved either, not a cardboard box, no bubble wrap, tissue paper, nothing. Nothing was different and I wondered what the deal was. Was she even moving at all? Why was everything still so secret?

CHAPTER 12

I wanted Ginny to let me out of the psychic awareness class, but since she was my chauffeur now, she wasn't about to let me. My car would be ready on Wednesday; three small, out of stock, parts later, and some wild explanation that only Seth would understand and somehow still probably blame me for. Why was I feeling I had to defend myself again? It was my car after all. I did have a warranty. Fuming silently to myself, I got in the car with Ginny, and off we went.

Stephanie had different pamphlets and book lists for us this time. Intuitive skills we could work on. Ginny again absorbed. I, again, felt like *get me home*. The last class had unnerved me. I wasn't sure where this one was going to go.

She did tell us a bit about each pamphlet and I got it that this was just an intro to so many other classes we could take. But this was all just so out of my comfort zone.

One pamphlet was on something called tapping, and had info on our energy meridians and all kinds of things over my head.

Another pamphlet described doing what they called rewriting your story to change your life. I mused over that one for a bit. If I could rewrite my story I would certainly have things work out a lot better for me. I mean I could rewrite that I was a multi-millionaire with everything I could ever want, but thinking like that often had the opposite effect on me. I ended up feeling worse than ever. Like I was making too big of a jump. But maybe what I could do, was rewrite one of the endless, *what the heck just happened here*, scenarios. The simple things that ended up being just a snarly mess. Like getting a simple license plate at the DMV! I could probably write for a couple of minutes in a notebook here and there, what harm could that do. I had zero belief it would actually work, but it sounded like something I could do for fun. Somehow I felt willing to give something like that a try. I felt so proud of myself.

Stephanie was already about four pamphlets ahead of me, but then to my shock, she turned to the class and started doing mini readings. Ginny was one of the first to be read and my shock quickly turned to fascination. For all my mother's readings, I only got whispers of what she was saying. She had always made sure we were out of the room and the doors were closed. My guess was she was speaking in a whisper just to make it more intriguing for her clients. She'd get their full attention and as a bonus the girls wouldn't hear a thing! So, to hear someone else's reading now turned out to be a little thrilling.

"Let's see now," she started on Ginny, "your fears are a little misguided. You're trying to please someone and that isn't what you need to do. You need to communicate with them. Something is off but it's not as far off as you think. You need to speak up." I saw Ginny squirm. Bingo.

Then she said, "You're also so stressed over work right now. It's not what you think. You need to say that to yourself — *It's not what I think.*"

Ginny nodded mutely and looked like she was trying to take that in, while Stephanie found a few more victims. I was spared that round, but I thought over what she said to Ginny. I was also trying to get my own sense on whether she was legit or not, but what she said, though somewhat vague, sort of hit home.

Ginny babbled on the ride home. I think it would take a bit for her to be able to actually do what Stephanie suggested and talk to Dennis about dinner, she needed to process that a little before we could talk about it, so I kept quiet and let her ramble. We both weren't sure what to do with "it's not what we think" with work, because we had played out every scenario we could think of. Which one did *we think*? I told her I was just glad she didn't pick on me tonight and waved my pamphlets like there was much to be studied! We only had one more class to go anyway. But I was actually intrigued by what she said.

* * *

Relieved to get my car back, I decided on Thursday it was my turn to take Ginny to our cooking class. We got into the classroom just as Anna was arriving. We hadn't talked to her since our dinner, and I realized we never set up the next round. Although at this point I wasn't really ready to volunteer, we were both still stressing over work, and this was now lower on our priorities.

"Hi, gals, that was a great time on Saturday I thought! Did Dennis like the leftovers?"

"He did indeed." Ginny smiled. Of course now I was thinking of the psychic but kept my mouth shut. "Meanwhile, Lainey has been having car trouble."

"Bummer! That can put a damper on everything. It was muffler trouble that lead me to borrow Gerry's car so I really know what you mean. Just think otherwise I never would have even known it was his plate!"

So, that had all been preventable, was my first thought, but then I realized it was over, the trauma was now over, and I wouldn't have to worry about that anymore. I'd more than bumbled my way through the dinner, but well enough, it was all over.

"Well, did you want to meet again at my place? I figure I got us into this, so we could swap, but I got the feeling that you don't want to be cooking with Dennis around. You liked the surprise element for him, and not having him underfoot, that kind of thing. Unless, Lainey, you want to have it at your place?"

"I think you have more space if you really want to know, that made it so much easier, do you mind if we keep doing it at your apartment?" With the grape incident over, I really didn't have to think about that anymore. Anna's place would be just fine.

"No, that works out great for me," she said and we all nodded in agreement.

The psychic never mentioned the cooking club or this class now had she?

* * *

Since we had decided on Anna's place for our club we also decided we had better switch off figuring out what the next meal would be. We liked the idea of trading that off since that was the tough part. Ginny volunteered to be next but then came by my apartment to figure it out and to at least look through cookbooks. She truly didn't have any. She also wanted to talk over what we should do about work.

I pulled out my computer and did a quick search for waitress jobs in the area. Nothing came up in our area and I said to Ginny, "Well, the restaurant chains probably have listings online, but not all the family owned restaurants do it that way. A lot of those are word of mouth. They are more of the *go in and ask* type places."

I also knew I'd already worked at several of them and had no intention of going back. Not seeing anything online that jumped out at me I said, "I vote we wait until…"

"Until the other shoe drops?" Ginny tried to finish my sentence.

"Until we know for sure," I corrected her.

She pulled one of the cookbooks over to her. "Meanwhile, let's see what we can find in here!"

"Ginny how have you gotten through life this far without a cookbook?" I asked in wonder.

"I get them off food packages. That counts."

"Didn't your mom ever use cookbooks?" I asked, remembering my mother's dog-eared books, all yellowed and stained from use.

"Yes, she did, but they were vaguely in the background, she did most of her cooking from memory, and we just learned by osmosis I guess."

"I'm guessing I know what to get you for your next birthday!"

"Cute!"

We started looking through my cookbooks for a bit, talking about the French cuisine class. I was saying something about how I didn't have any French food cookbooks when Ginny suddenly caught me off guard saying in a most distressed tone, "I've never been to France."

"Um, Ginny, me neither, but we can still take the class."

"It's just that it hit me, I've never been anywhere because I'm afraid of the food. Isn't that awful? I can't go anywhere because I'm afraid to eat the food there. Maybe I don't want to get a job in a more upscale restaurant too, because of the food there."

"Well, first of all, I have worked in a more upscale restaurant and I didn't *have* to eat the food, so you're okay there. And secondly, I haven't been to France because I'll never have enough money to get there, but okay, food could be another reason. But this seems like more than that, what's the deal?"

She looked at me very intensely. "It's a food phobia. That's what it is. I never realized it was a phobia. But I think it really is. This is bad." Then even stronger she added, "I'll never go anywhere."

This was something from our psychic awareness class kicking in, I just knew it. She had said something about phobias, and how to work with them on one of those pamphlets. She'd briefly told us about some kind of exercise to do if you had them. I didn't really think of myself as having phobias so I wasn't exactly listening at that point.

"Ginny, a phobia? Should we try the phobia work?" I surprised myself even mentioning it since I was doubtful it would work, but Ginny was so freaked out suddenly, at a level I wasn't used to with her.

"Do you think it would help?"

"What have we got to lose?" I asked, thinking this technique better be the real deal, or Ginny might end up with an even worse phobia. We were clearly amateurs here.

We still had one class left though, so if we really screwed it up the teacher should be able to help us out, I hoped, and not that she was just doing lip service to all this stuff. I immediately pictured

Ginny not being able to eat anything ever and suggested we wait until just before the class. Just enough time to see if there was any change but not long enough to get ourselves in trouble.

But Ginny said she didn't think anything would make her loose her appetite for what she did like, she'd probably been paying more attention than me during the class, and wasn't as afraid to give it a go right away.

I fished out the pamphlet and we got down to work.

We read that you needed to be very specific and to be very thorough, so we did everything we could think of for it. The technique included tapping with a few fingers, mostly on points on her face, and saying the problem out loud.

First, we tapped on the basic fear of eating unknown foods. Then we tapped on the fear of unexpected tastes, and for finding out she didn't like something, but how glad she'd be once she knew she didn't like it, or how sweet it would be if she did. At which point, I said, "Imagine if you'd never had sugar before, look at what you'd be missing!" Ginny laughed and suddenly seemed to wonder if that couldn't be true with other foods she was afraid to taste.

So, we did it for every aspect we could think of and basically just had a lot of laughs doing it.

We weren't sure if it had really worked or not, but Ginny didn't seem to flinch when I said, "Well, the real truth will be when we have to have escargot in the French cuisine class." She just laughed, which oddly irritated me. Maybe there really was something to that phobia thing. The pamphlet said phobias were just one aspect of things you could work on, but I felt I would need a lot more information to really feel comfortable with it. Granted, all of the pamphlets were *intros to... Intro...*was the key word here,

I had to remind myself, not a pro, just an intro!

Getting back to our cookbooks, we decided to try some roasted cauliflower as a side dish. Ginny had never had it roasted, but, of course, she'd had cauliflower before, so it wouldn't be any kind of a problem, and we still weren't trying anything exotic. But, maybe little by little, she'd have the nerve to get there.

"I have to say it feels like it was never really that big of a problem," she said talking about trying something new, "it must have been the whole sugar idea."

"Really, then you'll be going to France?" I asked.

"Well, now the money might be a real issue, you know — the potentially no job thing! — but yeah, I could go, if I wasn't afraid of the whole language thing!"

"Shall we tap on that too?" I asked.

"Umm, I don't think I will actually *learn* the language that way! I might have to take classes for that Lainey! Anyway, it doesn't exactly have the urgency the food thing did!"

Ginny taking French lessons! I shook my head, but also thinking France...vacation spot? Lainey, French lessons? No, not until we knew about the diner.

We made up some recipe sheets for all of us, like Anna had done, and then went off to the grocery store for our ingredients.

* * *

The next day we had our second cooking club, roasted cauliflower and mini meatloaves done in an unusual way with different seasoning, and a few different ingredients. Not as much of a stretch, but we were still making it up as we went along. We had settled on early in the day since I usually had to go in to work around three. Anna didn't seem too fazed by that and so we decided that would be great for all of us.

* * *

I called my mother later to ask about the new house and what was going on. I couldn't stand it anymore.

"Oh, that," she said.

Oh, that! What exactly did that mean? "What is it you're not telling me Mom? Are you moving? Or what is the deal?"

"Well, I don't know."

"You don't know? What does that mean?"

"It was Seth's idea, but I don't know."

"What was Seth's idea?" Seth. Seth's idea. Okay, now it was making sense. Seth was up to something with my mother! This must be what Jill had been sensing.

"We were going to flip the place I bought. But now we're a little nervous with the whole housing market. It could be a good investment, but I'm not so sure. I mean I liked the house, enough to buy it, but when Seth heard about it he thought we should invest more and *really* fix it up and re-sell it. Something I guess he'd been thinking about doing for a long time. So, he invested the rest for the renovations and then we would split the profit on the house.

"I became more of a consultant on the house, telling him what I would do if I really could afford to fix it up all at once."

"So you've invested in this house, you own it, and Seth came in and took it over as a renovation. Mom, do you still want the house?" I was half asking half trying to understand what happened. "But you have to sell to split the profit?"

"Well, yes, now it's a wonderful house. It's not completely

finished yet, but I'd love to move in when it's done, but now it isn't all mine. Now it belongs to Seth and me, and I really couldn't afford what he put into it as well. So, yes, I'd have to sell to split the profit and start all over, get something else, or stay put, or..."

What had Seth done?

"So are you worried if you sell, you won't get what you're asking now?"

"That's one thing. I'm also paying for two places right now and I can't keep that up much longer."

"Is there a way to pay Seth back over time, if you moved in?"

"Well, he wouldn't have invested if he wasn't going to make a profit right away. That was the whole point for him."

"So, you have to sell. But you don't really want to."

"Well..."

"Well what?" This sounded like it had been going on for a while. I was deeply confused.

"Well, I'm still thinking it over that's all."

I called Jill after I'd hung up with my mother but got no answer. I didn't want to leave any details on the machine about Seth so I told her I was just saying hello. A clear sign something was up.

CHAPTER 13

At work that night, I was on with Paula who told me Harold had been in again. No news on the plate situation but Harold was very keen on the whole grape plate coincidence. "Is he still interested in that?" I asked her.

"Lainey, not much goes without notice here, you know that. Once Meg heard about that one she wanted to know if you two would consider parking together once in a while," she said with an empty coffee cup in each hand.

"Again, how does Meg know about this and why would she expect him to come back here?"

"What are you talking about? He's here every other day it seems. We've all seen his car, we all know."

"What?" I said with an automatic hands-on-hips reflex.

"I guess you must keep missing him, but yeah, he's been back in."

Okay, this was just...I wanted to walk right back out the door and start all over again. This was not how it was supposed to go. Once I'd found him, that was supposed to be the end of that. I wasn't interested in this Gerry guy, even if he was a nice guy. It just all felt off to me.

Wait, he liked the meatloaf, I would go with that. He liked the meatloaf. His sister probably wouldn't go near it —that was probably the reason he was in so much!

Ginny came in later claiming all was good on the food front at home, at least for now, and she was still excited about the next few classes. Dennis had been thrilled with dinner of late. I was hoping we could keep the momentum going for her sake. Then I thought about the whole "communicate to him what she needed." Well, it was working right now, so I'd let that go.

* * *

The next day, we met outside the class a few minutes before it started, and Ginny had now lost all interest in this class. Naturally, she'd already had a reading! She said she tried to call me before I left but she must have missed me. She was going to go home and practice some other meal. My guess was Ginny had gone and bought herself a cookbook. I decided I still wanted to go to the class, curiosity getting the best of me, and said it was no problem that she was going home. We only had the one more class anyway.

I got in and the teacher did, in fact, go around the room and give little mini readings again. She got to me and said, "Hmmm, you've gone from very closed to very curious," she said and kind of laughed. "That's a good thing," she assured me before I could take offense from the laugh.

"Oh, okay, good," I said.

"Anyway, you've got a lot of external stuff going on around you that you really can't control, just let it all unfold. Don't worry about your mom, she's on her own adventure but it isn't going to end badly, so don't get overly involved or concerned. And I just keep seeing a sandwich... like a PB & J sandwich? Only it's on a roll. I'm not really sure what that means. Does that make sense to you?"

"Ummm, well, yes and no. I understand the reference but also don't know what on earth it means." There were too many bits to that. Peanut butter, that other license plate, or grape, was it grape jelly? I shook my head, and a sandwich, I was NOT getting together with the grape.

"Well, I wouldn't worry about that one, either. It seems to be a great sandwich. And it's all really sweet. Again, let it roll."

The only thing rolling was my eyes, as I absolutely didn't know what to make of the whole thing. That was really no info at all, just acknowledging the situation was what it was. Hmmm.

Then she was on to the next person and I just sat there wondering what help this had been after all? There was more to it than that, I just knew it, feeling my intuition must be kicking in. And then I laughed — so the class was working after all! By the end of the class, I had several more brochures of other intuitive things to investigate. It was true this class was just a tease to get you to take all these other classes. At any rate, my take away was I was to leave my mother alone. But I still had a very anxious feeling there.

As I left, I looked at my newest pamphlets and saw the one for rewriting your life was in there again. I put it back on the table. I had thought of doing that so maybe I should give it a try. I'd pick up a notebook on my way home.

* * *

Jill called me that night now suddenly confused about our mother and the house.

"Jill," I began slowly, "you know how you were wondering what was up with Seth? This is really why I called the other day…" I began twisting the phone cord around my fingers.

"I told you forget it, that was just a feeling," she said defensively before I got to the point.

"No. Actually, you were right. And what he isn't telling you, is that the house you found for Mom…"

"What? What about it?" She interrupted me again (granted I was trying to be as delicate as I could, thus talking as slow as humanly possible.)

"The house you found, that she doesn't seem to be moving into, is because of Seth." Poof. I said it! I pulled the cord off of my hand.

"What?"

"To be honest I'd prefer Seth told you all of this himself, but…" I inhaled deeply. "It seems after Mom bought the house, he talked her into upgrading it, so they could flip it and make a profit. But now Mom really wants to stay!"

"Oh. I didn't know any of that."

"So now I don't know where Mom's at. If she wants to say anything to him, or just have to find another place, or just forget about moving altogether.

"But maybe if you just want to have a get together with them," I continued, as the idea slowly started to work its way through my head, "maybe the two of them can work some of it out. I don't know if that's what she needs, or time to think on her own."

"Oh, sure, I'll do that. Memphis! Down, down, get off that, Memphis get…" she said in a loud whisper to me, "Let me get her schedule and I'll get back to you."

"Sounds good," I said hanging up, then realizing she meant I would be there too.

Jill mentioning Memphis reminded me I hadn't seen the calico in a while. I briefly thought what *was* up with that animal?

I took out my notebook that night. Rewrite my story. Did that mean my whole life as one big essay or the different things that happened each day? I went to find the pamphlet in a pile somewhere on my kitchen countertop. It was cluttered with all kinds of course brochures and paraphernalia, and I couldn't find it. I went ahead and decided it was a day-by-day thing. I would just rewrite what happened and see what it did for me. I would double check when I found the pamphlet.

So, what was going on? Well, there was a lot of confusion about the diner for one thing. I really, really didn't know what I was going to do if that closed, so maybe that was too big of a deal to start with. In a whole different direction, I could rewrite something from a few days ago. Like, that whole weird thing with that Gerry guy and the plate. That was all so uncomfortable and strange and why? That sounded like the perfect thing to just rewrite! I wasn't sure how I was supposed to do this exactly so I jotted down:

There is no weirdness in my life concerning my license plate, I have a very normal license plate.

I thought for a moment more and then added:

I am at peace with it and only good things happen because of it.

Okay, that felt good. It did feel good. Now I just had to let it go. I closed the book and really did put it out of my mind.

* * *

I had a computer class the next day and then work afterwards. The class was an update, new version of *Word*, just the highlights class, and while I was sitting there, a gal next to me said to her friend, "Wouldn't we get the same credit taking a *linda dot com* class?"

"Probably," the other one said, "but I wanted to get out of the office. We can go out to lunch here, why wouldn't we want to do that?"

"Oh sure," the first one said.

I had no idea what they were talking about and made a mental note to look *linda dot com* up when I got home.

* * *

I went back to my apartment after my class to grab something to eat before I went off to work. Calico was sitting on my doorstep like I'd summoned him just thinking about him the night before. He didn't seem interested in coming in or socializing, so I said hello and went inside. I was rethinking the tuna sandwich I was going to make and somehow wound up with a bowl of cereal instead. Calico was messing with my mind apparently.

I got into my uniform, a peach dress with a white collar and cuffs and a navy apron. We'd had white aprons for such a long time, but they got filthy so easily, and we were constantly having to bleach them. Once we got the navy ones it wasn't as big of a problem, although I'd been known to keep a spare or two at work. The waiters, all two of them, had peach shirts, again with white collars but navy slacks. They had the navy aprons as well. And to Meg's credit, the gals could have opted for the navy slacks ensemble if we really wanted to go that route.

We all had to wear badges with our names on them though, much to everyone's dismay. For a little bit we were using alias badges when Meg wasn't around. I don't remember whose idea that one was, but we had put on the badges all the names customers called us anyway: *Hun, Doll, Sunshine,* and *Sweetheart.* The guys had *Excuse Me* and *Over Here.* One surprise trip by Meg and that was the end of that, but I'd saved *Sunshine* as a souvenir.

Kitty was gone when I reemerged, so he really was just making an appearance. So, it was off to work.

I got there and saw the dreaded silver grape, er, GR8 PE, parked in the lot. Fortunately, there were cars to either side and I didn't have to agonize over parking next to him. I made my way to the back of the parking lot then braced myself before going inside. Just as I approached the door, Harold Burns popped up and opened it for me.

"Harold, good to see you. And what's the story of the day?" I said, sounding totally out of context, but wanting to shift away from anything I was thinking.

"I think the story is in the parking lot, don't you? I can't wait to meet the mystery driver."

"Well, he's not really a mystery to me anymore. Nice guy, a neighbor of someone I met in a cooking class." I tried to sound ever so nonchalant.

Harold wasn't buying it. "Oh, so you have changed your attitude."

"Whatever," I said now feeling a little confused. I wasn't sure I'd changed my attitude, just felt the whole thing was over. Maybe that counted.

"Well, I'm sure he's a nice guy. Let's go say hello."

"After you." I waved my hand to let him take the lead. I had to go punch in so I turned to go into the back rather than follow. I told him I'd be back in a second. Taking his hat off, Harold looked back at me and I'm pretty sure I heard him chuckle.

Meg started to seat him in his usual spot in one of the middle front booths. "I just wanted to introduce myself to the grape plate, which one is he?"

"Oh, over here," she said and walked him over to where Gerry was sitting. I noticed it was also in my section. Leave it to Meg. Leave it to any one of them, now that they knew who he was I'm sure they'd all been seating him in my section.

"Excuse me," she said to him. "You're the fella with that great license plate out there aren't you?"

"Nobody ever gets that it says great!" Gerry said.

I didn't think that was really what Meg meant, but she just went with it anyway.

"Oh, we all know; we've got Lainey here who has the JEL-EEE plate, we all thought that was so adorable. But anyway, this is Harold Burns of late night radio fame, and he's been doing a little segment on vanity plates."

"Oh, nice to meet you. I'm Gerry, you must get some interesting calls on that." Gerry extended his hand to shake Harold's.

"Like she said, it's late night radio so I get some winners, but I did find yours to be amusing."

"It really reads 'great PE' after the plastic parts I used to make. PE is an industry standard. Polyethylene. Anyway, that was the intention way back when! People outside of the business don't get it, but it was fun while I worked there." Gerry said.

"Well, we just loved it next to Lainey's. Nice when something happens like that, that just makes you smile. Anyway nice to meet you and give a call into the show sometime if you're ever up that late!"

"Will do."

Now it was my turn to say hello to Gerry. Fortunately, he was in my section so I could simply see if he needed anything. I went over and saw that he'd already been helped so I just said the usual hello, good to see you, and started to walk away.

"Lainey," he said and I turned back. "Would you be interested in helping me with something just for fun?"

"What?" Now he had my curiosity but then I immediately knew it would be something with our cars.

"Well, I just thought since we had the plates we might as well take advantage of them."

"Uh huh," I said, already not wanting to do whatever it was.

"It would really be just an hour or so. We could have them parked where I used to work. They'd all get it, and all the ones that thought I was crazy will get such a kick out of it...Anyway could I persuade you? We can leave the cars and I can buy you lunch over at this really nice restaurant I used to go to when I worked there."

"Ummm." I hated the idea.

"You'd really be doing me a great favor."

"Ummm." I thought back to the psychic and the sandwich. If I had a sandwich with him would this be all over and done with? Maybe that was the thing. Maybe that was what she meant. He seemed like a nice guy, but like that Steve guy, there was zero chemistry here.

"Lainey, say yes already," Meg chimed in.

It seemed there was going to be no end to this, no matter what I said. Clearly, I was just stuck with it.

"Sure, yeah, sure, okay." I *so* did not want this.

"Would Monday be okay? Are you free around lunch time?"

I didn't even have a class to get me out of it. "Oh, okay, sure.

Write down the address and…"

"No, just meet me at Karen's, or Anna's parking lot around 11:30, that way we can drive up together. It will be easier to make sure we can pull in and park together too. Monday's great because most folks are there, maybe not eager, but there."

"Sure," I said, thinking about how much he had thought this through. "11:30?" I repeated and realized I had someone waiting for me to take an order so I pointed to the other table and did a little good bye wave, reluctance just oozing all over me.

My customers were not too happy with me for taking more than a minute, and I got a good earful about them being in a hurry. They must have misinterpreted the wave. I hustled back with their coffees and nearly spilled it when I got back to them, thus getting another earful. Now I was mortified Gerry was overhearing the whole thing, but I was also apologizing for being all over the place. I could feel the *out of sorts* thing was just creeping all over me, probably for the rest of my shift. I just didn't want to do this. Why didn't I just say no. After I returned with their dinners, Harold got me, on my second passing by his booth.

"My dear, I hope it's a truly lovely lunch with your new friend. This is good. I know it."

Good old Harold. I smiled and thanked him. He did say it out of earshot of Gerry so, well okay.

Meg came by and asked us to come to the back with her again. We were now all anticipating info on the new management when she said, "Well, I have some bad news."

"Oh no," Ginny said. I looked quickly from Meg to Ginny and back to Meg.

"Well…" She seemed to be struggling to tell us the rest. "I

thought Walt, who was so interested in the building, was going to continue running the diner, but in fact he wants to turn the diner into some kind of vintage general store. He loves the structure, won't change that, but he wants to make it a store."

"What? No!" I couldn't believe it.

"Meanwhile, my daughter said yes to a huge project at work, since I told her I'd have so much more time to spend with my grandkids. I was so happy thinking about Walt taking over, and all my free time. Now I'm not sure what I'm going to do, I can't let her down, but..." She looked at each of us, then said, "Walt said he would like an answer from me by the end of the month."

I got home around midnight and was feeling devastated I could soon be out of a job. What on earth was I going to do? No matter what happened it would all be different. Unless Meg changed her mind. How much of a chance was there for that?

I was so confused as well; she wasn't giving us a definite answer and I wasn't sure what I should do at this point. Was there some kind of class I should be looking at? Something that changed my career path? I'd taken so many now, but nothing heading me in any real direction. Were these cooking classes doing me any good, or did I need to be looking at something else? Just don't sell Meg, don't sell!

Just as I was turning off the light, inches from getting into bed, I heard a crash outside my front door. I went over to the front window and saw a plant strewn across the porch, with bits of the planter all over the place.

How weird. It wasn't windy out, must be an animal, or someone had thrown something at it. I went over and cracked the door open with the chain on just to double check all angles and there sat the calico cat looking absolutely indifferent about the whole thing. *Not tonight, honey,* I thought and shut the door. Something was up with that cat.

In the morning, I went outside and cleaned up the mess, feeling bad I hadn't done it when it happened. Now I was feeling guilty I hadn't been worried about the cat. But it had just sat there like it was oblivious to what had happened. I thought about that for a second and realized I was letting the cat tell me what to do. How very wrong.

* * *

It was Thursday and I had a free night that I had been very excited about. This week our Thursday night cooking class had been postponed, but Ginny and I failed to mention that to Meg, so we both had the night free. I was enjoying the fact that this week I had both Thursday and Friday off together. Like a real weekend. I decided to take advantage of the time and treated the both of us to a romantic comedy. No decisions tonight, just a DVD, my place, and we ordered a pizza just to complete my pseudo vacation. No cooking! Bliss.

Anna called during our movie and I swear Ginny thought she'd seen us order the pizza, guilt all over the place. Anna said she was terribly sorry she was going to have to cancel the club on Saturday, she was way behind on some paperwork at work and it had to get done.

I, of course, was a bit relieved, because I hadn't figured out the next meal yet. I had planned on doing that on Friday. But there was so much on my mind now. Including that lunch thing on Monday with Gerry.

Chapter 14

Monday morning, all I could think was on top of everything else, what a weird day I had in store for me. Lunch with Gerry across from his workplace! What was that all about? Was this really a date? He hadn't actually asked like it was. It was more that I was doing him some kind of favor. So, no, I didn't think it was, which was good, but then the cars together – I really didn't want to do that. I walked into the kitchen and the phone rang. I *HAD* to get caller ID one of these days! Life without it was a constant series of letting the answering machine get whatever I decided was probably not worth answering, which had become most calls.

The machine picked up and I heard, "Lainey, are you there? It's Ruth." I looked at the phone wondering if I should pick it up. I knew I would, but I just wanted that one moment of not being sure. One good long moment of saying no.

Ruth was a friend from junior high school. I used "friend" for lack of a better term. Ruth was more like an obnoxious older sister I couldn't get away from. Not Jill obnoxious, no, way more intense than that. The good news was that she moved out to Texas when we were still in junior high school. However, what I thought would be the natural demise of a tricky "friendship," turned into a never-ending string of apprehension, obligation, foreboding, and dread. I couldn't shake her. I felt compelled to pick up the phone when she called because I would be besieged with calls from her until I did pick up. Ruth had a bit of an attitude.

One day in junior high school some kids were trying to torment me, calling my mother some kind of a witch, which really shook me up because I thought no one knew about her. Ruth came over, took over, and broke the group up. She told them they were the real witches and that was all nonsense about my mother and she knew that for a fact. Of course, she didn't know my mother or me for that matter, but they didn't know that.

At first, I was just too grateful and in awe of her heroics, that I didn't seem to realize what she was all about. So humiliated by my mother's newfound talent, and now confused because I really believed no one knew about it, I had become reluctant to bring my friends home. No unwanted attention. However, with Ruth I was off the hook, she had no interest in going to my house.

I must have thought she was helping me out, but bit by bit I realized she was simply overpowering me. It was always what she wanted to do, where she wanted to go, and doing what she wanted me to do *for* her.

"How about we go to the mall," she'd suggest and before I could answer it would be, "Yeah, that sounds good, let's go."

"How about we go for a bike ride?" *I'd* suggest only to have her veto my idea.

"No, what we *should* do is hang out at the pizza place," I had no idea what her reason really was. "Yeah, that's it, the pizza place."

Also, all the "Oh, Lainey, can you ask Mr. Spencer for last night's homework assignment for me? I have to help Mark after school." Mark was her brother who it seemed always needed help when she didn't want to do something.

And on it would go.

When I found out she was moving to Texas, I was relieved. I thought that would be the end of that, and so I was super nice to her knowing she'd be gone soon. Big mistake. Because after she moved, she would still call, and often the calls ended with some kind of errand for me to run for her. The "you just can't get those out here in Texas" errands.

After a couple years of that I did try to subtly let her know, it seemed you could get anything your heart desired online, *wasn't that amazing, from anywhere*, but she never got the hint. Who needed the internet when you could just call Lainey?

The bright spot was that she did seem to find one true love out there in Texas, and that was Bren. They started dating the last year of high school and both went on to go to college together. Of course, with Ruth he'd been in and out of the picture a number of times. But Bren must have really loved her because they were always back together again. I was always waiting for the news that they were getting married, yet somehow it always failed to materialize. And maybe I was really wishing it because when he was in the picture, I wasn't as necessary.

"Ruth! What a surprise," I said. "How are you?" and then I started calculating exactly how long I could be on the phone before I had to go meet Gerry at Anna's parking lot.

"Well, here's the thing," she began, "It looks like I'm going to be in town for a couple of days and I was wondering if I could stay with you. My family is all going to be there too, we're coming out for my cousin's wedding. They're all staying with my cousin's family, but I think I'm just that one too many for the house. Any chance I could bunk in with you for a couple days?"

"Oh, oh, that's a surprise!" I thought about my teeny tiny apartment and knew this would be more than a squeeze. Part of my brain told me I could say no. However, I heard, "Sure," come out of my mouth instead. I also realized she'd never been to my apartment. She had no clue how tiny it really was.

"So, I should be there on Friday. The wedding is Sunday. I say *should* because Mark is making the arrangements and well, that was the plan, but things tend to go awry with Mark, anyway, maybe late Friday I could come out. Of course, you'll have to pick me up at my cousin's. Then we can catch up!" Catch up my foot, but okay, let her catch up with me. All right, all right, all right, I told myself. One weekend. I could do this.

"No, no, that's fine. I need the directions to your cousins' place and all that, but fine."

"Sure, I'll call you back later in the week with them and confirm. So, great, I'll see you then."

I hung up feeling like I'd just been had. So, I was her accommodations. Wonderful. I would have to get her late Friday — I didn't usually work on Friday, but I never knew for sure. I supposed that could be arranged easily enough. Then would I have to take Saturday night off work to do whatever with her? Or would she be off with the family? And Sunday? That was the wedding so I was fine then, but then that night? I'd have to work that all out… I was a little flustered but I was sure it would all come together. Just a weekend. How bad could it be?

Pulling into Anna's parking lot, I saw Gerry standing by his car all set to go. He waved to me and I rolled down the window and he said, "Great to see you. Just follow me!" And he jumped into his car. It was a nice car. I had to give him that.

I followed along and we pulled into a really large facility with a great big parking lot. How on earth were his friends or ex-coworkers going to find our cars? Was this just a setup to go to lunch? I mean he could have just asked me to lunch, so now I was a little weirded out. He pulled into a spot near one of the main doors with a space beside it. How did he get these spots I wondered? Wasn't this prime real estate for parking? Then I saw the one-hour parking sign and got it. Okay, fine, he had a plan after all.

We parked with his car first to the left then my car next on the right, as you came out of the doors. Yeah it would get some notice. This was exactly what I never wanted to happen with the car, to have it be attracting attention for being so absurd, and here I was doing it. I hated this. Someone was already coming out the door. "Gerry? Good to see you."

"Hey, Jeff, how are you. Just giving my friend Lainey a tour of my old building."

Friend Lainey, sure, that sounded better than my sister's neighbor's cooking friend. But at least it was friend and nothing more.

Then I was thinking how did he leave here exactly, on good terms? Was he even allowed to be here? Wait, he was laid off, it must be okay since he wasn't fired.

Before I could get much further down that train of thought, he said, "So let's just get a bite across the street there, it's a great lunch place."

I don't think that Jeff saw either one of our cars. Awesome. We walked back through the very large parking lot and crossed over to a restaurant that was no doubt about to get very busy for the lunch hour, and got our table. This was all just a tinge beyond weird for me, but okay. The restaurant looked like your usual medium price range, okay food, sort. He forgot I worked in a diner, I wasn't blown out of the water, but it seemed nice enough. He suggested the club sandwiches but having served ten million of those at the diner, I spied the chicken parmesan sandwich and thought that sounded just about right. He got the club and we settled in for an uncomfortable moment or two.

"So, Anna never explained why you got that license plate, what's the connection?"

Oh, no. Now I had to go through this again. I thought for sure we'd established this part. Yes, I was pretty sure Ginny told him it was a mistake, but maybe he wasn't paying attention. "There is no connection. I just got that plate. I thought it was a mistake, like it was intended as someone else's vanity plate, and I told the woman, but she just dismissed me and that was the end of it. She wouldn't take it back."

If he said I should have tried again I was going to walk out right then and there, but he shook his head and said, "Oh man, I'm sorry, I really thought there was a great story behind it. But okay, it is kind of funny." He hesitated because he could see I didn't find it funny. I was still waiting to find it funny but no, it hadn't happened yet. Harold had tried to shake my feelings about it, but I was in my sulk again.

"Well my story, I might have told you, was, it isn't grape as everyone would like to think but Great PE. I won't bore you with all the plastics info but PE is polyethylene and they make tons — and I do mean tons — of plastic products with it. Just not *my* products anymore! Great, huh?" Anna had told me, that it wasn't grape and was this PE thing. So not everyone with a vanity plate was thrilled with their own choice at some point! I did feel better about that.

The waitress brought over our lunches rather quickly I thought, and once again I looked around to see if they were fully staffed. They seemed to be.

"So now you're job hunting, is that right?" I asked, changing the subject.

"Yeah, I think I've found something so it's not as bad as it seems. I'm interviewing. The company could have easily transferred me to another division here, but they were looking to make cut backs at this plant anyway. I didn't want to transfer to, you know Nebraska, or something like that, so I took the layoff. The thing is, that's why I wanted to do this with the plates. Give my friends a laugh.

"Anyway, yes, now I'm job hunting. Different companies but really the same plastics."

"Oh. I see. Well, then, the PE part will still make sense, that's good."

"You're right, it could transfer, which is nice. Anyway, I thought they'd get a kick out of seeing it as grape here instead of 'great PE' for a change."

"Simon!" Gerry got up and extended his hand to an older gentleman walking by our table.

"Gerry, that was your car! I thought so, how are you?"

"Good, I'm good, Simon, and this is my friend, Lainey, here," we both nodded. "How's everything going back there?"

"Well, the layoffs brought out a lot of the usual power trips in there." Simon's eyes said, *oh, what a headache.* "Phil and Stan vying for control, and well the whole thing just got so chaotic and stressful in there. You know, when they're at each other's throats the whole team suffers. It did calm down for a bit, but now we're back to stressful, so be glad you weren't caught in the crossfire.

"Anyway, so, where have you landed?"

"Ah, you mean besides my sister's couch? I've been looking at a few different positions, mostly I have my eye on one at PFP, I've been interviewing there, but we'll see. Anyway, I don't want to keep you from your lunch. Take care Simon, good to see you."

"Likewise." Simon went on to his table.

We finished our sandwiches and Gerry got up to pay the bill. I was now feeling somewhat apologetic. I shouldn't have felt so badly about doing him this favor.

We walked back to the lot and we both did a double take seeing a car a couple down from ours that read PNT-BTR.

"NOOOO," I yelped. "It can't be." It was in fact another silver car — BMW — the one Ginny had seen at the Home Depot. Now what?

I did and didn't want to find out. I mean right next to our cars, now he must have seen these too. "How do we find out who it is?" I asked Gerry, who was looking more perplexed than I would have thought.

"I can't go in," he said. "I mean I could, but I can't. It's too, it's just too... I can't explain why I'm here to anyone and I never meant to have to go inside, just wanted a few folks to get the joke..."

He was rambling and then he said, "And we have to leave, they really do tow you if you stay longer than an hour. I'm sure we've been noticed too. I'm sorry I just can't…"

"Look, I'm right here, this car is right here, I think I want to at least see who it is." I guess I had decided it was now or never, just go for it. I could just see who the person was, they didn't have to know who I was. "But it's okay, you can go. I'll just move my car to another spot in the lot. Really, you can go."

He seemed reluctant to my doing that, but I figured he couldn't make me leave. If I was in some other spot I could stay longer and see who it was. He was parked just beyond our cars but still in the one-hour parking, so I assumed he must be a visitor. Gerry had never seen the car before so it wasn't someone that had ever worked there while he was there. We both wanted to know what was the peanut butter connection?

Gerry said if I stayed he should stay too, although I kept saying it was fine for him to leave, he didn't have to. Truth be told I think I wanted him to leave. I didn't want him to introduce us to this person.

We both drove out to the outer parking lot area and circled around for a bit. It was becoming clear there was no good vantage spot to see who got in the car. We'd just possibly see the car moving and then what? This was starting to feel like a stake out and I was having all kinds of mixed emotions! Was I just going to follow the car until I could overtake it to see him? If it even was a him! Was I going to stop him, what was my plan? The longer I sat in my car, the dumber I felt until I couldn't stand it any longer. I got out of the car and walked over to Gerry and said, "This is dumb — I'm going to go."

But as I did he said, "Wait a sec, there he goes." And Gerry started his car to follow him. I didn't see him get into the car so

I was still looking to see what he even looked like. And, again, I felt like a fool standing there in the parking lot. The silver BMW made it to the exit before Gerry had circled around to follow him. I didn't get a good look in the car, too many trucks or SUVs in my sight line. As Gerry got to the exit I thought, what a ridiculous situation. This is absurd.

* * *

I had to get to work soon so I went back home to freshen up. A little grapefruit spray and I told myself I was feeling better.

At work the first thing out of Ginny's mouth was, "How did it go?" I gave her the shake of my head indicating not so hot, and she looked at me with surprise.

"Really, what was the matter?" she said.

"Oh, it was just dumb. But the weirder thing was PNT-BTR showed up."

"What, are you kidding? The same one I saw? What was he like, how did that go? Seriously Lainey that's so cool."

"Um, no it really didn't go...I never met him, I didn't even see him, just a car driving off, but it had been parked near our cars at the building Gerry used to work at."

It was half feeling like Gerry had planned all that, but it bumbled so badly it couldn't have been. "We had to leave the parking spots we were in, I don't know, it's like this car is taunting me, but I don't know why, or what the message is, or if there is one," I managed to tell her, still thinking it's just stupid, it just feels stupid now. That damn plate, it's just so stupid!

* * *

Since the whole thing with Gerry had even happened, I felt like

I had to defend myself. It felt like everyone was trying to set me up with him, and why? There could be other plates out there. (Did I hear myself?) Why did I have to be setup at all with a matching plate? Even PNT BTR, that was not happening. This was nuts.

Two hours later, I was still rehashing the whole thing in my mind when I heard Ginny calling, "Lainey, kitchen quick."

I ran into the kitchen, and one of the cooks was attempting to get up from the floor, after what looked like a huge batch of minestrone soup had fallen over. I hadn't heard the crash, usually that was the signal. But Dillon was on the floor, covered head to toe in small veggies. He looked more mortified than hurt. "Must have caught on the spoon," he was saying out loud, but not really to either of us.

"It's okay. He's okay. It wasn't hot," Ginny was now saying and he was nodding. "The worst is the mess. Get a mop and stuff." *Stuff* meant figure out the best way to clean that up. I got the mop but also a dustpan, wastebasket and paper towels and started slopping it onto the dustpan and then into the bucket. Ginny was helping Dillon get up, more slippery than anything else, and trying to get some of the slop off of him into my bucket.

"Righteous," Dillon muttered to himself.

We were trying to decide how to proceed, send him home to change, or find clothes for him here, or get someone to get him something to wear. If he went home, we were short staffed, and while we could fill in, it would leave us short out front. We asked him if there was someone he could call to bring him another set of clothes and he said sure, he'd call his mom, looking absolutely humiliated.

CHAPTER 15

Covered in minestrone, I too was wondering about going home and taking a bath. Cleanup ended up being more on me, than in the bucket. Unfortunately, I really didn't have that choice about going home, and I changed my apron hoping that would do some good. My white sneakers were on the disgusting side but I'd wiped them down a time or two. As long as they didn't squish or anything. Ginny didn't seem to be in bad shape after she helped Dillon out. I was hot and sweaty now that I'd mopped every inch of the kitchen, trying to clean up around the other workers and not get underfoot. This was the "if you only knew" part of the job. The pretend and move on part. I hated that part.

I went back out to see what the customers I'd now been ignoring were up to, and as I made my way down my section I saw the back of Gerry's head in one of the booths. Oh, come on. We were done. I walked past him and turned and then pulled out my pad to take his order.

"Well, hello again," I said. "Something I can get you?" I didn't try to make small talk and didn't even try to smile. I was tired.

"Lainey, I wanted to apologize for today. I don't think that went as I had planned and I just wanted to say it was probably a dumb idea. Not the lunch part, that was nice, but the whole car goof."

Goof? Did he say goof? "Wait did you know about that other car, was that part of it?"

"No, oh, no, that's just what made it so awkward, even after it was already a little weird, so no, that was just...I don't know what that was. I was curious who that person was too, but no, I had no idea."

"Fine, it's all fine," I said wearily. "We can just let it go. Did you want anything to eat or did you just stop in?" Didn't we just eat a couple hours ago?

"Oh, sure. I'll have some coffee and maybe something light, how about the soup? What's today's special?"

"That would be minestrone."

"Great, I'll have that." Naturally, how was he to know?

"Coming right up."

* * *

Calico was sitting on my stoop that night and I let him in. "Did you break the plant on purpose? Were you trying to get my attention?" I asked him fully expecting some kind of reaction, but he just sauntered into my living room. Why was I even letting him in? Was I now attached to this little animal? I absentmindedly turned on part of Harold's show just to entertain the cat really. I wanted a shower after the soup fiasco. Harold was all into "how they met" stories tonight. How couples met, any good magical moments that kind of thing. He was getting some grocery store moments that didn't really take my breath away, but the people were all having a good time telling their tales. Calico curled up on my couch and proceeded to go to sleep.

After my shower, I spotted my notebook half tucked under some papers on my dresser and pulled it out and reread the bit about all things being good with my plate. Umm. Okay, that did not go as planned and it certainly didn't go as rewritten. That went horribly wrong in fact. I tore out the paper and ripped it up and thought clearly I just did it all wrong. Forget about the plate thing, I would rewrite a bit about Ruth. She could be a little demanding of me and I was always trying to accommodate her. Maybe I could spin that around. Maybe I was supposed to rewrite a longer term issue, so this would be good. The plate thing, that was too new, and such a fluke anyway. So maybe that was the problem there, because rewriting that had only made it worse.

I wrote:

I always have a wonderful time with my friend Ruth. I love catching up with her, and it's always so much fun to do things together. We have a great friendship and I look forward to seeing her.

Okay, that felt good. Yes, that was how it should be. I did want to have a good time when she got here and maybe it would be fun. Hey, this was really feeling good. I tossed the book back on the papers.

The next morning Jill called and said she'd have us over for dinner at her house on the following Friday, after Ruth's visit. I told her I had to double check my schedule but I thought it was fine.

I was so back and forth with Fridays being my day off, especially with the class on Thursday, that I always had to check.

Scheduling could be so easy going or turn on a dime into a nightmare, it just depended on what was happening. Fridays themselves were always so busy in the diner, great tips, and guaranteed exhaustion!

· Chapter 16 ·

It was still my turn to figure out the menu for Ginny and Anna. I'd put it off the week before and hadn't thought twice about it since. I kept going back to Walt not wanting to keep the diner open. What was my new plan? So many odd things seemed to be coming up keeping me distracted. Gerry and that plate thing, now Ruth coming for a visit. I couldn't focus on what I needed to do.

If I started now, I'd be well ahead of the game with the menu. This time Ginny and I were both due into work at three-thirty that day. I pulled out one of my favorite cookbooks and looked it over. Everything was so familiar. I realized that was not the point of this cooking club.

I felt so frustrated. And I also started to wonder, was cooking as an occupation something I should be taking more seriously? Would that help me somehow? Could that be a direction for me that I just didn't see?

I knew I didn't want to do anything French, leaving that up to actual class, but now I couldn't decide which way to go for the club. Comfort food with a twist was what I kept coming back to. But what would that be?

I went online to try and find something to stir up some creative thoughts but I kept nixing everything I saw as too complicated, too normal, or too blah. I needed a little more inspiration so I decided to go to one of the grocery stores I never go to. Maybe one of their readymade dishes would do the trick. Not the organic store, but the jazzy out-of-my-price-range small grocery store that had all the fancy pastries as well. Couldn't hurt to get one or two of those while I was there.

I landed in the parking lot and spotted AOK2DA. It was a scruffy brown pickup truck and I decided it had to be "A-okay today" since I couldn't think of anything else DA was supposed to mean. After Gerry's GR8 PE I knew there could be some other weird interpretation but I wasn't willing to try and figure it out. I was also annoyed feeling I was *supposed* to figure it out now. But then, "A-okay to do anything" hit me as I walked into the store; pickup truck, errands, chores, it all made sense. Did that also mean me? I shook my head and said, "Just stop!" to myself as I was walking in and the guy in front of me turned around and looked at me. "What?"

I looked up at him and said, "What, what?" and then it dawned on me I was talking out loud. "Oh, sorry — thinking out loud." He gave me a look that told me he wanted nothing to do with me from this moment on, and I walked into the store now a little confused as to why I was there.

The smell of the bakery jolted me back to reality. I was there for something yummy. I looked in both the cases and on the display racks. I found I had to have the chocolate chip cream cheese brownie along with some of the lemon squares. Something cinnamon was in the air as well, and it took over every sense of control I had. Some kind of gooey roll that was sure to be all over my face without my even knowing it. At least with the lemon bars, I would probably only have confectionery sugar down my shirt. I resolved to keep the rolls in the bag until I got home.

My purchase in hand, I paid the gazillion dollars and proudly walked back to the car. Halfway through the lemon square I remembered that I was there to look for something to make for dinner. I shook off my shirt and headed back in now feeling a little self-conscious. Really, Lainey, really, I thought. My memory completely erased by desserts!

I wandered over to the pre-made dinners, and maybe it was that I was feeling satisfied from the lemon square, but nothing really looked all that inviting. My big chance and I was blowing it. Then I spotted what was being called pizza lasagna. Okay, this could be something. I looked again and thought, now what was my plan? I'd have to go back home and find some kind of recipe for this. Okay, I could do that. I wondered if I should really get it, now doubting my decision. I didn't think there was a chance on the planet that I wouldn't actually like it so why not? I got the dinner for 8 more gazillion dollars and headed home.

"Okay, Lainey, here's the deal..." I was greeted with a lengthy message on my machine from Ruth when I got home.

"Mark intended to use one credit card for our tickets, one that he wanted all the mile points to go on. That was why he volunteered in the first place. But then midway he remembered that he'd used the card for some extensive work on his car, so he figured he could only book three flights on that card without quite maxing it out, then he was going to get the other one on a different credit card." I heard a bit of a *humph*. "Of course, he paid for those and then didn't get back until much later that day for the last one, and the flight was no longer available." Her voice rose a little. "So now, I'll be coming in late Saturday. Rather than meet with the family first, I was wondering if you could pick me up at the airport?"

Talk about getting tickets close to the travel time, was all I could think. No wonder he couldn't get them all together. And I'm sure they were the priciest of the lot! I looked at the machine knowing I should probably listen one more time, take note of late Saturday, and then delete the message, because surely there was no room left for any other messages!

I still didn't have her cousin's address but now I probably wouldn't need it if I was just getting her at the airport. That would be fine. The airport I knew.

I called back and left my message. "Sure. Time and flight, all I need."

Now it was time to start cleaning up for the visit. Saturday night would be here fast. I looked around. I should do the bathroom last I thought, but my kitchen needed help, and where again was I going to put her?

My apartment was on the first floor of what was originally a duplex, but now it was converted to three units, so I had half of the first floor, which was also just half of one of the duplexes. The conversion in my place had an odd configuration. My bathroom being hit the hardest. Ummm, my bathroom/walk-in-closet that is. An odd combo of a room, that was larger than my kitchen. And so strange for the bathroom to be the catch all, hall closet, bedroom closet, extra space room.

So, I had a small kitchenette, and a large room. The bedroom/ living room area. I had a daybed that doubled as my second couch, a bunch of toss pillows by day, tossed to the floor by night. Easy maintenance. A trundle bed tucked neatly underneath, that was used exactly never. It was a bit "cozy" in there — cozy meaning cramped.

I had one neighbor above me, and then on the other side, an older couple had both the first and second floor.

Roger was the upstairs neighbor: he was quiet, kind of a goof, but a nice kid. He was in his early twenties and worked at the hospital doing some kind of maintenance. I was never sure in exactly what capacity. Building, grounds, whatever. Every time he started to tell me, he somehow switched over to some other story, usually about one of the nurses he had his eye on, and he never got back to telling me what he did. He shared the front door and a hallway with the up and downstairs neighbors, and I had my own entrance on the porch.

I was now looking at my options as to where to put Ruth. I had my daybed with the dusty trundle, and then the couch. Pulling out the trundle would just cram up the space even more. I was leaning towards putting her on the couch. It was a comfortable enough one, and roomy. Either way, I had to get it all straightened up. Roomy also meant papers and books and magazines and catalogs strewn across half of it.

Ginny knew to toss them to the floor. Ruth...no.

I went into the kitchen and mindlessly started the dishes with the intention of scrubbing everything down after, cabinets, counters, then get the floor. I was so immaculate at the diner but here I was a little less than stellar in my chores.

Somehow, I'd managed to accumulate a large collection of things related to all my classes lumped together. For the kitchen collection, there were also catalogs and pamphlets and books. I had all the other things in the main room, all the kits as I called them. The little art kit and the floral kit, and the many crafting kits staring me down, as I thought about cleaning up the place. Now I was wishing I'd taken an organization class and that would fix this situation, but it was way too late for Ruth's visit for that. I was also glad I hadn't volunteered my kitchen as the cooking club's main gathering place because knowing me, it would now be chuck full of spices and all kinds of things I would use once and then have it sit here forever not knowing if I would ever use them again.

After the first go of scrubbing, the clutter was still intact, but at least sitting on a well-scrubbed surface. I wondered if I was going to do the clutter part or just end up ignoring it.

I was just about to pull some of the books and pamphlets out — I figured I could at least sort them and maybe actually put them on a bookshelf rather than the counter when I heard a knock at the door. There was Roger with his back to me, looking out onto the street.

"Oh, hi, Roger, come on in," I said, and he turned back to me. I looked with a full on stare.

"What? What is that all about?" I asked in wonder, as Roger was sporting exactly half of his beard. One side of his face was clean-shaven and the other still had his red haired beard. "Roger, what is going on?"

"Lost a bet. Do you like it?"

"Do I... Roger, ummm, most unusual I will say, and now how long will that last?"

"Oh, hard to say. I don't know. I may grow to like it."

"Yeah, well good luck with that."

"You don't like it?"

"Um, Roger, come on. What kind of bet?"

"Oh, just the usual." So, he wasn't going to tell me.

I was going to chalk this one up to a temporary lapse of sanity. Just part of his goofy charm. Roger was the tall and thin, lanky type, with that very red hair. Ordinarily he would be down to borrow something that I would, or wouldn't, ever see again, which for some reason didn't really phase me, thinking eh, that's Roger. It was never anything big or irreplaceable. Batteries, super glue, etc. If I really needed it back, I'm sure at some point I could suggest it be returned. Seemed more often than not he just could not be bothered to go to the store for a few items that most folks just had in their junk drawer.

"So what's up?" I asked, expecting the usual.

"Any chance you know where I could find some nice candles? Nice scented ones."

"Do I detect a date in your future?"

He gave me a *but of course* smile, and slightly nodded.

"Ah, then you are off to Shine Bright on Elm." Shine Bright specialized in all things light. It was a relatively fun store, that had all kinds of cool theme type lamps, along with mood lights and salt lamps, light bulbs and flashlights, and candles, lots of candles. "Either that or you can go to the card store next to the supermarket."

"Awesome, thanks."

"Roger, does your date know about the whole beard thing here?" I said, pointing to his face and then pointing up in the air.

"How do you think I got the date?!" I just shook my head and watched as he headed out to his car.

I looked at my stacks of books and pamphlets and decided to put all the pamphlets in one of the square cloth baskets I kept buying and never used. After I'd sorted and filled about three of them I put them back on the counter where they'd been but at least now they didn't look as bad. One small nook done, I felt I'd done enough. It was already time to get ready for work. I grabbed a sandwich and looked at my pile of laundry. Tomorrow. Ah, yes, tomorrow.

I had made sure I had this Friday off to get Ruth. But now I had to go and switch it with Saturday, since this all got bumped. I thought I would get a few disgruntled remarks from Paula, since Ginny was already scheduled that night, and I couldn't switch with her. But, instead, Paula surprised me.

"Well, I certainly need the work. This is killing me. I've left my resume at six other restaurants and have been to a bunch more than that, and *no one* is hiring right now. I'm flipping out."

"You're already looking?" I said, amazed.

"Of course, I am! You're not?" she replied, equally amazed. "Lainey this is our job and it's about to be gone! I have to have a job, something I can count on."

"And no one is hiring?" I said, feeling suddenly uneasy.

"No one so far. You know how it is with this business, some places have a lot of turnover and a few like ours don't. Anyway, none so far, and I'm getting really anxious about it. I've even starting to look at the fast food joints. Heaven help me!"

"But we don't even know for sure..." I said, hoping somehow it would be okay. And very dimly my thoughts flashed to the plate AOK2DA.

CHAPTER 17

Saturday's cooking club was tomorrow, and I had not in fact gotten my recipe for pizza lasagna. I'd had the dinner, and it was pretty good, and then I promptly forgot to do my homework. But, really, it was a lasagna with pepperoni. Maybe a spice or two? Pizza lasagna. Make lasagna, add pepperoni. When I looked online, however, I found just the opposite of what I'd had. I'd had lasagna. I found pizza with lasagna ingredients. Hmmm. The order. That was it. Pizza lasagna was the lasagna and lasagna pizza was the pizza with lasagna ingredients. That was going to get confusing. But, either way, both sounded good. What would the gang be more inclined to like? I knew the whole point was really new dishes, and this was one or two ingredients different on a very familiar dish. I felt like I was cheating, but easy had been part of the plan too. Discovering one or two new ingredients for any dish. Wasn't that equally important?

I pondered my brilliance or laziness and decided on the more lasagna, not pizza version and wrote out my grocery list. I printed out the recipes for the group at the same time and then went off to get the ingredients. Easy enough.

I set off for the grocery store with my list in hand. I then realized Ruth would be in later that night and it would be a great chance to show off the recipe. Tell her all about the club and how we'd learned to cook new dishes. I was psyched for dinner. But as I thought about telling her, I could already feel her cool breeze of indifference. Well, she still might like the lasagna.

* * *

"Are you a baker?"

I heard getting out of my car at the supermarket. She was pointing to my plate, and I thought, you know I really need to come up with something other than the truth. I shook my head and was about to say, just a mistake at the DMV, when she continued, "Oh, I was hoping you made those jelly cookies, you know the apricot ones or, oh! The raspberry ones! Oh, those are really good."

Did she think I had them in the backseat?

"Although, I like those chocolate covered raspberry sticks, have you ever had them? I think Trader Joe's carries them and they are awesome. Orange ones too."

Apparently, I had no need to answer any of these questions, or actually speak for that matter, although I was thinking that I had *seen* the chocolate sticks.

"But I also like the chocolate espresso beans, now those have a kick," she continued. I was very slowly nodding and also very slowly walking close to the car wondering if I was going to be able to get away. I did need to get into that supermarket.

"Mawwwwwwwm," I heard coming from one of the cars further down and she turned towards it saying, "Soccer time."

Oh, thank goodness! She was off. I was able to get into and out of the store without further incident and took my groceries home.

* * *

Saturday at the cooking club, they loved the idea of the pizza lasagna. I still felt like I was cheating but they thought it was brilliant so we were all happy. Besides, it was lasagna!

Ginny said over and over again how this would thrill Dennis to no end. Then I remembered her mentioning *one good lasagna* to that woman in the class!

We'd met at Anna's apartment once again — this time at 10:30, our now established club hangout. Ginny brought coffee and donuts for all of us.

"Ginny, you're spoiling us."

"No, I had nothing for breakfast this morning. I have to go grocery shopping, so I needed something before we started cooking, so I wouldn't go crazy! I also wanted to ask if they were hiring. I really don't want to, but I do need to get a feel for what's out there."

"Oh, no, you too?"

"Well, Lainey, it looks like it's inevitable."

"I know, I just... I just keep hoping." My fears turned into total denial.

"That's all well and good Lainey, but in reality... Anyway, they're not hiring at the moment but I left my info."

Anna had been silent looking from me to Ginny while we rambled. Ginny then told her how the buyer Meg was thinking of selling the diner to, wanted to close it.

"Oh no! I'll keep my ears open at work. I tend to overhear a lot of conversations in the reception area. You never know what might turn up!" she said trying to help. Ginny and I looked at each other for a second with hope.

"Well, at least our club is food related... you know, maybe even educational?" she said, trying to lighten the subject. Something told me I should pay attention to that point.

We had our donut party and coffee, and didn't get going on our cooking until around eleven. Anna also told us she usually got her coffee at the Café of Coffee, and felt a little guilty at the sight of any other cup, but she would get over it. We promised to stop into the Café of Coffee on our next visit.

"Are they hiring?" Ginny asked.

"I don't believe they are. It's just a couple of retired doctors, but I'll ask next time I go in!"

* * *

Full, I left with my lasagna and headed home again. We'd done a good job. We still had a couple of Thursday night French cuisine classes left, but the club was becoming more fun than the class. Fun until it was my turn to figure out the meal again. I knew that was going to be tough. It shouldn't be, but I kept second guessing what I thought they'd like. So far we'd all liked everything.

I put the rest of the lasagna in the fridge and suddenly could hear really loud music from Roger's apartment. Most unusual. He must have a date tonight, getting all psyched up. Then, I remembered the beard thing and just shook my head.

Ruth's plane wasn't due in until 7:30, so I did one more round of straightening up. Fluffing pillows, moving magazines, and realized that without a complete makeover nothing was going to look any different in my apartment. More space was about the only thing that might do the trick.

I left around 6:30 to get to the airport. It usually took about 40 minutes to get there, and if I ran into slight traffic that would probably be just about the right amount of time. I pulled into the airport garage and circled a few times before finding my spot. I didn't come to the airport all that often, it was rare I went on a trip, thus my need for a real vacation, but it was also rare for me to pick up anyone else there either. So, it took me a bit to figure the whole system out.

Stopping at the arrivals and departures sign, I checked on her flight and saw it was delayed by two hours! 9:30. What? NO! Now I had to find something to do for two hours. I went over to the newsstand for a book. They did have the rent and return ones but I was hoping I wouldn't be there *that* long!

Maybe I should just get a magazine. Well, the average article was what, a five-minute read? That wouldn't last for two hours. I eye-balled all sorts of mysteries that were just not to my liking even though some of them I'd heard people raving about. Same thing happened with TV shows, I would hear customers all excited about some new show and I'd feel I was missing out until I actually watched it and found I didn't like it. Let's face it: I was a wimp with anything gruesome or frightening.

I reached over for what looked like a lighthearted novel and started to read the back. "Lost in the gentle breeze that evening, Jasmine squelched a scream..." Okay, no thanks!

Now, I'd been here too long and was feeling self-conscious and I needed to make up my mind. I grabbed a romance novel. I had issues with those, too, but decided I'd let that go for now. I also grabbed a *Home and Garden* magazine to put the book in, lest anyone actually see me reading a romance novel. So about $20 later, I found myself a nice chair to read my novel.

Then, after about ten minutes of trying to settle in, I decided to go back to the arrivals/departures sign and get the latest before I got too comfortable. Maybe it was back on track.

Cancelled. Cancelled? What was I seeing? I looked in my bag for my phone only to discover the missed call from Ruth. Yup, she'd found out it was cancelled. I called her back and got her voicemail. She was probably having a fit there in the airport, but I just said, I got the message, and asked if she had found another flight, or what was the deal?

I plunked down in my chair again and my phone rang.

"Weather — we are having weather in Atlanta. Just rain, just lightning, just perfect. Anyway, it looks like I'm not getting out of here tonight, so I'll call you in the morning when I get in. They're saying it's going to be an early flight, so I may be in around 8ish."

"Wow, just for rain. Okay, well, yeah, I'll get you in the morning, this time I'll check from home."

"They're adding this flight so it may not be listed. Why don't we just say 8ish."

"Oh, okay. I guess that's fine," I lied. ""See you then."

The morning, are you serious? I took my bag of reading materials and went back to my car.

"Is that your plate?" an elderly man asked me as I was opening the door.

"Yup, yup, it is."

* * *

I set my alarm for 6:00 just to be safe, leave by seven, and get there around 8ish. It wasn't until I was on the road and realized it was Sunday morning and there was absolutely no one on the road that I would indeed be quite early. I also had failed to get the flight number from Ruth and looking on the board I didn't see anything coming from Atlanta this morning. She did say they added the flight, so maybe it wasn't on the board. I went to the information desk to ask. I was assured there was a flight and my best bet was to wait at the baggage claim area. It should be in at 8:20.

Down I went to the baggage claim area. Not a lot of seating there and I still had time so I went back up to my seating area near the newsstand from the night before, grabbed coffee on my way and had my bag with mixed reading items and sat down. Today the place was a lot less crowded.

I made it through a chapter or two and headed back down to the baggage claim. At long last, I saw Ruth coming towards me. "Lainey! You're here, excellent! I thought I'd never get here! That was by far the worst. The wedding is today, and I'm so tired and rumpled and oh, this was not what I had in mind! That Mark, he should have booked us all together. I bet they didn't have any trouble getting in, even with the weather!"

"Wow, well, Ruth, wow! How long has it been?"

"I have no idea. What time is it again?"

"It's about 8:40," I said as we stood looking for her bag.

"What time is the wedding?" I really didn't want to ask that one.

"Well, that's the thing: it's at noon. Do we have time to get back to your place so I can take a shower, get dressed and get to the wedding?"

I was now realizing I was transportation for the whole event.

Actually, it might have made more sense for her family to come to the airport and then go right to the wedding with her. I wished I'd thought of that last night.

"Sure, yeah we can make it, I think. Where is the wedding exactly?"

"I have the invitation on me somewhere. I'll fish it out at your place. Wow, what a whirlwind huh?"

When we got to my car, I took her bag to put in the trunk. "What's that all about?" she asked, looking at my plate. "I mean it's…I don't get it…what is that? What does that mean?"

"Yeah, tell me about it. DMV. Mistake, bad karma, I don't know, but they wouldn't take it back and now it's my plate."

"That's awful!" she said and I felt like she was waiting for me to make it better somehow.

"Yeah, I know. Now, we should make good time this being Sunday morning and all."

She looked like she wanted me to comment further on the plate, but I had nowhere to go. Much to my surprise I found I was checking out all the plates as we left, some teeny tiny part of me was looking for the one that made me feel better, a "hey it's all going to be okay" one.

On the ride back, she vented what seemed to be 100 years' worth of frustrations about her brother, Mark. He should have booked them all together once again, he should have given them a little more time, he should have thought about the return trip, which she had made for Monday morning so our little visit was basically this moment now and on the ride back to the airport, which I hadn't heard about before this moment, somehow assuming she'd be back with her family then, but that was not the case.

It would all be over soon I told myself. Very soon.

We got to my apartment and I brought in her bag and set it down in the middle of the room. "You can just put that in my room," she said to me and I looked at her.

"This is your room, and my room, and everything else in between. Couch or daybed is the selection."

"Oh, sure, the couch is fine," she corrected herself very quickly. I was a little impressed. "I just need the shower anyway."

She took her suitcase into the ample-sized bathroom.

After her shower, she emerged in a blue crepe dress that seemed to have withstood the whole traveling ordeal pretty well. Note to self — crepe for travel.

Somewhere on the ride to the church, she asked if I wanted to go to the wedding, that I'd have a great time. Did she reply with a plus one I wondered? I looked down at my jeans and T-shirt, and then told her I had to be at work at three. I wasn't able to get the day off, but I would be home again around 10:30 that night. I'd somehow managed to get a little time off at the end of the night, pretty rare, but she didn't seem to catch on that that was a big deal. I told her I could pick her up after ten-thirty at her cousin's house or if one of her relatives wanted to drop her off at the diner that would work. She opted for the latter and I gave her the directions, which she put in her phone. I let her off at the curb near the church.

"See you tonight. Have a good time!" I said. She waved and she was off.

• CHAPTER 18 •

I went back home and changed for work and noticed Roger had the music up loud again. Maybe he was up to a third date, I mused. Really, was that whole half beard thing working for him? Part of me was wanting just a hint of a nap but I knew I'd never wake up if I went back to bed for any length of time. The music would probably keep me up anyway. *Just more coffee*, I thought. That and maybe a little pizza lasagna.

I pulled into work and there was a space right next to GR8 PE. What was he doing here again? Begrudgingly I took the space — it was Sunday and Meg would love it. I strolled in looking for Ginny to vent to first. Both Harold and Gerry were sitting together up front, in my section. This was going to be a long, *long* day. They already had their coffee, so I was going to let Ginny continue to wait on them.

"Lainey, did you hear about the new Italian restaurant? Fabulous pizza, I hear! I'm going to be there for the opening Wednesday."

"Oh that's great Harold," I said. "No, I hadn't heard about it, but at some point I will be sure and check it out."

"Are they hiring?" I heard Ginny quietly ask Paula from somewhere behind me.

"No. All staffed up," Paula whispered back.

"You should come by Wednesday," Harold continued. "There's going to be a lot of promotional stuff going on. TV coverage and the like. It's always so much fun when they bring in the media."

It would be a three-second blip on the news, but yes, it did stir up a lot of excitement from the locals.

"Balloons and the like?" I said, being a little facetious.

"Really, Lainey, you've got to get into this stuff. Things happen. There's always the potential."

He did have a good way of looking at life. I probably should listen to Harold's show more often. I was at least trying to look for the potential of the diner staying open.

Gerry hadn't said a word and was just observing my take on Harold's news, but he gave a nod with *potential* and a raise of his coffee cup, which I was taking as a salute and not a, "how about a refill?" moment.

"You need your own restaurant," I said offhandedly to Harold. "Imagine all the events you could hold!"

We both smiled and I went off to help another customer.

When I ran into Ginny again, I pointed to Harold and Gerry together. "Best buddies?" She smiled.

"They arrived at the exact same time so it only seemed fitting to say table for two? They didn't object, and yup, best buds."

"Why does that worry me?" I said in a distracted far away voice.

"Oh, don't be silly, Lainey." She glanced at me. "Oh. How was Ruth? Did you have a good time last night?"

"No, her plane was cancelled last night. I picked her up this morning. I barely said hello to her and now she's leaving tomorrow morning. Her family will drop her off here tonight though, so you'll get to meet her for probably all of a second!" I was trying to remember exactly how much I had said about Ruth to Ginny or vice versa. The awkward meeting of two different worlds! Nah, it would be fine. Ginny was just that way. And with Ruth, I probably never had the chance to even mention Ginny.

About an hour into my shift, I saw a group coming in, dressed very formally. At the back of the group, I saw Ruth. It was only four o'clock. That was fast. And weren't they all going to go back to the cousin's house afterwards?

Meg was seating them in Ginny's section and I went over to find out what the deal was. Ginny had the side tables and you could seat larger parties there, pushing smaller tables together. After I said hello to her folks, and her brother, all of whom I hadn't seen since junior high school, I said, "I'm surprised to see you all here. I thought you were going back to your cousin's house."

"I mentioned you work at the diner to everyone. We used to come here all the time, back when we lived here, so we thought we'd all stop by. Well, that, and the bride got sick," Ruth said.

"What?"

"Really sick."

"Oh, that's too bad," I started to say and realized I had never asked if her cousin was the bride or the groom. I didn't know her extended family at all but I was immediately interrupted by her brother.

"She threw up just as she was about to walk down the aisle."

"Wait, what?"

"Yeah, she got pretty sick." Ruth took over again, and my stomach lurched a bit. I was not immune to this type of talk even with my own horror stories from working at the diner. "So everyone told her to go in back, sit down for a bit, cleanup, and we would try it again when she was ready. Some poor soul went to clean up the mess." *Poor soul.* Okay, she was either showing some compassion, or being glib.

"Which lead to more gaging and such," the brother continued, now just grossing me out.

"Anyway, I guess she had a few more spells in the back room. We waited. Next, they were trying to decide if they should postpone the whole thing. But of course, the whole reception was paid for already, and it wasn't that she was backing out, she was just sick.

"So after about an hour she came out again, looking really disheveled, but wanted to go ahead with it. Tim, my cousin, looked a little scared but they somehow got through it. Everyone looked a little queasy when the minister said 'you may now kiss the bride.' Let's just say it was short and sweet, to be nice. Anyway, they made it all the way to the reception hall where she got sick again.

"Tim got up and said, 'Friends, family, Margie and I are going to excuse ourselves, but please enjoy your dinner and some dancing.' And they left.

"So, we stayed but it was so uncomfortable. No one really felt like eating, but they fed us right away. The band was good however, so there was a little dancing, and we didn't want to go back to Tim's folks' house right away, since we weren't sure what was going on and so, well, here we are."

"Wow. Well, they are going to have a wonderful story to tell once she gets over how hideous it was!" I was quick to point out.

"Yeah, I'm sure that's going to be a while. Tim told us they're going to reschedule the photos, which doesn't really make sense to me, it was today after all, but I guess they do want one good photo, pretending that's how the day went!"

Suddenly remembering I was at work I asked, "Well, would you all like some coffee or anything? It looks like I have to get back to work for a bit, but if there's anything I can get you?"

I got the coffee and soda orders and brought them over. They had all just eaten so I didn't think they would be ordering much of anything but they surprised me, all wanting dessert. They told me no one wanted to cut the cake at the wedding, so they left it intact. Now that seemed like a total waste of a good cake. Someone had suggested just taking the top layers off for the bride, but the staff didn't seem to want to do that.

Anyway, they said they were just regrouping here for a bit and then they might go back to the cousin's house and see what the deal was.

* * *

Ginny called me to the side and said more as a question than statement, "They're still here?" I was going to answer with *they really just got here,* but then I realized she meant Harold and Gerry, who were still deep in conversation. They'd had dinner, and then coffee a couple of times now. I'd even topped off their coffee once.

"Yup, best buds." I was just glad I hadn't gotten dragged into the conversation there so it was all good by me.

"Lainey," Harold said waving me over. Okay, I'd put the thought out there, and here it was immediately coming back to bite me.

"Yes, Harold," I said.

"Gerry and I were wondering if you'd like to come with us to the antique car show. It's really an impromptu car gathering at the west side of the mall parking lot on Thursday nights. I don't know why I hadn't thought of it sooner."

"Ummm... I—I have a class on Thursday nights, so I don't think so, but thank you," I answered really slowly. Now I was completely confused. What was the game plan here? Me and Harold and Gerry, at the car show, because obviously I had such a fascination with cars? No. So, then because we were in search of...not PNT-BTR. That was a silver BMW — hardly an antique, and otherwise...I really wasn't looking for...Harold had some weird sense of humor was all I could think.

"Oh, that's too bad," he said and it sounded genuine.

"But, maybe you might want to ask Meg," I said, thinking that might actually be a good thing for Harold.

I went on to another table and as soon as I could, I caught Ginny to tell her. "Hey, that sounds like fun," she said.

"I would say, you should go too, but we have a class!"

My dessert party seemed to be breaking up and I went back over. Mark announced, "We're headed back to Tim's folks' house, to see if anyone else made it back there, see what's going on, and if no one's there, we're going to go sightseeing for a while."

"Oh, that sounds great," I said. "I hope you all have a good time, it was so good to see everyone again. Even if it was just at work!" They all got up to leave but then Ruth sat back down again. "Aren't you going with them?" I asked.

"Oh, no. Who knows when they'll be done, and I don't want to make them come back here after all that."

"Oh, Ruth, go with them, you don't want to sit in the diner for hours! Trust me on that one. I'll come pick you up tonight after work," I volunteered and then thought what am I saying? I am going to be a zombie after work, I got up at 6:00 a.m. this morning. Then I couldn't remember, 6:00 or was it 5 or was it 4. The longer the day, the earlier I was inclined to make it in my head! I will no doubt get hopelessly lost trying to find the cousin's house.

"You're right, that sounds better," she said and then ran out after them not waiting for me to reply.

"Wait, wait," I said and had to run out myself to catch her to get the address of the cousin's.

They all seemed to have different reference points to tell me how to get there, and I hoped I'd remember some of them! I wrote down the address and just one or two of the references on my order pad.

When I went back into the diner Harold and Gerry were leaving. They were swapping business cards, Gerry crossing something out on his, probably the old work number, and I'm sure putting down his cell phone. Maybe his old business cards said GR8 PE on them too and he couldn't bear to part with them!

The diner seemed empty after all "my people" had left, even though the seats filled back up relatively soon after they did.

"What is this?" one customer was asking and pointing at his dinner. I told him it was the chicken pot pie as he had ordered, and he said, "Did this come from a vending machine?"

"Excuse me? A vending machine? No, no we made it in the kitchen."

"Tastes like it came from a vending machine."

I offered to get him something else and he said, "No, the tasteless food would be fine."

My "getting out early" was a bit of a joke as there was always something else to do just as I was leaving. So, at nearly 11:00, I got in my car and automatically started to drive home. Then, I had to turn around to go by the directions they gave me which now started at the diner. A good 40 minutes later, I passed a small convenient store and I couldn't remember if they had said to go by it, or you've gone too far if you go by it.

I kept going down the road anyway. It turned into one of those ultra-dark roads with trees on either side and nothing else. The darkest trail through a forest I had ever been on. It twisted along with lights spaced just far enough apart to be in pitch black for a while before the next one emerged. The lines on the road were also extremely faded and I was just so thankful it wasn't raining. Were there houses here? If so, they were completely secluded in hidden driveways. It was more likely I'd stumbled into a state forest. I kept going wondering at what point I should turn around, or where would it be safe to pull off and call Ruth. Part of me kept saying *hey, it's late you're just weirding out, I'm sure it's just up a little bit further...all roads go somewhere don't they?* At that point I was wishing my cell phone was a smart phone and I had GPS on it. But at least I had the phone on me this time.

Finally, the road ended, turning into a "T" at the very end. At the stop sign I decided to pull over a little and I pulled out my order pad. According to my scribbled directions, there was no mention of a "T" so it was *not* the road I was supposed to be on. I thought I was seeing some kind of lake just beyond the trees ahead but it was so still and so dark I wasn't really sure. There had been no mention of a lake or water of any sort during the call out session. I thought I'd better call Ruth, and at least let her know I'd taken a wrong turn. They must have said, if I saw the convenience store I'd gone too far.

But, she didn't answer, it went straight to voice mail, so getting new directions was out of the question. I did see the irony of the out-of-towners having to give me directions. She probably wouldn't know where I was, or where I took a wrong turn! I changed directions and proceeded back through the dark, dark forest trail again. I made it back to my landmark after another tense ride, just trying to watch the road. There hadn't been another car on the road the whole way back and forth and I was delighted to see headlights when I'd reached the store! Deep breath.

I pulled into the parking lot and took out my scribbled directions once again. This time I was a little calmer reading them and redirected myself. A few minutes later, I was at the correct address with nary a light on.

So, this didn't look promising either. Was I about to wake everyone? There was a rather large garage and I couldn't tell if everyone was parked inside, or no one was home.

I pulled in the driveway, called Ruth on her cell once again, hoping not to disturb anyone if they were all asleep. Once again, it went straight to her voice mail. I then worked my way up the walk to the front door. It was now long after midnight. The party was over and here I was at the door. Doorbell or knock? Please just shoot me.

I was just about to knock, figuring it would wake the least number of people, when I saw the headlights and car pulling in the driveway. Yay! Pulling in the driveway blocking me in thank you, it was a two-car driveway, and I parked on the far side!

I turned to walk back to the car, and two people got out from the back doors. Two guys, it seemed to me, and they were laughing and started towards me and then the car itself backed up and left.

"Hi," I managed to squeak out, in a voice so timid even I didn't recognize. "Do you know if Ruth is here?"

"Hey, yeah!" one of them said as he got close. "You're a little bit late aren't you?"

"Do you know if Ruth is here?" I said again, slightly louder and in a voice I would say was mine.

"Ruth?" he echoed, sounding a little confused.

"Ruth, she's with her family, Mark's her brother, and..." My mind went blank. I had called them Mr. & Mrs. Stone my whole life, what were their first names? "Her parents," I finished with, good enough, I guess.

"Oh, I thought you were here to cater the party!"

Cater the party? I looked down at my uniform, oh of course. But did they cater the after party? Wow.

"No, oh, no. I'm Lainey, Ruth's friend."

"Well, nice to meet you, Lainey, come on in and we'll see if Ruth is here," one of them said, but failed to introduce himself. Uh-oh, was I past finding out who these people were? Was I just randomly going into someone's home with strangers? That would not be good.

One of them turned on some lights. Before me was one of the grandest homes I'd ever been in. I was in a massive foyer, with an ultra-formal living room to the side of it. This place was seriously deceiving from the outside in the dark. He called out "Anyone home?"

That didn't feel so good. There was no answer. "Mom? Dad?" Much better, now I knew these were brothers of the groom. Or one was anyway.

He went to the kitchen and more lights went on and then he said, "Oh, dear."

I went into the kitchen and he was listening to his cell phone. After listening to his voicemail he pointed to the phone and said, "Cell phones. Dad's mortal enemy! He insisted we keep them here so no one was texting during the wedding. We promised to be on good behavior and he still wouldn't hear of it. Anyway it was Mom," he said more to what I now assumed was brother number two. "So it looks like they've all gone to the hospital. Margie slept for a while after the ceremony and then woke up only to start throwing up again and Tim got really worried and took her to the hospital. Most of the clinics were closed. Of course, he called Mom and Dad and they all went down. Margie's folks too. I'm sure she's just got the flu or something but everyone's there."

"Do you think we should join them or just wait here?" Brother number two asked.

"No sense going down. I'm sure they'll be back soon." Brother number two looked at me as if waiting for another answer. I wanted to ask him if he wanted to go but didn't want to offend brother number one's remark.

With so many of them there I had absolutely no business being there, except to bring Ruth back to my place to get up at, oh, no... I didn't have the flight time. Was this going to be a no sleep night? I'd gotten up at what—3 a.m. this morning? This was not happening.

I got my timid voice back and said softly, "Did you want to go to the hospital?"

Brother number two said, "You know, it might be more than the flu. You don't know."

I was wondering now why Ruth had never called me to tell me where she was, unless she'd been banished of her cell phone too. If her uncle didn't want them using them...she probably turned it off. Was this her mother's brother or sister? Her father's brother or sister? No clue. Not that it really mattered, but I didn't even know their last name to match it up somehow. If it was the same name, I was dealing with her dad and his brother, but otherwise all bets were off. It just seemed rude to ask, *who the hell are you people?*

My vote at this point was to go to the hospital and rescue Ruth and get at least an hour's sleep. If we stayed and waited for them... well how long would that be. The mother hadn't said.

"Let me check with Ruth," I said. "Maybe she can tell us some more." I called Ruth's phone one more time and it still went straight to voice mail. I told her I was back at the house with her cousins, and even as I said cousins, I wasn't 100 percent sure they were, (but no one corrected me as I spoke,) and we were waiting to hear how things were going.

I put down my phone and looked at them. "Oh, do you know the name of the hospital? Maybe we could page them."

"Oh, I think I know, let me try." Brother number one called, and asked if he could speak with Joan LaMorton. She'd be in the waiting room. Okay, so it was not Ruth's dad's brother. No, no one there. So, now, it was either another hospital or they had left. He tried another hospital while we huddled around the kitchen island.

Amazing kitchen. The all coordinated black, white, and grey granite countertops, with the matching mosaic focal point master- piece, and backsplash, and all the stainless steel appliances.

(Everything I'd ever seen on eat your heart out TV remodeling shows, it was all right here.) I'd pulled up a stool as had brother number two. Brother number one got up once in a while to do some pacing.

We sat there for, I'm gonna say an hour, but it might have only been fifteen minutes. Then we heard car doors closing and we knew they were back. Many doors. Must be two cars.

The front door opened and three people I'd never seen before came in, I was guessing mother, father and a sister. Then my crew with Ruth somewhere in the mix came in. There were about four conversations going at once, but Ruth made her way over to me and said, "Oh good, you made it."

I glanced at her, annoyed, but I didn't say anything. Everyone spilled into the formal living room, and they all took what seemed to be their assigned seats as every one of them knew exactly where to go. All but me, of course, and I heard someone say "And who is this, is this your friend Ruth?"

"Yes, that's Lainey," she replied for me.

"Hi," I said again in my new meek voice. Too many of them at once.

"Have a seat, dear," I heard from somewhere, maybe Ruth's mom, I wasn't sure. So, I found the last remnant in a plush footstool and plunked down.

They all went over, what for them must be the millionth time, how lucky she was it was only the flu, and how distressed Tim had been. Although it was clearly a severe bout of the flu, but nonetheless...

Tim's mother was asking if anyone wanted coffee, and I might have had a look of horror on my face as I tried to communicate to

Ruth that we most definitely should go. Fortunately, Ruth's mom had the sense to say she thought she should call it a night as she had a plane in the morning. Unfortunately, her father had decided that since he was getting up at four to get to the airport, he might as well stay up and have coffee now. I looked at my watch. It was now almost 2:00. Her mother looked crestfallen.

"What time is your flight?" I asked Ruth.

"Oh, I got the one right after them at 8:30."

Oh, lucky me.

"So we need to leave by at least 5:45 to give you enough time?"

"Yeah, that sounds good."

"Okay, then we need to leave now," I said, sounding very authoritative. Go Lainey!

"You girls are welcome to stay here," the mother said.

"All my stuff is at Lainey's, but thanks," Ruth said.

She offered us to stay there? Had she offered that to Ruth before? Wasn't there *no room*? I was having something of a hard time working that one through.

"Well, I think we're off then," she said, sounding very disappointed to leave, and said her goodbyes to the family.

I wanted to ask why again she was staying with me, but couldn't do it. I was tired, and I'd probably get angry and it wouldn't help me a bit at this point. Instead, I went the other way, be cordial, be nice.

"So, besides the hospital, where did you all end up going?" I asked as we made our way back to my apartment.

"Oh, we had a great time sightseeing. It's been so long since we've been back here all together, we drove by the place we used to live at, and where other friends and family had lived, and basic sightseeing of the area, noticing so many of the changes around here."

"Sounds like fun with the family!"

"Of course, everyone had a different opinion on what used to be where, how it used to be and all that. My father goes way back. He's still busy noticing changes that happened before I was born. They all go on and on about things you know nothing about, and you just have to let them ramble!"

"Well, I'm glad you got to the diner then, I'm not supposed to tell the regular customers, but it seems Meg is thinking of selling it to someone who wants to turn it into some kind of general store. So, it's possible it won't be here next time you come back." There, now I was facing it. It now sounded true.

"So you'll be out of a job?" she asked.

"It's looking that way," I said and this time I really felt it. I was going to be out of a job.

Wait, for a second there it actually sounded like she was concerned. It was very strange because I had seen such a different side of her today, not so much with Mark, but with her family. She seemed to cater to them. I was so mixed up. I'd never seen that side of her before.

We eased up to my apartment somewhere close to 3:00 a.m. and I noticed Roger's lights were on. Ruth was either still on central time, or working on adrenaline as she didn't seem all that exhausted. Maybe she was counting on sleeping on the plane. Meanwhile, I was calculating when I could get some sleep myself. Maybe from 9 to 2, if I could fall asleep then, that way maybe I'd make it to work on time, and be half alive.

Calico was sitting on the porch railing as we approached.

"Oh, you have a cat?" Ruth asked, very surprised. "I think I'm allergic to cats."

"You think?"

"Maybe, I just don't like them. I'm not sure. They don't like me."

Ah-ha.

"Well, no, it's a neighborhood cat, very friendly."

Calico watched from the railing, only its eyes moving, going back and forth from me to Ruth, over and over again.

We got in and I went to set my alarm for 6 but it was already set there from earlier that day. Then I realized, no, we *leave* at 5:45. Get up at...my mind went a little fuzzy.

"Do you think if I got married they'd all come out for my wedding?" she then asked from somewhere out of the blue.

"Are you getting married?" Finally, I thought, it's about time. Bren, you are my hero!

"I'm just wondering if they'd come. You'd come, right?"

Now, I felt trapped. I didn't want to lie, but why on earth would I go all the way to Texas to be her personal assistant? If she had it here, that might be another thing, but... "I would certainly try." I offered my best possible compromise. I would be punished for that answer, I knew it.

"I knew you would," she said confidently. "I'm just going to take a shower now. I don't think I'm going to get any sleep, anyway."

She shrugged. Then, she looked as if she'd just remembered something she meant to tell me. "Oh, and Lainey, why don't you just buy the diner? You're such a natural there, I bet you'd really enjoy that."

"I could never afford anything like that!" I cried. "I'm not exactly living in the swells you know. I don't think that would even be possible."

I started thinking of loans and bills and my head started to swim. Besides, she already had the offer.

"Lainey, a long-term sale. Haven't you ever...? You take over the business, but Meg continues to get most of the revenue as pay out until the sale is complete. Thus, the long-term. She may not want to do it, but it could be an option. Just ask her."

She said it like it was the most natural conclusion there was, and with that, shut the bathroom door.

Would Meg ever go for something like that? I wondered if that was even possible! And was that something I could even do? The questions started pouring into my head as I tried to even comprehend what she'd said.

All righty, then. Sleep was out of the question.

CHAPTER 19

I did manage to get just a couple hours sleep *after* I dropped Ruth off. I woke up at one o'clock to the sound of Roger's music again. What had this woman done to my otherwise quiet neighbor? I had some cereal and coffee and now was thinking I should have had lunch instead, but well, I'd have something at work on my break.

My head was swirling about the idea of buying the diner. Ruth had gone over once again what she meant and how it worked, and I tried to take it all in.

I did know all the ins and outs of being a waitress and how the diner ran, but I'd never been on the managing side of it. I'd seen Meg in action with most of it, and on the few occasions when she was out, Ginny and I handled a number of things for her. But it would be a huge responsibility. Was it just that one step too much for me, or was I just being timid? Or maybe this was the thing I needed, the step, the direction that would pull everything together for me. I could almost see myself doing it. It felt a little exciting. Scary! But exciting.

Then I thought of Ginny and Paula. Would either of them want to do something like that with me? Paula had so much going on all the time with her kids. I could mention it, but I doubted she'd be interested. Too much time, way too risky... Ginny on the other hand, I didn't know. Either she would feel overwhelmed by it or... It was so much to think about.

* * *

"So, that was a fast visit wouldn't you say?" Ginny began when I got in. She was asking too many questions, because I hadn't really processed what had just happened with Ruth's whole visit either. That whole idea about the diner... but also I believe I'd turned my schedule all around just to take Ruth to and from the airport and I'd spent some time with people I didn't know in a very nice home I would never be able to find in daylight. And what was up with Bren? Was she hinting she was getting married or was that something else? What had just happened?

"Lainey? Lainey, are you okay?"

"Sorry, Ginny, I must still be exhausted." First, I told her about being out all night after work. Then I looked around to see if Meg was in earshot, and noting that she wasn't, I said in much quieter voice, "Then, after all that, just as I was this close to telling Ruth to find her own way to the airport," I gave her the inch between my thumb and index finger reference, "she said, 'Why don't *you* buy the diner?'"

"So she's delusional too! Wow!" Ginny laughed. "You told her that would actually take money, right?" Her voice was a little louder than I would have liked.

"Yes, I said that." I brought my voice level down again. "But she said something about a long-term sale. I have to look it up to see what that really means, but it was such a shock to hear an idea so completely far-fetched to me, and yet, to her it seemed so absolutely possible! I know alone I'd be a nervous wreck to actually do it, but then I thought, what if I teamed up with Ginny..."

"Whoa!" Ginny said, throwing her hands up as if to say "Stop!" She took a little step back. "Whoa!" she repeated, but softer this time. I guess she'd need to process that one!

* * *

The following morning, I was feeling a little more like myself. I didn't have any classes so I was free until work. I started doing some research on what a long-term sale meant and even though I was feeling way, way out of my comfort zone, I was starting to feel, if Ginny went along with me, maybe this was something I really could present to Meg.

And some part of me felt maybe, just maybe, all those classes I'd been taking for so long, all the "prep" work, was for this.

Around noon, I got a knock at the door. I was fully expecting to see Roger, who I was going to mention the increasing volume on the music to, maybe barter whatever he was going to borrow for some peace and quiet, but to my utter surprise, it was my sister.

We hadn't had our great get together with my mother and Seth to hash out whatever they were doing yet. Jill told me Seth had finally told her in detail all about wanting to do some house flips, but knew it was risky. He'd asked our mother if he could use this opportunity to try it out and she was willing to help out. He didn't want to hide it, but he wasn't so sure Jill would be on board either, so when our mother was investing in a house he couldn't resist the chance to at least try and do one. "He was too chicken to tell me the real story at that point," she went on as we settled in on the couch.

"Does he know she wants to stay there?" I asked her.

"Oh, no, no. He didn't mention that!"

I decided Jill would have to figure out if she wanted to tell him that or not. It would show him what a position it put our mother in, and I didn't think he meant to do that, so I didn't know who I wanted to feel bad at this point.

"You know what? I think I'm going to reschedule our dinner Friday. I'll talk to Seth and let him talk to her first himself. We'll reschedule after that, how's that?"

I could hear the psychic's words kicking in as I nodded my head yes in reply. *It wasn't going to end badly, and not to get overly involved or concerned.* I also thought, good, then I can tell them when we're all together about Ruth's idea, once I'm a feeling a little more sure of myself and know what Ginny's thinking.

"Anyway, the real reason I'm here, is to borrow something for Janie's 'pajama day' party at school," Jill told me.

"Why didn't we have silly things like that when we went to school?" I asked.

"Somehow, I don't think it would have gone over as well back then. Parents would have had a fit."

"Hmmmm. I don't know. It feels like it's more the other way around these days, but, hey, still sounds like fun."

But, what did I have? I wished she'd called and I'd have fished around for stuff, although okay, maybe not this weekend!

"What about the bunny slippers I gave you? Do you have those?" she asked me. I got up and went into my bathroom-closet and saw them sitting on my shoe rack. How could you throw out bunny slippers?

* * *

Meg called us into the kitchen when we came in. I wasn't at all ready to ask about the long-term sale, and needed to talk to Ginny about it seriously, so I felt a little apprehensive. Instead however, she told us that Harold had called her and asked if he could reserve the diner late on the following Tuesday night. That way most of the dinner crowd would at least have come through. And while some diners were open 24 hours and got a lot of the drinking crowd, after the bars closed, the ones who were then wanting breakfast; we didn't get them so much, since we closed at 11:30.

"So, he's having some kind of party?" Ginny asked.

"Well, he said it was a gathering of some of his special listeners. You know how he does all those 'how they met' shows and things like that."

* * *

I seated a woman who seemed vaguely familiar. She took the menu and then with a wispy voice said, "Oh, I remember." I looked at her. She remembered, but clearly I didn't. "You're in the class too, aren't you?"

"Which class?" I asked, handing her a menu. I'd taken too many of them. But looking at her, I made a quick judgement that she was from one of the art classes. She had a long scarf around her neck, and lots of necklaces underneath. Long curly brown hair, a large shirt dress with black leggings and a macramé pocket book that could have easily been a hand-me-down from the sixties. Yes, definitely one of the art classes, but I couldn't remember which one. Did she have that bag in the class?

"Stephanie's class," she said.

"And what one was that?" Wait, was this a current class?

"She's the intuitive, the class was psychic awareness but I think it was really just an intro for their new line of holistic programs. Holistic health, holistic healing. I think they wanted to get people interested that would never have thought about it before."

Okay, so I was completely wrong. Now, was she talking about me or just people in general that never would have been interested? Probably people in general, I didn't want to be put off by her so soon in our encounter.

Then she blurted out, "Oh, I get it now!"

"What?"

"The sandwich! Oh, that is funny, no?"

I knew she meant my mini-reading but...and then I was trying to think, did she get a reading as well? While I was fascinated with the readings I couldn't put a face on a one of them. I was too busy wondering, is this what my mother does, how close does she come to hitting the mark? Is she vague with lots of interpretations? And why have I never once asked her about it? Or Jill for that matter. We never once said a peep. Okay, you know what, that had to change!

"You work in a diner! Oh, that's so funny."

Oh, okay. Totally wrong context.

"It was positive too, right, like a great sandwich or something, you must be good at your job! Oh, she's good. I had a private reading with her and she saw things I never would have put together for myself. I think she's going to be having some different type of classes in the new program. You should look them up..."

Ginny walked by and the woman smiled. "She was there too!"

Ginny nodded and said, "Oh, hi, from the class, right?" In my defense, I took a *LOT* of classes.

I wanted to pull Ginny over and swap places with her now but I just smiled and nodded.

"Yes, she was. Okay, then, let me leave this with you," I said, tapping on the menu. "I'll be back in a few."

"Thanks! I'm Shawna by the way."

"Well, Shawna, I'm Lainey and I will be right back to get your order."

"You have a name tag," Ginny said as I walked by her.

"Shut up."

* * *

I had to have a talk with Roger. What was up with the music lately? Was it the girlfriend or did he just get a new sound system? In which case, why weren't our neighbors to the side all over him? It was so random and sporadic, it seemed each time I was about to lose it, he would turn it off again.

I was mulling over whether or not to march up and put him in his place when the phone rang. Now in a fairly irritated mood I didn't even wait for the machine to kick on. I answered and knew any telemarketer was in for a rough day.

"Hello," I said in my snarliest voice.

"Lainey?"

"Oh, hi, Mom." My whole being sunk. Wow, I thought, shaking my head no. Mom got the full wrath of that one!

"Lainey, are you okay?"

"Yes, just, yes... what's up Mom?"

"I was calling to invite you to lunch one day this week. I know dinner is usually so much trouble for you." Weren't we scheduled for a dinner on Friday before Jill cancelled the whole thing?

"Oh, that would be great, sure." Was she ready to dish on her decision, or would I have to pry that out of her?

"How about we meet around 11:30 on Tuesday?" Tuesday, Tuesday, what was up with Tuesday? Oh, right, Harold's thing at the diner. But that was late that night.

"Oh, that's fine, Mom. I just have to be to work by 3:00 or maybe 3:30 I'll double check, but that should be fine."

We decided on a restaurant to meet at and then she said, "Great, see you then."

Hmmm. She hadn't "invited" me to lunch in a while. Sometimes, we would do lunch but it was more of a going out to lunch because I was visiting. She didn't usually "invite" me per se, either. It was usually, *are you coming by this week...* something more along those lines. There was something formal about this. Maybe this was because it was supposed to be a dinner at Jill's. And Jill cancelled. Well, there was no telling with Mom. Hmmm, maybe this was the time to tell her about the diner too. Maybe telling her first...forget waiting to tell them all together. Get her input. It really was a big idea. I almost felt proud of myself.

I put down the phone and the music stopped. What the...? It wasn't *that* loud but that I could hear it at all was the problem. Was I now going to wait until the decibel level was intolerable and *then* I would speak to him? Better yet, somehow just casually slip it in next I saw him, wasn't that the original plan?

I looked over at the living room window and saw the calico sitting on the outside ledge of the window somehow. How did it do that on just a sliver of a ledge? And wouldn't it have made more sense to be on the inside of the window looking out? People logic, not cat logic, I guess. I went in to grab a sandwich and instead went for the rest of the pizza lasagna. Ruth's loss.

Ruth, I should give her a call and see how everything turned out. Was the cousin's wife okay — it was just the flu, right? We had exactly no time to actually sit and talk. What was the deal with her? Argh. That whole other side of her too, so considerate of all her other relatives, just had me baffled. And then the idea about the diner, I should at least thank her, even if it was scaring the daylights out of me, it was a solid idea.

I reached for the phone again and then remembered the time difference. It was only an hour earlier there, but what was I thinking? It was a work day; she'd be at work now. That was not going to happen. Sometimes I was too out of sync with the 9-5 people.

A serious crash outside the front of my apartment stopped my rambling mind. I ran to the door and saw Roger's car crumpled alongside a tree outside. He'd hit it on the passenger side.

"Roger," I screamed as I ran out to check on him. "Roger, are you okay?"

Roger looked completely dazed as I got to the car — the airbag had given him quite a wallop and he was staring off into space.

The neighbors came running from both the house and the house next door. No one else was in the car with him, just Roger.

I opened the car door slowly half thinking he would fall out if I went too fast. Hadn't I just had a little tirade in my head about his music? He was heading towards the house, which made no sense since he couldn't possibly have gone out and come back in what, the last three minutes? I hadn't heard him leave, although the music did turn off after I hung up with my mother.

"Roger, are you okay?" I repeated myself not sure what else to say.

"Yeah, I'm…"

He was clearly still dazed, maybe talking wasn't the answer. He unbuckled his seat belt. I was glad it wasn't all mangled up and un-wedged himself from the airbag to get out.

"What happened?"

"I swerved to miss a cat. Then, I got confused because I wasn't sure what direction it had taken off in. I tried to turn around and the tree was on me before I knew it. Wow, did that do some damage!" He looked out at the car. The neighbors had all formed a semi-circle around the front of the car so he'd walked to the backend and looked over at the side.

"Cat?" I asked, looking back at my apartment and saw it was no longer there. "Tell me it wasn't the orange cat."

"Orange? No this was a black and white one. Well, it might have had orange too. I don't remember."

"No, it…never mind, as long as you're okay," I said.

The neighbors had started interjecting that Roger should get some medical help just in case. We heard the sirens in the background, apparently one of them called when they heard the crash. Police came, and an ambulance. Roger was too dazed to object and let them check him out. I was impressed that they didn't even seem to look twice at the whole half beard thing — naturally they'd seen it all.

Roger was pronounced okay, and there was just the car mess to deal with. He took a couple of pictures of the car with his phone and the neighbors began to disperse. He called to get it towed and we both went and sat on the front porch waiting for the tow truck. I knew I'd now missed my opportunity to talk to him about the music. And since I couldn't do it now, and well after it had already gone on for a while, yeah, I was stuck with it now and forever.

"So, how's it going with the new girlfriend?" I asked, trying to change to something uplifting.

"What new girlfriend? Do I have a new girlfriend?" he asked, a little eager.

"Oh, oh, I just figured the date the other day went well." I was now squirming. I had assumed way too much.

"Nah. After the two-second novelty of the beard wore off, it went straight downhill."

"Oh, oh, sorry about that." I could not end this fast enough. "Well, hey, how about I make us some coffee while you wait for the tow?" I said eager to do something, anything else at the moment.

"Oh, thanks that would be great."

"Cream, sugar?" I had no cream, only milk.

"Black."

I tried to think of anything else I could do. I knew he was going to be roughed up a bit from the airbag for a few days, but the medics had told him what to expect, so I went in and made the coffee.

When I got back out he was still sitting on the stair but the calico had saddled up beside him.

"So, no hard feelings for the cat?" I said, handing him the coffee.

"What? Oh no, this...did you think it was this cat?" He asked, probably now remembering I asked the color.

"I hoped it wasn't. Do you know whose cat this is?"

"No, I just see it around. It's very social, but I don't know who it belongs to."

No help there.

After the tow truck came and he dealt with the car, we disappeared back to our apartments.

But ten minutes later, he was down at my door again.

"Any chance I could get a ride to the drugstore? I'd ask to borrow the car, but I'm not sure you'd want me driving right now."

"Oh, um, no, I wouldn't," I said tentatively, I had to be at work in an hour. I looked at my watch wondering how long this would be. "Okay, but it has to be quick. I have to go to work." I felt a pang of guilt.

"Awesome."

I managed to get back to the diner in time, and I was now all flustered. I took over my section only to find Shawna sitting there.

"Oh, hello again." Was it possible she had on even more necklaces today, this time with the matching bracelets?

I could see she had already ordered so I started to walk away when she said, "I was hoping you'd be in. I brought some of the pamphlets for the new courses they're going to be having at the college. I know the course booklet has them listed, but these really tell you what they're all about." And she handed me a half dozen pamphlets.

"Thank you?" I said more as a question than anything. She'd mentioned them, but had I indicated any interest? I didn't think I had, but okay. I took them and put them in my apron to put in the back room.

* * *

Later that night, when I was home, I noticed my notebook sliding off the stack of papers it was on. I opened it up and reread the bit about things going so well with Ruth. Okay, that did not work. But maybe it was just too much of a leap. I looked for the pamphlet I'd originally gotten about rewriting things, but couldn't find it there. Then I pulled the new pamphlets out of my apron that Shawna gave me and flipped through them but it wasn't one of the ones she gave me either.

Hmmm. I'd do that rewriting thing one more time, I thought. Something in me wanted it to work, wanted me to get out of my own way and have things feel more at ease. But I'd have to word it differently, or change the tense or something because whatever it was I'd done, had really been making things worse. Maybe I needed to start with something easier. I wouldn't dream of touching anything so complicated as work. I could not screw that up! So, what would be easier? Something that would already be fine, I'd just spruce it up a bit. Maybe this was all done in baby steps. I thought about Harold's party. Make that really fun. Harold was such a dear. That would be a great time. This wouldn't be so hard and yes, make that a really great time! This was a no brainer.

I grabbed a new pen, different color, and decided I was now talking about a specific *future* event. Could I do it that way? Or maybe that was the key. Yes, yes, maybe I was supposed to do it that way. Now I really felt good. No doubt, I'd done it backwards the other times. So, I thought it out and proceeded to write:

Had a wonderful time at Harold's event. He draws a really nice crowd for all of his events. He brings together people who have interesting tales to tell and it's always a good time with lots of laughs. I really enjoyed myself. We outdid ourselves for this event, and everyone was talking about it on the radio for days to come.

Oh, now that was great. And, I'd made it sound like it had

already happened, and okay, that must have been the key. I was liking it. I felt good.

Once again, I ripped out the last page, the one about Ruth, and shred it. I put the notebook on the newest stack of pamphlets. I had a feeling I'd finally turned the corner.

* * *

Saturday, we had our cooking club and Ginny had already supplied the recipe, jumping in when it should have been Anna's turn to figure it out. I was so surprised but Thursday night after our French cuisine class she said rather excitedly, "I have this week's idea!" It was for a taco potato and it was clear that she had done exactly like me, just mixing up what we normally ate, but I had no objections to that because it was fun. We were as far from "exotic" as we could be, but if Dennis was happy, we were all happy. And she seemed to think Dennis was going to love this.

That week the French class had been some kind of veal stew and she showed no interest in ever making some version of that for Dennis. As it turned out, she had never had veal before. But she did eat some of it in the class, just a small amount but she still had some. I was so impressed she got that far. But I didn't want to make a big deal of it, for fear she'd remember how much she hated trying new foods.

"So, Ginny, what do you really think about the idea to buy the diner?" I managed to ask after our club, as we were loading up our cars with our carefully wrapped taco potatoes.

"Well, I mentioned it to Dennis," she said, putting her food in the back seat, "but we haven't really discussed it yet. I think this is a real sit down type talk, and we haven't done that yet, so I don't know," she said as she shut the back door. "But I am giving it a lot of thought. Do you think we could really do it?"

"See, I keep thinking and thinking," I answered. "I'm at the point where I feel I really won't know until I do it! I know that sounds backwards, but given all my classes and all the jobs I've ever done, nothing has screamed this is what I want to do. But right now, I know I don't want the diner to go away. I want to stay there, and maybe, just maybe I have to step up. But I know I would need help. Maybe after a few years I could do it on my own, but I don't think I'm that ready just yet. So, that's where I'm at."

"Yeah, Dennis and I need to talk it over too. It's risky, Lainey, but, yeah, it's down to *am I all in, or not.*"

• CHAPTER 20 •

On Tuesday, I was off to meet with my mother at the restaurant at 11:30. I had a funny feeling about the formal invite and all, but I just never knew with her. It could be nothing. It was a nice restaurant, a little closer to me than her. I think Paula mentioned applying here, and they were full up too.

Once we'd settled in and ordered, she said, "I don't know if I've mentioned my friend, Sam, to you, have I?"

"No, I don't think you have," I said in my most casual voice.

Wow! No! Sam! No! What?! Mom has a new man in her life. Wow. Never thought I would live to see the day!

"He's in the construction business." I was getting a little more daylight here. "And he's been helping me with the house renovations with Seth. He was the one to recommend the crew we got to work on the house. Nice bunch, they've all done such a great job."

"So, where are you with that now? Have you made any decisions? Are you going to sell?" Oops, I sidelined the Sam info. Wrong move.

"Well, the thing is...I didn't want to tell you, because, well, because I think I am going to keep it. Well, um, me and Sam."

Did my eyeballs fall out? It sure felt like it. Whoa, okay, so that was the real deal. "Oh?" Mom, un-freaking believable. "So, wait, you did this whole 'flip' thing with Seth but now the house is for you and this Sam? That's a little fast, isn't it?"

"We met Sam in the process looking into all the different people to help with the renovations. He's legit, don't worry. I've got a lot of references. They've done a wonderful job. Anyway, yes, through the process we've been seeing each other."

Seeing each other was one thing, but moving in together on a house you're renovating is a whole other thing... "And you haven't said a word about this all this time?" I was so stunned.

"Well, I didn't know how you'd react, especially with the invest-ment, thinking that I was just doing it on the spur of the moment. I knew you'd get all upset. I do know you've always been wary of Seth, that's pretty obvious, so I had no idea how you'd react."

"When did you decide this with Sam?"

"Oh that was very recent. He saw how upset I was to lose the house, and now dear, at first he was going to just help me out, but at our age... we just decided you know what... let's do this."

"Well, wow! But, okay, I get that. How much does Jill know?"

"Well, she did help me find the place, but that was about all. I wasn't sure what Seth told her about wanting to invest in it, so I didn't say anything, and no, she didn't know about Sam..."

"But Seth must have known..."

"I don't think Seth knew we were dating, just very friendly. But Jill knows now. But only since she called to cancel the dinner."

"Does she know you two are moving into the house?"

"Yes, she does. But I'm afraid Seth doesn't know about the

house quite yet."

"So will Seth actually make a profit after all this, or just recoup his renovation costs?"

"We'll get the house appraised and Sam will figure that in with the renovation costs."

"So, when do you think the house is going to be done?"

"Well, it can go pretty quickly at this point."

"This is all so sudden it seems. So, when do I meet him?"

"Oh, I hadn't gotten that far."

"No, Mom, the gig is up. I need to meet him! This whole thing has been such a bombshell!"

"Don't be so dramatic."

"Mom!"

"Okay, well I didn't want to say anything if it wasn't working out. I like to keep things to myself, you know that."

"Yes, I do know," I said very slowly.

How on earth could I ask this next one? And should I?

"Say, Mom, does Sam know that..."

"That I read Tarot cards? You wanted to know if he knows that? Yes, he knows it's stories people buy and he's on board. So, there you have it."

As I sat there, I had a sudden realization. The anxiety I was feeling in the psychic awareness class; this was what that was all about. I resented her saying she had seen signs, I resented thinking that somehow she knew what was going to happen with my dad, and didn't do anything about it. My ten-year-old mind had turned that resentment into blaming her for what happened, for not saying anything, and at the same time I knew it wasn't true. There was no way she wouldn't have done whatever she could have to prevent something like that.

I couldn't believe what I was feeling. The twenty-five years of bottled confusion spilled out.

"Mom, were you ever *really* psychic?"

"Of course not, you know that! What did you think? I do read the cards, that's all. And people really, *really* enjoy that," she said, defending herself.

"You know, I never really knew. And Mom..." I took a long pause. "I think as a kid I thought you were, and I held it against you."

"What are you saying?" She looked at me totally confused.

"Back then, I think I thought you really knew dad was going to be in an accident, and never said anything."

"You what?" she said, looking horrified. "Lainey, oh Lainey, how could you think that?" She stared at me in shock.

"I really didn't know I thought that," I said equally stunned at my realization. "I think I blamed you in a way. I just had this sense that something was always wrong."

"I'm so sorry you thought that, no, I never knew."

"But you talked about ignoring the signs. You thought something was going to happen," I said remembering the bits and pieces.

"Lainey, I did not know something was going to happen. I kept saying I *wished* there had been signs, I hoped I wasn't ignoring signs, I *wished* I had some kind of knowing, some kind of gift. And that's when folks started telling me the only way to see the future would be to read the cards. That was probably the only way to know. I was so distraught I actually tried them. I tried them on myself and felt like I was just telling myself what I already knew.

Then one by one I tried them on friends, and with each reading I knew it was the person's interpretation of the cards, they were just taking away what they wanted to hear. But they really enjoyed that. I just read what the cards were supposed to mean. But when they started paying me, well, we really needed the money. I didn't think we could get by on my grocery store job alone. So, it stuck."

We were quiet for a little bit. "I kept feeling this dread when I went to my psychic awareness class. I think that was what it was. I just never knew."

"In what class?"

"Oh, it was nothing, just a tease, it was called psychic awareness."

"Do you think I'd like the class?" she asked, totally breaking the serious tone we'd been in and making me laugh. I shook my head no.

"So, what's going on with the diner? Any news?"

"Well," I hesitated. Should I tell her? "Ruth gave me this crazy idea about buying the diner." There, I'd done it, I set the whole thing in motion.

"I'm sorry, what?" she asked.

"She said I should think about asking Meg to sell it on a long-term sale. I know, I have no money, but Ruth said that's the beauty of a long-term sale. Providing of course, Meg was willing."

"You what?" she asked again slowly tilting her head sideways, either in confusion or about to give me a lecture.

"So I would slowly take over the business. Give Meg a chance to ease into retirement. She'd have an income from the diner, and, eventually, I would own it. I asked Ginny about it too, thinking maybe she'd want to do it with me." Now I was wishing I'd gotten an answer from Ginny before I opened my mouth.

"You really want to buy the diner?"

"Well, once I really thought about it, it all started to make sense."

I was expecting, "You don't know the first thing about business. It isn't just some class you take on a whim." And now that I'd said it out loud to her, my mind started filling in all the terrible things that could possibly go wrong for me. It was perhaps the worst idea I'd ever had.

But Mom, surprisingly, didn't negate the idea. Instead, she said, "Well, I didn't know about flipping houses before I did it with Seth, but you know what, now I do."

* * *

That night I went into work almost forgetting it was going to be Harold's event. He hadn't been in all week which was unusual.

Meg put up a sign saying the diner would be closed early due to an event and sorry for the inconvenience. We would close it at 8:00 because there were always people still eating that you didn't exactly want to throw out, but you had to let them finish. At 8:00 with only two couples in there, we started doing a deep clean on all the booths, sweeping under the tables and getting it all prepared. No matter how much we prepped ahead of time there was always something that needed to be done, or done again.

At twenty to nine, Harold came in to situate himself nicely before the event. He had a few bags with him with what I guessed would be prizes or something. Harold loved giving out prizes. Usually T-shirts, saying something about "The Best." Generic ones, *Simply the Best*, and sometimes custom... Best how they met, best novelty store finds, best story about ghosts/ hunting/ sailing/ vacations/ doctors' visits /apartment nightmares/ house buying... basically you name it, because he never ran out of themes for stories.

I hadn't caught which group would be in tonight. My hope was it would be one of the stranger types, just for variety, to hear some of the wilder stories. I also had to remember it was the midnight to 4 a.m. listening crowd. So, no matter what, my guess was it would be an odd bunch.

At ten to nine however, the next person to join Harold was Gerry, which surprised me. "What did you say your group was Harold?" I finally asked.

"Oh, well, I decided to bring the vanity plate folks all together to see what interesting a group we could get. Gerry and I went to the car show and recruited a bunch from there. Now those are the hardcore, classic car, classic plate, I've got something to say folks!"

"Oh, Harold. What have you done?"

"I brought them all to you, to show you what a great bunch of folks they are!"

"I'm sure they are..."

I thought he'd been happy I found Gerry's plate there. I really thought we were done with this. This was never going to end, and I was forever going to be at odds with everyone over it. Seriously, what did I need to do?

They started to trickle in. Gerry was on photo detail, out in the parking lot getting pictures of the cars and their plates. I'm sure mine was there and no doubt Harold would have a big display of the car plates at yet another function.

I could feel myself getting more and more humiliated as they all came in. I did not want to be in the company of these "like-minded folk" because we were not like-minded. I did not want attention drawn to my plate, or my car or my life or anything else for that matter. Do not draw unnecessary attention to yourself.

I could hear them all talking about who they were and why they had chosen such and such. A bunch were just their name, so obvious, and some of them were cute, some were very clever... But not for me. That was the point — not for me. I didn't want to partake in this conversation. But of course, to my horror, Ginny and Meg eagerly told people all about my plate. I shrank a little more with each conversation I overheard.

I sat people, I took their orders, and avoided Harold for as long as I could before it became painfully clear I *was* avoiding him.

I had a tray of orders when he got me, and was saying to one older fellow beside him, "Lainey, here, well she just got a great one by the luck of the draw, didn't you, Lainey?" He wanted me to play along but it was almost excruciating.

"JEL-EEE," I eeked out and then said, "Excuse me, orders to get out." I gave the tray a little nod and quickly went to serve them. I didn't even ask what his vanity plate said.

I ducked into the ladies' room for a moment just to get away but then I could feel my stomach turning. Oh, no. Oh, no, I was going to be sick.

I had to keep it together. Water on my forehead. Then I heard Harold's boom above the din of the room, "and for the best use of the letter 'Z' is CRAZII," and no doubt he was giving them a gift bag. Water on my forehead did nothing for nausea.

"And, oh, where's our very own Lainey here?"

That did it. My stomach said *no freaking way* and I got sick.

I was starting to sweat as well. This was bad.

"Lainey, Lainey? Where did Lainey go? All right, well, let's go on to the best use of some numbers here, we'll start with..." and his voice faded out.

There was a soft knock at the door. "Are you in there, Lainey?" Ginny said. "Harold's been calling for you."

I opened the door slightly. "Ginny, I gotta go home. I'm not feeling well."

"Lainey you look awful! Oh, sure, I'll let Meg know. Are you okay to drive?"

"Yeah, of course," I answered without really knowing for sure.

I looked back in the mirror and I was some kind of pale version of myself with wild hair. How did that happen too? It all came on fast and strong. Could this all just be a reaction to the plates? Somehow, that just seemed too excessive. I had eaten out with my mother earlier, that could be the culprit right there. Wonderful timing!

I excused myself and got out to my car now feeling shaky as well. It was dark, but the lighting in the parking lot seemed to shimmer on the cars. I looked around at the plates, almost glowing, and something in me just let go. Next thing I knew Ginny and Meg and people I didn't know were standing around me.

"Lainey, Lainey, are you okay? Meg saw you go down in just a whoomph. Lainey, we got so scared. Are you okay?"

"Should we call someone?" Someone else asked.

"Does she need a doctor?"

"Is this a 911 call?"

"Did she hit her head?"

I heard all different voices prescribing all different things. My head was a little fuzzy and my stomach was still turning and I was now afraid I'd get sick in front of a crowd, how charming.

The more they spoke the louder the voice in my head was saying, *let me go home, leave me alone, get away from me.* But all I managed to get out was, "I'll be okay. I just need some rest."

Ginny helped me up. "I'll take her home."

"Oh, I don't know," Meg said, looking at her diner full of customers, "Maybe...Gerry..." Of all people, Gerry? "Gerry would you mind taking Lainey home? Or else we could..."

"Sure, I'll take her. Is that okay with you, Lainey? We'll get your car tomorrow."

See, *car* was the word, and I felt so sick once again.

Gerry got me home without a word. I stumbled out, waved a thanks and made it into my apartment just in time. Eventually I staggered into bed fully clothed. If I went and thought about it, Gerry had been very kind to me, but I wasn't thinking, I was busy feeling both humiliated and still fuzzy, and sick.

I woke with a nasty headache to add to my discomfort.

Maybe it was the bride's flu come to get me a week later. Didn't seem probable. And "bride's flu," was that like the "bird flu?" Yes, I was still sick alright. I didn't feel as nauseous as the night before, but I was still iffy and the headache didn't help. I stumbled out of bed and got out of my uniform to put some pajamas on. I was working in reverse order here. I went out for aspirin and then fixed myself a cup of coffee. Thinking about the parking lot, as the next round of humiliation was about to set in, I heard the knock at the door. Could Gerry really be back this early? I wasn't sure I was even ready to get my car back today at all. I was definitely calling in sick, even if I ended up feeling better later today. My mortification level was through the roof.

I opened the door and there stood Roger.

"I didn't see your car. What happened?"

"Then how did you know I was home?"

"I didn't."

"Oh, I'm not feeling so hot, Roger, but what did you want?" I wasn't up for small talk.

"I wanted to borrow your car, but that doesn't look promising. What happened again?"

"I'm really sorry, Roger. I don't feel so hot. Can you come back later?" And I closed the door without waiting for an answer. He must have seen the glazed look in my eyes. I also had no intention of explaining everything to Roger right now. I went back to the table and sat down.

Being in the spotlight with that plate was killing me. The attention was getting on my nerves, but it was more because I didn't feel good about the label. Jelly. I might have many interests, but somehow getting this one as my moniker was way too much for me.

As I went to all the associations of jelly, I was just doing more damage. Squishy, goopy, syrupy, sickeningly sweet, all so drippy gross, but then on a more positive note there was also tasty, but, oh, heaven help us, not on my license plate! See? Nothing was working.

Maybe it was my being sick, but the problem suddenly felt even bigger; things were not right for me. I was going to have to ask Meg about the diner, and I would either fail miserably with that, or be out of a job. And according to Paula it was slim pickings at the moment out there. I was woozy but owning the diner felt right. My place, my decisions, all my skills working for me...

And I really loved being there.

I called Meg at work. "I really don't think I'll be in today."

"Oh, I didn't think you would," Meg said. "You'll probably need to take the rest of the week off, don't you think? I don't want everyone else getting sick too."

"I'm hoping it's just a 24-hour thing but I'm off tomorrow anyway so I'll call you and let you know about Friday, how's that?"

"Okay, but don't come in if you're sick. Rest up."

"I should be good, but thanks, I'll let you know."

I thought I heard a hint of jealousy in the "rest up" part. Meg must have had a long night with Harold's group. She must be looking forward to retirement more and more.

I circled the kitchen. I realized she was right. Let me get back to bed and just sleep this thing off.

As soon as I laid down, the phone rang. I let the machine get it. It was Jill wondering how the thing went last night. I didn't remember telling her about it, but I'd call her back later.

Ten minutes more and the phone rang again. Telemarketer. I just about started to doze and one more time...I wasn't this popular when I was well! This time it was Gerry. He was sorry to call, hoped I was feeling better, and left his number, which I was pretty sure I had from the whole lunch car thing, but said to call when I needed to get my car. Okay, that was nice.

At three o'clock, I woke up famished. I was hoping that was a good sign but when I opened the refrigerator nothing looked good. I was out of a few basics. No eggs, no bread. Toast was about all I was wanting right now and there was none to be found. I think I was going to go grocery shopping either today or tomorrow, and hadn't been too worried about it. I settled on a can of vegetable soup and sat thinking about my next move. *Rest up* wafted through my mind and I took the soup to the couch and turned on the TV for a bit. Absolutely nothing was hitting the right cord and off it went again, but I settled in for my next nap. I would be awake all night at this rate..

• Chapter 21 •

"Did I leave my belt in your apartment? It's white with a round silver buckle?" Ruth asked me on the phone the next day.

"I haven't seen one," I said and moved into the main room to have a look around. "No, I don't see one here. Are you sure you brought it with you? Maybe last minute you didn't pack it or something? Have you already asked at your cousins'?"

"Yeah, they didn't see it either."

"So, I feel like we never really got a chance to talk. How's everything going?"

"I'm okay. Work and more work."

"How are things with Bren?" There, I'd boldly asked. Pretty sure I wasn't supposed to.

"Yeah, it's all good. So, I have to go, but we'll get in touch again soon."

"Sure, fine. Oh, and I meant to say thanks for the suggestion about buying the diner. You know, I think that could have some potential."

"Oh, good. Anyway, I'll talk to you later."

Seriously? Not even three minutes. No time for chit-chat. Wow, and yet I continued to put up with Ruth's behavior, why did I do that? And I *did* just thank her for the suggestion, didn't I? Even that... I was thankful, but...? Wow she confused me.

I'd called Meg to let her know I'd be in work on Friday but now I had to get my car back. Gerry had offered but I decided to give Ginny a call instead.

"Hey, Ginny, would you mind swinging by here and dropping me off at the diner, to get my car before our class tonight?"

"No problem. Are you better?"

"I'm okay now. I intend to go to our class tonight and would never go feeling queasy, so I'm good!"

"Excellent."

"Oh, hey, did Anna call you? She got me last night when I was still on the couch half-asleep. She wants us to decide on the meals when we're all together. So, I guess she hasn't thought up anything for Saturday yet. Or, maybe she wants something more creative than our slight variations. I don't know. I seem to like our slight twist on everyday stuff."

"No, she didn't call, but we can figure something out tonight. Maybe tonight's dish will inspire us. Who'd ever have thought those words would come out of my mouth?!"

"Great. Okay, well, then, see you when you get here."

* * *

I hopped in her car later and she turned to me and said, "Okay, but on one condition."

"What? What are you talking about?"

"We don't change the menu just yet."

"You want to do it?" I could hardly believe she was game.

"Dennis and I talked about it. It actually made me talk to him about all our dinners too. You had a sick day, but I had a long day with Dennis! He promised to start taking me out for dinner at least once a week too!"

"Oh, Ginny! That's such good news! On both counts!" I wondered whether it would work. "Do you think Meg will go for it?"

"Tomorrow, when we go in, why don't we just ask her then?"

"That sounds great! I also think maybe we should look at some of those classes again, maybe we can find some business type ones to give us a little help!"

"Excellent idea. Dennis said if we do this, and at some point we really do make a profit, we're putting in a staircase to our basement. That was all I needed to hear!"

When she dropped me at my car, I ran into the diner just to confirm I'd be okay for Friday. Meg handed me a business card and said there was a man asking about my car. He said he wanted to speak to me. She asked him what it was about and he said, "Well, about that plate of course."

She tried to get more out of him but he just smiled and handed her the card and asked that it be given to me.

I told her thanks, and put the card in my bag. Part of me wondered if I would call him at all. I was so done with the plate, hadn't that sent me home sick for a day?

I mulled that over a couple more times and then put it out of my head as I parked at the community college for our class. Anna came in a bit late so we didn't get to chat before our class. We were making Chicken Cordon Bleu roll-ups tonight and this one felt like a stretch for our meager culinary skills. Not so much the meat and cheese but the pastry part. Pastry was a big word to us novice chefs. Having that, *this could go very wrong* feel to it. This was one where left on my own, or the cooking club, I would use a store bought pastry shortcut. But, the class didn't take the shortcuts. We had made crust for our quiche, but this one somehow felt much more delicate!

After the class, I got the latest catalog. I was pretty sure I had one, but grabbed another anyway, now on the lookout for any business classes. We took our leftovers and decided that for Saturday we would do something much simpler. Ginny suggested we each think up just one addition to a cold pasta salad and we all seemed fine with that. So, it wasn't that we weren't fancy enough for Anna, that was good. Anna would get the standard groceries and we would each bring that one, or two, extra ingredients. We could make different batches see what we liked best. And in that instant, I saw myself testing batches we'd experimented with for the diner.

Friday I woke to the sound of Roger at the door again. Could he borrow the car? He was hoping to get his on Saturday, at least that's when they had told him it would be done. As I scrounged around my handbag for the keys I remembered the business card in there. "Drive safe," I called after him and shut the door.

I pulled out the card and read: William Deballen, Deballen Corporation. Was I really going to call this man? I was curious, but I also didn't want anything to do with something that in any way, shape, or form, connected me to that plate.

I punched in the number on my phone.

"Deballen Corporation."

"Yes, may I speak to William Deballen?"

"He's in a meeting right now. May I take a message?"

NO, no, no, no, no. You may not…Did I have to describe this outloud?

"Actually, Mr. Deballen contacted me, so I don't know what this is about. He left his card for me where I work." That was all I was going to say and I left my name and number. He could contact me. And now even that sounded bad to me. I was now giving out my number to some random stranger, if I wanted to get all paranoid about it. Oh, whatever.

"I'll have him get back to you," she said, having taken my info.

"Thank you." I don't even want to hear from him, but yes, thank you, anyway. Thank you for taking my full name and phone number and violating my privacy. Thank you for allowing me the discomfort of having someone else yet again make a mockery of me for the damn license plate that the DMV would not take back. Yes, thank you. I winced.

Wait, Roger had just taken my car. Now as I sat at the kitchen table I felt like a sitting duck for some ridiculous reason. Maybe Mr. Deballen wanted to buy my plate. Maybe he was the person it was intended for all along and by some sheer coincidence I got his plate and now he wanted to make it right. He wanted the JEL-EEE plate because he invented some kind of jelly, spice jelly, no he was an investor in a giant food corporation, obviously! No, *his* car was PNT-BTR and he wanted this for his wife. Of course, it all made sense.

I had leftovers from last night's class for breakfast. Nothing like Chicken Cordon Bleu roll-ups first thing in the morning. Fancy breakfast! Anyway, it was fine. I was fine. Everything was fine.

Mr. Deballen was going to rescue me from my plate and I wouldn't have to buy a new car after all. I did like my car. I had no objection to the actual vehicle.

I got dressed and spritzed on my happy grapefruit essential oil spray. This was fine. It was going to be a fine day, I decided.

By one o'clock, I was getting a little bit nervous about Roger. Just the post office?

At one-thirty, the phone rang. "Mr. Deballen for you."

Did he have his secretary call me? Wow. Who was this guy?

"Miss Evans, this is William Deballen."

"Yes," I was about to say sir, but then felt totally weird about that. "What can I do for you? I heard you were asking about my license plate."

"Yes, Miss Evans."

"Lainey please." I usually only said that when they called me Lorraine first.

"Yes, Miss Lainey," he began.

Miss Lainey? Okay, worse than Lorraine.

"It seems my son has embarked on a project writing a book, and he's collecting tales of eccentric possessions or what he's calling our 'wacky stuff.' Not to say your plate is wacky or eccentric, but not everyone would have such a plate. It is out of the norm."

"Well, yes, it is. But..." Oh, dear. Here we go again. "I hate to let your son down, but this is just..." Must I say this again? "...a mistake."

I'd really hoped this was something else. Anything else, my whole litany of could-bes, but no. "I really hate to disappoint you here, but I do know someone who knows a lot of stories like that. Have you heard of Harold Burns, the radio host? He has a late-night program and is always looking for the best stories about well, you name it! He just had a party for other people with weird vanity plates. I'm sure he's the one you want to talk to. Or, your son at any rate. He could call him at the station or even stop by the diner, although Harold has no set schedule that he comes in, just frequent is about all I can tell you."

"Perhaps, I should stop in and leave my card with the hostess."

"The hostess is the owner, Meg. If that's who you mean. That was who you left your card with before."

"Well, then, I believe I will do that. Thank you so much for your time. And you're sure there is no other story behind your plate, no connection whatsoever? I really believed that would make a great story for him."

"*NO*. I mean no, no there really isn't." The rant continued in my head though…I've been trying to hide that plate since the day I got it. I do not enjoy being linked to jelly. There's no connection.

"But, you do work in a diner. So, there is some connection." Here we go again. Like those people whose last names end up being their profession. Is it chance or are they being nudged into it. Family profession since the beginning of time? Roof, Carpenter, Baker. Was that fate?

"Mr. Deballen, I could just leave your card with Meg, I already have it. I'm sure Harold will be in sometime this week."

"Thank you so much, Miss Lainey. My son will be so pleased."

Roger returned with my car not long after I hung up. I wasn't sure if I was irritated with Roger, or the Deballen thing now, but I was feeling short with him.

"Oh Lainey, chick magnet!" He had started to let the beard grow back in on the naked side. I guess that bet had ended and he wasn't going to continue with it. Interesting enough but...

"What?"

"Your car, that plate, total chick magnet."

"Really, did you have a good time?" I said, the resentment growing every minute he spoke.

"Did I? I have a date tonight. Oh, can I borrow your car?"

"Roger, I have to go to work. That would be a *no*."

"Oh, but Lainey, this was the trigger. You gotta let me have it just for tonight. This girl, she was all, 'whoa, where'd you get that?' and I'm like, 'Isn't it sweet? I would have done toast but that implied way too many things!' So, first she took a selfie with it — we got a good laugh at that — and next thing I knew we were on for tonight."

"And then what Roger, after that, the NEXT date and the one after that. Turns out I need my car too!"

I could see he was slowly catching on but I had totally bummed him out. And somehow, I was now feeling guilty for not letting him have it. Really, why did I do this to myself?

"Hmmm. Total chick magnet, what a waste," he said, shaking his head and turning to go upstairs.

"Roger, you might want to get a vanity plate yourself if it's such a big deal," I called out after him. "I don't think they cost that much for all the attention you'll get. Really think that over."

"Hey, that's not a bad idea," he said, still walking off but clearly his mood was lifting. "I wonder what I could come up with?"

Oh, the attention. And now this other man wanted to put my plate in a book of wacky things people owned. Wacky. Chick magnet. Really. I mean, really?

Oh, no, what had I done with Roger? I put the idea out there, and what if he did get toast? Jelly and toast, in one driveway. No, he didn't like that one, but he could really do some more harm, or people would just think a bunch of kooks lived here. That wasn't so bad. I didn't have to interact with people who just saw it as they went by, it was all the attention at work, and every other single place I went *in public*.

Half the time, they didn't even need to say anything, the looks alone. The last time I'd been to the bank I saw some guy take a picture of it and I wanted to crawl into a hole. It just wasn't fair.

Chapter 22

My mother called and told me she hadn't been feeling so hot the other day. When I told her I'd had a bad reaction to something as well, we suspected the chicken salad we'd both ordered at the restaurant. We had a thousand do's and don'ts at the diner about food, and Meg was a real stickler. Today, I was ever so glad she was!

She said she'd give them a call at the restaurant and ask if others have been having the same problem. It was too late for us, but a heads up to them wouldn't hurt.

My mind flashed back to the bride and her wedding, and wondered where she'd eaten the night before. Probably a rehearsal dinner and they all would have been affected in that case.

Then she told me she'd talked to Jill. Jill said she would have us all over for dinner to meet Sam. Jill hadn't met Sam either, so this would be most interesting.

* * *

Roger was back at my door again. What was the deal?

"Your car will be done tomorrow, right?" I asked, trying not to sound too annoyed.

"That's what they said. They told me the part they ordered wasn't coming in until today, and you never know if that's true or they just messed something up that they need to redo. So any chance I can borrow yours again now?"

"Gee, Roger, I'm going to work in like ten minutes. I don't think that's going to work for me." I know I'd already said no to tonight.

"How 'bout if I go to work with you and then return it to you there?"

"Then, how are you going to get home?"

"Oh, that's no problem. From the diner I can catch the bus. There's a line right down the street from there."

That was actually good to know if I ever needed it.

"Well, I guess," I said, giving in. "Wait a minute, how about you take the bus now!"

"Not going where I'm going this time."

"All right, give me a minute and I'll be ready to go."

As we pulled into the diner, I saw that same girl, Shawna, getting out of a small beat up car. She saw me too and then she saw Roger.

"Oh, hi there," she said with full interest on Roger.

"Hi, Shawna was it?" I asked double-checking the name.

"Yes, it's Shawna," she said with a big smile. Not such a wispy voice today.

Roger gave her the once over and said, "Roger here."

"Oh, hi, Roger!" She smiled. "Do you go to the community college too?"

"What?"

"I know Lainey from the school. Do you go there too?"

I was pretty sure Roger had zero knowledge of my community college classes. I'd seen him more this week than any other time in our history.

"No, no, I don't. And what is your major there?"

"Oh, I just take the continuing ed. classes there, I'm not enrolled. Lainey and I met in the psychic class."

No, just no. Roger gave me a very complicated look like he'd just met me and said, "Oh, sounds like a great class!"

"It is. You should come sometime. I bet you have skills you don't even know you have." Then she gave me a look like she was sorry she'd stepped over the line with Roger.

"You two might have a lot in common," I said to try and let her know yes he was available. But, then, I handed him my keys and she stepped back a bit.

"Roger's car is in the shop," I said, again trying to let her know he wasn't my boyfriend dropping me off at work. No, *have a nice day, dear* and a peck on the cheek.

"We're hoping it's fixed real soon, aren't we Roger?" If I were a winker that would have been the moment.

"So, tell me about this class," he said to Shawna, not even remotely aware of me now.

Excellent. I was done there. "I have to go. Drive safe," I said again to Roger.

"Hey, look at the plate on your car," Shawna said, aware of it for the first time.

It's not Roger's car was all I could think, but Roger went right into chick magnet mode with, "Cool, huh. The Jelly-mobile. You want a spin?" She laughed and I walked away not wanting anything more to do with this conversation.

"Would you look at that!" I said to Paula when I got in. "I've become a matchmaker."

"Who are they?" she wanted to know.

"A customer and my very odd neighbor. Odd in a good way though. At least I hope. I think. He is kinda odd though." I trailed off but then found myself back at it. "I don't know. Did you notice the beard? Said he lost a bet but again? Friendly. I think he already has a date tonight... What can I say?" I was totally rambling.

She looked amused but didn't say anything.

Today there was a strong cinnamon scent in the air. "Are we making cinnamon rolls?" My face lit up.

* * *

When Ginny got in, we decided this was going to be the time to ask Meg about the diner. We asked if we could talk to her, and she waved us to the back with her and into her little office.

"My friend, Ruth, made what I thought was an outlandish suggestion until I thought it through. Then Ginny and I talked it over and..."

"And we think this is just a great idea." Ginny couldn't stop herself from saying.

"And we're wondering if you would consider the idea of selling the diner to us." I began telling her about the long-term sale idea, and how it would just continue to be income for her rather than one lump sum, and that instead of closing it as Walt would do, we would continue to run it as the diner.

She listened intently, and then very slowly said, "Oh, I don't know about that, girls. That's... I don't know. I'll have to get back to you on that."

Ginny and I looked at each other, feeling a little bit defeated, and started to walk out of the office when she called back to me, in a much more upbeat tone, "Oh, and what did that man want? Did you get in touch with him? He seemed so distinguished." She was asking about Mr. Deballen.

"His son's writing some kind of book on the unusual items people have. I told him he should get in touch with Harold. And that I'd give Harold his number."

"Well, you're in luck. Harold said he'd be in later tonight so you can give it to him then."

"Oh good." Odd she knew that Harold would be in, but nonetheless, I would be happy to get this guy and his son all out of my hair.

A little later, still feeling somewhat defeated, I found a soda spilled all over the back of the table. I was cleaning it up when Roger came back with my keys. The ice was still melting as I mopped and draped rags on the seat. The floor was that brown and white checkerboard linoleum stuff, so you had to be thorough, soft drinks could often become invisible on the brown tiles.

"Hey, living the dream," he said as he plunked the keys on the table.

"You or me?" I asked sarcastically, but it was lost on him as he immediately breezed out the door again.

I looked out the window as he left and saw him get into the passenger side of Shawna's car. Well, that answered that!

* * *

Calico was on the porch when I got home.

"Hey, cutie, what's the deal? I haven't seen you in a while."

I wasn't sure if I should let him in or not but when I walked to the door I saw he had some kind of gash on his ear. Upon further inspection, which wasn't so easy, I saw that was about the extent of it, but it looked nasty. I opened the door and he wouldn't go in at first so I went for the tuna again. This was the kitty brand I had gotten just in case! I put some down inside the door and opened it and just kind of talked to him for a bit. That seemed to work although he didn't actually want to eat. Once I got him inside I called Jill and asked her who her vet for Memphis was. I told her this calico from my porch had a nasty gash.

"You realize you woke me for a cat that isn't your own?" she said, a little gruff. Okay, I did wake her. I didn't even think about the time.

"I know, but he's hurt."

"Take him in in the morning if it isn't an emergency. They'll charge you extra if it's the middle of the night. Which it is! Also, if he is someone else's cat...Now think about this, what if you had a cat that went missing for a day and then came home with say a bandage around its ear. Wouldn't you be extremely concerned about what happened to him?

"Anyway, there must be one closer to you than mine is. Mine is a haul away from me here, even further away from you. Have a look online first."

"Thanks, Jill, sorry to wake you."

In the morning I went online and found the closest vet and took him in. I also called Ginny and explained I'd be at the vets this morning for a bit, and I asked her to explain it all to Anna, and to start the club without me, that I'd be there as soon as I was done. We were both feeling pretty lousy about Meg's reaction to our plan, but we didn't want to assume the worst just yet. She did say she'd think about it. I was one marble away from losing it and knew I had to keep it together.

I wrapped the cat up in a light throw blanket, loosely tying the ends together like a bib around his head, not too tight, not touching the ear, and so he could see out but hopefully wouldn't wriggle out if I was lucky. It was all I had, so I went with it. For the most part he was content with the ride.

He was admitted as Calico by the receptionist. The vet came out to see him, and she explained to him that he was a stray I'd found. He looked at me and I immediately noticed his eyes, almost the same grey blue that I had, but he had black hair. Then he looked at the cat. "Wait a minute. I know this cat. He's got a chip. Hold on a second." He came out with a little scanner and scanned the back of the cat's neck between his little shoulder blades.

"You know Calico? What a neat little gadget!" Gadget. Probably cost more than my car, and I call it a neat little gadget. Wow. I must have been a little flustered by the vet.

He grinned a little and then went over to his computer and a few minutes later he said, "Well your friend here is named Jasper, and Jasper has a home. I'll phone them and see what they want to do about the ear."

"You can just do whatever you would do for the cat. I'll pay for the visit. Somehow, I feel like it happened on my watch."

"I really just have to clean it, it should be fine." He smiled.

"He's been on my porch every other week. But, if you want to just to let them know he's okay, and I suppose if they want to pick him up. Or I can call and return him myself — either way." I found myself rambling at an uncomfortable rate. The vet kept giving me this intense look, which somehow made me ramble all the more, I could feel myself becoming flushed. I was *way* over explaining my relationship with the cat to the good-looking vet.

He called the owner who said she would come by and pick him up, and said to thank me for taking him in, he'd gone missing a couple days ago and they were all worried.

I wanted to wait until she got there to pick up the cat. I also wanted to get over to the cooking club, but I'd wait as long as I could just to make sure Calico, or Jasper as they called him, was okay. I also felt there was something else I should explain about the cat to the vet, but sat quietly. Around 11:30 a woman arrived for the cat.

She thanked me profusely and asked if there was any way she could repay me.

"Just happy he's okay," I said and sadly left the cat knowing he probably wouldn't be around again, the woman had said he was an indoor cat that kept getting out when the kids weren't paying attention. I had a feeling she'd be more careful from now on.

We left the office and I walked over to her car with her, just to make sure it got in the car okay, and then as I turned to leave I noticed a rather nice car with the plate ROL-LLL on it.

Seriously?

CHAPTER 23

Roger was sitting on the step when I returned. Gee I wonder if he'd be needing my car again today?

"The calico was an indoor cat," I told him.

"What? How'd you find out? Did the owner come by looking for him?"

"I brought him to the vet, he had a nasty tear on one of his ears."

"I bet he got caught on that fence wire in the back yard, something like that," Roger said.

"I really don't know, but he had a chip and the owner came to get him. Said the kids kept letting him out."

"Okay, that explains it then. So, tell me more about Shawna," he said, totally changing the subject.

"I don't know all that much about her Roger, she was in a class and I didn't even notice her to be honest. Then she showed up at the diner. Somehow I'm thinking at this point you might know more about her than me, am I right?"

"Oh, it sounded like you were friends from the class. Now what class was it again?"

"It was some psychic awareness class. It was more like an intro to psychic awareness. Just an intro. Ginny, the gal I work with talked me into it." I told him knowing he knew next to nothing about my interests, beyond cleaning out my junk drawer. And vice versa.

"So, I don't see your car yet? Did you need a ride to get it? I've got a little bit of time here, till I go out tonight."

"No, I'm good. Shawna is taking me to go get it. I really just wanted to know what you knew about her."

"So, the car's done, that's great." She was taking him! Wow, he did move fast.

"Yeah, I think they should have had it back a lot sooner, but like I said, if there was still something wrong with it, well, you'd want it fixed right. Anyway, yeah it's done. And now I can go get my sound system fixed. It keeps short circuiting, volume all over the place. I was going to give in and get a new one but Shawna knows a good place to get it fixed." And with that he picked himself up and went back upstairs.

Short circuiting, that was it! I kinda liked that as a description. I'd had a few short circuits myself. I looked around knowing Calico was probably not coming back, and suddenly thought I might need to get myself a cat.

Hmmm, not a bad idea, and then I'd bring it back to that really nice vet and...hmmm. I then found myself thinking about the plate I saw at the vet's. ROL-LLL. Now that was either the vet's plate... Made sense, *roll over*, or it was one of the patients. Made more sense for the vet, but did it matter? What was the big deal? Except, except, jelly-roll made me laugh. I shivered. That was the most absurd thing I had ever thought. Why would I do that to myself? Jelly-roll made me laugh while the grape there really irritated me. Really? Yeah, I definitely needed a cat or something to put my mind back in its place. I was clearly losing it.

• CHAPTER 24 •

It was "meet Sam" night at Jill's tonight. I was very nervous getting ready. More than anything else, I was worried that I wouldn't like him. He'd be some kind of nice guy to my mother, but a jerk to everyone else. Or else he would be the charmer that you knew was up to no good underneath it all. I was terrified I'd just get a bad sense about him and then not know what to do. Mom would get swindled out of her savings on this house deal with this stranger, and we would have all sat by and watched it happen. Now, I was convinced I wasn't going to like him. Or if I did, I still wouldn't trust it. No why should I — Mom was going to get hurt here. That was what this was all about, and now what could I do to stop it?

Lainey, you haven't met the guy yet. Lainey be good. Lainey, give him a chance.

Somehow, because she'd met him through Seth I got a bad vibe. It must be the Seth connection. But Seth had been good to Jill and Janie. I really shouldn't react so poorly to him. He just rubbed *me* the wrong way. I found him to be a know it all, that didn't know it all. So pumped up with himself I didn't trust him. But he was good to them. He hadn't cheated or lied or abused them.

Wait, was that my definition of *good*? That was a very poor definition. Still, he wasn't any of those awful things. I just kept suspecting he could be. How mistrustful of me, but I couldn't help it.

I put on a very casual sundress and sandals with a little bit of a heel. I was trying to look sporty. Be a good sport. After I arrived, I could already feel myself starting to sweat. I was really uncomfortable.

Memphis greeted me at the door. Hmmm, maybe Memphis could tell me what the real deal was. Didn't dogs have that people sense ability? Although, this was Seth's dog too. So all bets were off.

My mother and Jill came to the door.

"Lainey, come in. I'd like you to meet Sam," my mother gushed.

Sam stood up, a rather tall man with pure white hair, who gave me the impression he could have been a doctor. "Lainey, I've heard so much about you, nice to finally meet you." I couldn't say likewise; I'd just heard of him. Thanks, Mom.

"Well, my pleasure," came out of my mouth instead. I put my pocketbook down on the living room couch.

"So, your mother tells me you work at Milly's Diner. I used to go there years ago. I mean *years* ago when Milly was still the owner." Sam sat back down again and we all started finding our seats.

"What? You're kidding me. There really was a Milly?" How cool was that?

"Of course. And her husband, Mike. The silent partner! Well, Mike started the diner for Milly. It was Milly's dream and Mike was the business side of it. But Mike died shortly after they opened, I think it was a heart attack. Milly was so devastated she sold the place about a year or so later. Her heart wasn't in it without Mike even though he'd really done it for her."

"Oh, that's so sad." I bet that's why Meg never talks about them.

"I haven't been back since then. I guess it didn't feel right at first and then I just never thought about it again. I'll have to go in sometime with your mom and see how, did you say Meg? How Meg is running it. I'm sure it's a great diner still."

"Well, she's run it great so far. But now she wants to sell it and they'll probably be closing it as a diner."

"What Lainey? You didn't mention that part!" Jill said.

"I know that just came about. But did Mom tell you? I'm thinking of buying it myself, with some help from Ginny."

"What? No, no she didn't say. How could you even do that?"

"Ruth came up with the idea of a long term sale. Ginny and I proposed the idea to Meg, but she hasn't decided anything yet. But she had told us the person she was thinking of selling to was going to close it."

"Oh, I'd hate to see it close altogether," Sam said.

"Well, that's what I thought too!"

"Oh, it would be such a shame." My mother said, and I thought about my mother coming to the diner, she never did. That alone was a weird idea. Interesting, but totally weird.

"And, yes, you should come by," I told Sam. Now, see, it wouldn't be weird for my mother to be there with him. That would just be normal. Hmmm. The benefits of having a new boyfriend.

Oh, that sounded so absolutely wrong with my mother. A new boyfriend. I couldn't use that term, but nothing else seemed to work either. Partner? NO, it was too soon for that, even though they'd been together a lot longer than I was aware. Anyway, her new man friend. Oh, she'd hate that. But, her new man friend could bring her into the diner and it would be fine.

I noticed Memphis had settled back in his bed very much oblivious to all of us. I guess he didn't have any secret animosity towards this man, maybe I shouldn't either.

"Well, speaking of dining, why don't we all go in and get settled, dinner is just about done." Jill got up and waved her hand towards the table and we worked our way in there.

Seth had been absent for this part of the conversation and emerged from the back room. I hadn't even asked where he was. How wrong was that? Janie must have been at a friend's house.

"So, how's the new place coming along?" Jill braved the question.

"Oh, great," Seth said first. "We've just about finished doing the dry wall in the living room, that was a disaster in there. There had been a leak but that's all been taken care of, it wasn't as extensive as we feared, and we should be painting in a few days. You see so many places set back when they open a wall and find everything that could go wrong has, but we're moving ahead. I think this was a really good investment wouldn't you say." He nodded to my mother who also nodded back without saying anything.

Sam also said nothing. Oh, no, they still hadn't told Seth they were keeping it!

Jill brought out some kind of casserole for dinner and everyone changed the subject to how wonderful it looked and smelled. It was a broccoli and chicken pasta casserole with some kind of creamy cheese sauce. We all got back to wanting to be able to easily whip up something like that and I mentioned my club. I hadn't realized

I'd never mentioned it before. I guess I thought the class on cooking was mention enough.

"So, you each invent something new for dinner each week?" Jill asked.

"Well, we find something new. Inventing would be a stretch for us, but it just seems we eat the same thing over and over again.

"But even finding these new recipes it seems we still use a lot of the same ingredients no matter what we're making. I swear bread, cheese, beef, tomatoes, have been used fifty times now. Okay, so we've only met four or five times but it really seems..." They all laughed.

"So, your mom tells me you have a most unusual license plate." Ah, the food segue, and here we are...

"Mom!"

"I guess this is not your favorite!"

"No, I don't enjoy all the comments I get from it, I don't enjoy everyone telling me I should have returned it, when clearly I tried to, and they seem to think they would have done a better job at that than me." I glared at Seth. "I don't enjoy that I now look at every vanity plate out there like it's a sign for me! Like I need to connect with, or find the plate that goes with mine. Am I destined to find Mr. Right or something with this abomination? Grape! I have been on a date with someone with the plate grape. This is the most humiliating thing to have to deal with day after day. The looks I get, the comments, I can't stand that plate. I want it gone. It's making me crazy. Harold has contests to find the best plate. Meg has me parking out front for the publicity. I am so done with this plate."

I couldn't believe I'd just vented like that to someone I'd just met. Some guy my mother was what, about to move in with? This could be my stepfather at some point, and I was sounding off like a lunatic. Did I say find Mr. Right? I didn't say things like that out loud. Oh, that damned plate. Then, I thought of the vet for a split second and almost felt guilty.

But instead of looking at me like I was crazy, he said, "Yeah, I get it. I had an address like that once. I mean I didn't notice when I took the place that it was just so wrong, but once I did...Village Lane. You'd think that would be nice, sounds incredibly friendly. But it was 8-A. A duplex. 8-A and 8-B. You don't even think about it. I didn't put the number with the street name together right away.

"And then it happened. Someone made a crude cannibal joke about it and I was stunned. 8-A Village Lane. Every time I had to write it out anywhere after that I just cringed. Those labels that come to you in the mail, seemed to be tormenting me. Every piece of mail I got, I saw it.

"Eight anything could be odd if you think about it. Eight Rocky Road. Eight Maple Street. *Eight* anything and you've got a setup. It could be very funny or very irritating, just depended on the name of the street or your point of view! But '8-A' that was downright cruel."

And I laughed. I actually laughed. Okay, that could be worse.

"So, how long did you live there?"

"It was about four years. A long time for an address you weren't crazy with! But, I did eventually learn to ignore it. I really liked the area and that house, if not the address. When I left I felt a pang of loss! Sad to leave the house, but not the name!"

There would be no pang of loss when I was done with my plate, but I gathered he made some sense. If I could just accept it, instead of resisting the fact that it existed, I wouldn't be so mad each and every time it was mentioned. But this was an easier said than done deal, and I couldn't seem to get there.

Seth had been quiet through my rant and now was smiling with the address story.

"Oh, so you lived on the east side of the town," my sister said, completely ignoring the whole number story and focused on exactly where he had lived.

"Yes, it was a good spot that's why I never noticed the number when I got the place, just liked that street, seemed like a nice place to live and it was, except for the embarrassment at the way it sounded. It was a long time ago."

"Of course, the difference here is people think I asked for this plate, that I identify with it. At least they didn't make that assumption with your address, or at least they shouldn't have!"

"True. But it was cringe worthy none the less!"

"But you work in the diner so you could make a connection to the food." Jill started saying.

I was about to say my usual, "I do not *want* to make a connection" when Sam said, "Lainey, your plate!" rather excited.

"Yes," I said, all slow and suspicious.

"Your plate! If you buy the diner, *THEN* your plate really will be an asset. Now you just work there, so I get it, but if you own it... You are your own advertising. You could even add a bumper sticker that said '*Milly's Diner*'"

The man had a point. I was a touch loathsome about it, but he had a valid point.

If I owned it. What a total change of perspective.

So, Sam had won me over it seemed. Damn, I was fully expecting to hate him.

Jill brought out hot fudge brownie sundaes with strawberries for dessert and everyone got lost in them for a while.

"Well, thank you for dinner," my mother said, and Sam said the same, and I guess we were all wrapping it up there.

Then, I heard Sam say quietly to Seth, "We need to go over a few things about the house, so why don't we meet on Monday?" Okay, I was right.

"Very nice to meet you," I said to Sam as I was leaving, and found myself delighted to be sincere.

CHAPTER 25

When I got home, I curled up on the couch and thought about how much the dinner had caught me by surprise. I fully expected to dislike the guy and be very defensive. Things never worked out like this. Why was that so painless? Did I miss something? I really did like him. The whole thing about his house won me over. The random chaos that these things create...

And my plate. Did my plate have a purpose after all? Or if Meg sold the diner to Walt would this just be a bitter, bitter reminder of what could have happened?

The phone rang which startled me, since it was close to ten o'clock. Didn't Jill just give me grief for waking her at midnight? She was probably calling to get my take on Sam. "Hello."

"Hi, Lainey, it's Ruth." She sounded totally wired.

"Ruth, hey, what's up?" I said, sitting up a little bit straighter.

"Lainey, this is so exciting. I'm getting married and I want you to be my bridesmaid!"

"Wow, congrats, Ruth, that is exciting," I said automatically. "Congratulations!" Or was it best wishes for the bride? Didn't matter. So, she *was* getting married! "Wait, what? A bridesmaid?"

"Oh, absolutely! You have to be one!" she insisted.

Bridesmaid. Hmmm, don't know about that. Wasn't that a whole lot of responsibilities, planning a shower and stuff? And was it here or out there? If it was out there, it would be out of the question to do all that. Oh, and all the flying! No that wasn't going to happen. If I were going to fly somewhere it would be that proper vacation I was promising myself. No. This was a no.

Besides, I was probably about to be out of a job, Meg didn't seem very receptive to the idea of selling the diner to us, so I really needed to be careful spending money right now. I needed to watch every dime.

"We're going to have the wedding here." Damn! "Bren doesn't have all that much family here. They're scattered, so we thought we'd do something simple and if they can't come they can't come, that's okay."

"But you have a lot of family here, don't you?" I said trying to let her know here would be the better place to have the wedding.

"I know, but same thing, if they can't come they can't come, and that's okay. I doubt they will but, like I said, it's going to be simple and small, and right away. We're going to have it next week..."

"Next week?" I said in total shock.

"I know it's completely short notice, but we figured we've been together so long now, absolutely no need to wait. So, I'm gathering up my bridesmaids. Just wear lavender, anything will do. Do you think you can make it?" Bridesmaids, oh, oh, wait a minute, thank goodness, I was thinking maid of honor. I was in the clear!

Can I make it? Like ASAP? I had absolutely no idea! I couldn't just leave Meg without any notice at the diner. *Next week*?

"Let me see what I can do," I told her, trying to organize too many thoughts at once. My whole being was screaming *no* and yet I felt myself almost just blurt out yes. What was wrong with me?

And, oh, did I forget, the whole *flying* thing? Tickets would be at a premium. I'm counting every penny right now. *She* was all amiss about not getting a flight with her family, and look at what she was doing to me! Flights in an hour...no problem!

"I'll have to check, and I'll let you know." Good for me. That left me an out. No, it didn't. Who was I kidding? I knew I was going. I could feel it. I felt like I'd been setup when she asked me before.

* * *

I turned on Harold's show to take my mind off the whole thing before going to sleep.

"And what kind of things do you find people collect the most of?" Harold was asking.

"I think there's nothing people don't collect! And, I mean, even beyond the normal collections like dolls, candles, stuffed animals, toys, hats, and sporting paraphernalia, and cars... Essentially if more than one item exists there's someone with a collection of them. Seriously, collections of soda cans, and empty packages, gum wrappers."

"Are you talking trash?" Harold laughed.

"Well, for some it might be!"

"Okay, listeners, let's hear them. What's your collection all about? Do you have several, or is one taking up half your living space?"

"How about awful thoughts?" one caller asked, taking the show on a turn for the worse there.

"I think that might be a topic for another show." Harold

rebounded quickly and upbeat. Harold had said he sometimes had to signal his producer to take the call and speak with the caller off the air. Some of those calls got transferred to a crisis hotline. You just couldn't be sure anymore. The late night crowd was truly a special group.

"I've got a collection of vintage signs," the next caller was already telling him. "I know you can get them all over the place at different general stores and online catalogs but mine are really vintage. Real antique stores and such."

"Excellent, excellent. And does that fill up half your living space?"

"All my wall space, does that count?"

"See? These are the collectors!" Harold sounded as if he was beaming.

"My garage is filled with old license plates," another caller began. "I was trying to get one from every state, but I seem to keep getting them locally."

"Any vanity plates?" Oh, Harold! Still?

"Hmmm, a couple could be read that way, I don't know if it was intentional. You know LRG-222 or NVR-81. Those types. Got lucky with some of them."

"I believe it was a vanity plate that lead me to you, Harold," his guest interjected, "my dad saw this one the other day and told me about it. He thought it would be a good story for my book. JEL-EEE. I think you know the gal."

"We're going to take a quick break here listeners, be right back after a word from the good folks at Lasting Memorial." Harold was quick to end that topic.

It was the guy. He mentioned *MY PLATE*. Nightmares do come true.

* * *

"So, you're going to Texas?" Ginny was giving me the once over, leaving out the *in about an hour* part.

"Doesn't she know you're about to be jobless." She added quietly, glancing around for Meg.

"She probably thinks I've actually bought the place by now." I said in an equal whisper, "Reality runs a whole different path for Ruth." Granted, she probably didn't even think about my situation at all.

"I suppose you could think of it as a mini vacation before our lives get thrown totally upside down." She said now, taking the up side of the situation, "Besides, it could be fun, no?"

"Probably no. I told you what happened when she came out here. I got zero sleep and zero appreciation for chauffeuring her all around town. It won't be any different. She'll have me doing her bidding there too. But if I look on the plus side, I've never been to Texas. Seriously, I've never really been anywhere. And a vacation does sound good!"

While Ginny had seen the sweet side of Ruth, all cheery and concerned about her family, I had informed her of the Ruth I knew. The one that treated me like her personal servant.

"So, you should go. Just go. You could still have a good time there, just not with her!"

I frowned. How could it not go as I expected?

"Otherwise, Lainey, it's time to cut the cord. If she's making you crazy, she's got to go."

"Oh, I know, I just can't. I keep remembering how she helped me out in junior high school. I was prey to some older kids and she knew how to stand up to them. I didn't. So, she kind of took care of me then."

"But then it sounds like she's the bully now!"

"Oh, you don't understand." I knew anything I said here I would just be making up. Ginny was 100 percent right and I was getting bullied by my "friend." But she'd helped me back then, and now she'd gone and helped me out again! There was no one right answer.

"Maybe I'll say no. Maybe I'll make an excuse," I said with little conviction, and more to myself than to Ginny. And by her raised eyebrow, I could tell she didn't believe me.

Gerry walked into the diner. More things I was done with. I nodded and showed him a table, then handed him a menu.

"I already know I'll have the meatloaf and coffee. I'm celebrating." He handed the menu back.

"Meatloaf is how you celebrate?" I asked, astonished, instead of asking what he was celebrating!

"Yes, well, yes, today it is. I got the job at PFP, the plastics and foam company, and I start on Monday so here I am celebrating!"

"Ah, last few days of freedom."

"Well, I guess you could look at it that way too. I thought I was celebrating getting the job. Different points of view!"

"Sorry. I just...Congratulations!" I said, sounding all weird now. Gerry was not interested in me. Gerry was just out having a meal he enjoyed. I had been way too harsh on Gerry.

"Thanks," he said, sounding equally weird. "Yeah, meatloaf and coffee. Karen is going to be thrilled when I'm finally able to move out, and horrified when I tell her the name of the company."

"Horrified?"

"You do not mention the words foam or plastic around Karen." He laughed.

"Has it been that bad?"

"No, but I think she needs her space back. It was hard when I realized it just wasn't going to work any longer in my apartment. Karen came to my rescue and had me move in before it got ugly!"

"Well, then, congrats on all the changes about to happen. I'm glad you found something you like. You do like the new job, don't you?" I'd made an assumption there!

"Oh, yes, this is going to work out fine. It took a while to get but yeah, I think it's going to work out."

"And you'll keep your plate? The grape?" I asked, and also made a quick glance around realizing I'd probably been at his table a little too long.

"For now, yeah. Who knows what it will lead to!"

"I know last night on Harold's show he mentioned them yet again. The guy who's doing a book on the weird things we own or collect was on," I told him.

"I didn't hear it. I keep telling him I'm going to and never seem to remember at that hour. Too busy sleeping! We are going back to another car show if you're ever interested. Meg came last time. I know we should have let you know it was a vanity plate gathering before. Harold was afraid we made you sick."

"Just a bug. But thanks." Meg went! Okay, maybe she did like Harold after all!

I heard the crash in the kitchen and said, "Oops, gotta go!" When I got there Paula was on her knees trying to gather whatever she could of the dinner mess. It looked like she'd had a full tray going before the crash.

"Oh, they're going to kill me."

"Who?"

"The family at table 12. Lisa left the table with me when she went home. So, that upset them. Then, they were complaining that everything was taking too long, and now they're going to have a fit."

"Sorry, Paula. You know what? Why don't we just give them one of our 'emergency maybe this will fix it' coupons for the delay."

"Can you do it? They've already yelled at me twice. They had ordered coke and asked for it in coffee cups which I didn't know, then I automatically went to top off the cups with coffee and they went crazy! It's a tough, tough table. The dad."

"Sure, I'll let them know. I'll bring them the coupon too, for next time." Maybe in a coffee cup!

I went over to the table and told them I was so sorry for the inconvenience and that there had been a problem in the kitchen, dinner was delayed by a few moments and gave them the coupon for next time. The father took the coupon and then said, "A lot of good that does us. We have to go now. I'm posting a complaint online."

"Truly, I'm so sorry," I said, a little confused about how they would have had time to eat if it were ready. I started to explain to them it shouldn't be too much longer and we certainly could make it to go for them, knowing it was already being prepared again for them.

"We're done," he said and proceeded to stand up. "Thanks for nothing."

"How'd it go?" Paula asked when I went back to the kitchen.

"Yeah, that was fun. They left. They're posting a complaint. 200 happy customers today, one unhappy one. One posting…"

"Oh, no."

"I don't think they would have been happy even if they stayed. Don't worry about it."

"I just hate when that happens. It ruins your whole day. I've just been so stressed about the diner closing. I just didn't want to let it get the better of me. Lainey, I've been to a dozen other places looking for a job and I haven't found one yet. This is serious."

"You do know Ginny and I asked if she would sell the diner to us. If she takes the offer we'll all still have jobs," I said trying to sound like I knew what I was doing.

"I know, I guess I just assumed she wouldn't want to do that. I've been a wreck since this started."

"I know, it hasn't been easy on any of us," I told her shaking my head. "Oh, I'd better get Gerry's dinner to him." I had taken so long with the disgruntled folks while Paula cleaned up the mess, I nearly forgot Gerry's order.

"Hope it's celebration worthy," I said when I finally got back to him.

"It's organic, right?"

"Well, some things are. I'm not sure if..." Oh, no, not trouble with Gerry too now. Sometimes, they asked that and we had a few assorted items I could recommend, otherwise it wasn't always feasible.

"I'm kidding, sorry, I'm just kidding. Karen won't let me eat anything that isn't, and to tell you the truth, some days I just don't care, that's all. I just want a cheeseburger and fries. I don't want to have to know the pedigree of the potato. I just want the fries."

I'd totally missed his sarcasm in my mood.

"Okey dokey, then. Want ketchup with that?" I smiled. Gerry wasn't so bad.

Chapter 26

It was decision time for the wedding. I knew if I was going to go I'd better get something to wear. Was I going to go? That was the question. I still hadn't really made up my mind. Ruth wasn't going with traditional bridesmaids' gowns, how could she with zero notice, but she said just wear something lavender. The dress and style was up to us. I knew I had something lavender in my closet, but that dress hadn't seen the light of day in ages. I pulled it out, and gave it the once over. It needed a cleaning. "Dry clean only" prominently labeled at the back. I'd worn it to a party that Jill had given when they bought their house. I thought that was going to be a very casual party and next thing I knew she told me it was a formal party. I had obliged. I was completely overdressed.

Next to it was a black and white dress that I loved. Now that would look nice for a wedding. Very simple, mostly white with a small geometric black design. It was so sophisticated. Then I looked at the lavender one. A totally different feel. It wasn't *that* bad. It was also simple, a sleeveless V-neck but with some kind of puffy bow on the side. The front was just below the knees, with a little ruffled trim on the bottom, but the back went slightly longer giving it an even more formal evening feel. The bow was kind of drooping and needed a little poof to it.

So, I had two options. Try and find another lavender dress or take this to the cleaners. Normally, shopping would have been fun, but no, it was way too close. It would probably end up costing the same. There really was only one decision since I'd never find something else in the given week. And lavender, that was a tricky color to just happen to find. Then there was option three. I considered it as I was getting into my car; just don't go.

So, it was off to the cleaners. There was a nice one that I went to every once in a while, when one of my uniforms had had just one too many weird spills for me to deal with and I knew it was time for help. Most things were ready in 24 hours and I would definitely need it that fast. I went in and the woman ahead of me was picking up some kind of wedding dress. I laughed thinking, oh, it must be in the air, it was some kind of sign. I didn't even flinch thinking "sign." Wow, something had shifted.

"Acid free," the owner was repeating as she paid for it. She turned to me and I thought I recognized her, but I didn't know from where, must be a customer I thought.

I pointed at my dress and said, "Mine's for a wedding as well!"

"Oh, I remember you!" she said and kind of startled me a bit. "You were over the night of Tim's wedding. Ruth's friend."

"Yes, of course. Wow. Was that the bride's gown?" I asked pointing to the dress. "Was she okay after all that?"

"She's okay, still upset and all that, but no, this isn't hers. I guess Tim's wedding brought out some nostalgic thread in me. This was my mother's, and then mine. I was having it restored.

It had yellowed pretty badly. I must say I was worried it wouldn't come out but they have done a really nice job with it." She looked at the dress, shook it a little, and then looked back to me. "And, so now you're going to a wedding, how nice. Did you hear Ruth is getting married too, next week?"

"Yes! This is for Ruth's wedding!"

"Oh, how wonderful!" she beamed. "Well, then, dear, you'll have to come and stay with us at the lodge! We always go there every time we're in Texas visiting. It's the most wonderful lodge, and we usually rent a cabin there. It's an amazing place to stay. Better than a hotel, and they treat you like family. Do say you'll come. We'd love to have you. It's so spacious and gorgeous."

They were going to the wedding! On that short a notice too, wow. That was very impressive.

"Oh, I couldn't impose."

"No, dear, it will be fun. It's no imposition, we get the cabin anyway. We could use some new blood there."

New blood, kinda scary expression. "Are you sure? That really sounds like I'd be intruding on your vacation."

"No, no, it will be fun. It's not vacation, it's a family get together. It's always great to get a group together for these things. Do you know where you're staying yet?"

"No, I haven't gotten that far."

"Have you been to Texas before?"

"No, I..."

"Oh, that settles it, if you don't know the area, no, this is my treat, you have to stay with us. You're like family.

"Okay, here's my number," she continued, clearly not going to let it go. She wrote it out on a slip of paper with her name, "I want you to call when you know your schedule and you know your flight. We can come and get you at the airport. We'll be staying for a while ourselves, so it's no problem."

Now, I couldn't decide if it was rude to say no, or rude to accept. This woman was planning my whole trip and I didn't believe she actually knew my name yet. Why did she want me to stay with them, just being polite? This place sounded expensive, but it was a cabin with them so I was just one more bunk bed right?

"Well, I'll give you a call when I have it mapped out. I'm Lainey by the way!"

"Then, it's settled, Lainey. I'll tell Ruth's mom and she'll let Ruth know. Ruth gushed over how you took care of her during Tim's wedding. I'm still not sure why she felt she had to stay elsewhere, we had plenty of room at the house. But, she was probably just wanting to see her old friend! I'm so glad you're going!"

Okay, that is not what Ruth said. But, I did remember this woman asking us to stay that night. And excuse me, Ruth gushed… she had barely said ten words to me since. This woman seemed nice, but new blood. Just an expression, but it had murder mystery gone wrong written all over it. Yup, I was a goner.

* * *

What have I done, what have I done? I hadn't even decided I was going, but now I felt locked in.

And, that would mean a gift. Well, even if I didn't go, I guess I should have thought of that.

I headed home again. I had so much to figure out and no time to decide. How long should I go for? Meg was about to give Walt her answer, which meant she would also be giving us an answer soon. It was make it or break it time, and I'd be somewhere in Texas. But, it was also a long flight, I didn't want to just get there and then turn around and come back. Maybe four days. One to get there, one to come back. The wedding and an extra day before. I didn't want anything to go wrong like it did for Ruth. So, if I left time for something to go wrong, it would be alright. I'd be staying in a cabin, so maybe this really was a mini vacation.

When I got home I booked the flight. It had been slim pickings in the good flight department, not a direct flight in the batch, but at least it was done, and I was all set.

I sat there looking at my flight confirmation. I had told Ginny I might say no, didn't I? Yet, here I was all set to go.

Now, would I have this woman pick me up at the airport? Then I would be traveling with them for the whole event. How many were going? Brother number one and two and the sister? Okay, that's already five in the car. Or, was it just the folks?

I should rent a car. It was really more expensive than I was ready to spend after the tickets, but I also had that whole day free. I put in the reservation online and called the woman Joan back to get the address of the lodge.

"No, really, I insist, we can come and get you. It's so easy for us. I'd hate for you to get lost. Besides we always get the roomy van for everyone. What time is your flight dear?"

I caved and gave her the info and then sat back and thought this is just so very strange. Why was driving to the airport easier than giving me directions?

I didn't wait for work. I called Ginny to tell her if I went missing this was exactly why. "What is wrong with you?" she wanted to know. "You weren't even going to go to this thing, right?" I heard the sarcasm.

"Okay, that's not the support I was looking for. You're supposed to tell me she's just being nice, she doesn't want me to have to pay for a car and hotel. She's family to Ruth, and is thinking of me as family. *And* she isn't good at giving directions." All the things my second round of thinking got me.

"Well, if that's what you think why are you asking for support?"

"Because I'm probably wrong. Anyway. Whatever."

"Lainey!" She was holding back a lecture; I could just feel it.

"Well, sadly it will be a lot cheaper to go with them. They all seemed very nice at their house that night. I don't think it will be as bad as I'm imagining, I just…"

"What does your gut tell you?"

"Haven't a clue. That's why I called you! I really can't tell."

"Okay, well, it should be fine," she acquiesced. "You'll have a good time, maybe some laughs and, hey, you won't have to face Ruth alone. Besides, now you'll be with the people she's extra nice too, maybe she'll be extra nice to you too, maybe Lainey you'll come back actually liking her! How's that?"

I hung up with Ginny now feeling foolish.

CHAPTER 27

By Thursday, I was as ready as I was going to be. I'd found a gift — make that a gift card. I knew I didn't have enough time to think of a gift that would do the event justice. She hadn't registered anywhere, she said, because she didn't have time. She'd emailed me the info about the wedding, but somehow I couldn't believe I was going all this way with a little email print out, and not a formal invitation, but there it was. She'd gone to her cousin's wedding, decided "me too" and here it was!

I parked at the airport that morning knowing it was going to cost a small fortune for four days, but it ended up being better than my other options. Ginny had offered to drop me off but said she wasn't sure she'd be home to pick me up and I didn't want to have to call Jill or my mother.

I started to walk past the ATM machine and even though I was all set for cash I thought, you never know, a few more dollars to be safe. I'd better have a job when this was all over, because all the extra costs were killing me!

I arrived at the San Antonio airport eager to get away from my fellow passengers and had to get my bag. It was only four days and

I had a very small bag, which probably would have fit on board, but unlike most everyone else, I didn't like the idea of having to stow it on board. It seemed like such a hassle bumping up against everyone else getting theirs, and the last time I'd been in a plane, now eons ago, it felt like it was stashed four rows back and I had a miserable time getting it. There was just no room up there! My dress was the only thing I worried about — I should have gone with crepe. Oh, right, *lavender* crepe, if I'd had more than a week to plan, I might have actually found such a thing!

As I stood in the baggage claim area, I overheard one woman growling, "Hey, be careful with that." She was one very angry woman, with very long, extremely brittle-looking bleached hair, and a beige outfit that lacked a single wrinkle. She was now shouting, "That's expensive you know! You can't handle it like that, you have to be very careful." There went his tip. I wanted to say, "This is luggage. That's what happens to luggage, it gets handled." But, I wasn't about to take on that woman! Hmmm, perhaps it was all a ploy not to tip. My discount bag would be out any minute now.

I saw Joan out of the corner of my eye and turned to get her attention. I waved an *over here* wave to let her know I didn't have my bag yet.

"Oh, there you are. How was your flight?" she asked.

The flight. *"Why do we have to go?"* screamed the kid behind me, kicking my seat. *"But WHY? Why are we on this plane? Why isn't it flying yet? Hey, I have to go to the bathroom, where is it? Hey, where are my raisins?"* Then he got lost in a game on his tablet, and was fine until the descent and it started all over again.

"A little bumpy here and there, but otherwise fine," I replied.

"Oh, it's usually over the mountains, the air pressure change and all that. Never worry about that."

Good to know. I didn't travel all that much so I had nothing to base it on, now I would always just think mountains, bumpy. Even if she was wrong. Did I even go over mountains?

Joan waved over her husband Frank and reintroduced him to me. I thanked them both for coming to pick me up again not really sure why they were doing this for me.

We left the baggage claim area and headed out to the car. We passed a car that said "HOTTEE" on the plate and Joan let out a disapproving sigh. "That's just so wrong."

"Maybe it's a typo," I said, feeling a strange hit to the gut. I did a quick, tell them about mine, or don't tell them and decided, don't tell them. Maybe they saw it the night of Tim's wedding. But I should just be quiet.

"I doubt that," the husband said, and I knew I picked the right answer.

"Hmmm," was all I could manage to say.

Looking at the plate, I realized I'd been thinking about that ROL-LLL plate more and more. What had happened to me? Since Sam had mentioned the plate being a tool for the diner – should it become *my* diner, I'd really softened on the whole idea. There was some kind of oddball humor in Jelly-Roll that I liked, and yet at the same time hated in the whole PNT BTR or GR8 PE scenario. It had to be the vet. Nothing to do with the plate, I just liked the vet.

From the backseat, I could see the scenery all around. I wasn't really following how we ended up at the lodge but it had a great presence coming in. It had sprawling grounds and small ponds and you could see the cabins all lined up by the water. The lodge itself appeared rather regal and I could see why they loved it there.

Old worldly was all I could think, massive and yet comfortable looking.

Joan brought me to the front desk. She said to the staff, "This is our friend, Lainey. She's with us, and I believe she has the room across from us." The woman handed me the key and asked me to sign in.

I repeated, "I'm with them," a little hesitantly, and the woman said, "Of course."

"Oh, I thought you said a cabin," I said to Joan.

"Usually, we do, but it was such short notice this time around, they were booked, but don't worry dear the rooms are even nicer!"

Frank grabbed my small bag, waving the porter away and Joan led the way down a series of hallways. He plunked my bag down and said, "Here you go."

I opened the door to an amazing room. It had a leather couch and club chairs, a feather bed and dark wood furniture with brass accents. It had built-in bookcases and books and shelves everywhere that went on for miles it seemed. If I thought my bathroom at home was big, I was in for a surprise, as this one had a Jacuzzi tub, and a separate massive shower. And a storage system with built in shelves and counter space that no guest could fill. I could move into the bathroom comfortably.

"Isn't it wonderful?" Joan said and I had to admit it was not a normal hotel room.

"Ummm, this is too much," I said, suddenly feeling like the poor kid on the block.

"This is the Executive Library room. They all have fun names. We'll let you get settled. We're across the hall over there, the Executive Break room." She pointed to the next door diagonally down the hall. "We'll be going to dinner at 7:00 in the main dining hall, if you want to join us, or, I don't know, are you going to be out with Ruth?"

"I was going to give her a call now. I'll let you know."

"We'll be at the pool for a bit. That's down to the end of that hallway," she pointed once again to the back entrance. "There's also a nice spa at the other end, Frank and I prefer to lounge at the pool these days though."

I looked towards the hallway. I had not brought a bathing suit. The idea never entered my head. As for the spa, it sounded amazing but that was way out of my league.

I called Ruth to see how she was doing. I had called her when I booked the trip to let her know I would be coming, and that I was going to be for the most part, in the company of Frank and Joan. She had said something weird like, "Oh, of course, that's great." Really, I thought? "Of course?" Really, did everyone just adopt strays like this and it was normal?

She told me that beyond the color of the bridesmaids' dresses, she had forgone with any formalities. Her coworkers had had an impromptu party/shower for her about two days after she announced her engagement. But there was no rehearsal dinner, none of the normal traditional events, there had been no time for any of that. A week, who does a wedding in a week?

However, she did have a few things to take care of. She said she'd be lucky if she got everything done in time. Basically, I got the, "see you at the wedding, thanks for coming," speech.

I was now thinking that at the church, besides showing up, and going wherever someone pointed, (hopefully someone would point), I had no idea what I was supposed to be doing. I told her

I would get to the church a little early, and apparently, that was "perfect."

So, I was free for dinner. But, instead of the pool I decided to wander aimlessly through the lodge. I checked out the dining hall, I took a peek in the spa for a split second, found several conference and function rooms, and then I went to the gift shop.

It was a large room with all the overnight supplies you could ever want and a couple of shelving units full of magazines and books. Several large clothing racks with T-shirts and sweatshirts with the name of the lodge on it. Then a rack with more upscale clothing. Dress slacks and silk shirts, a couple of dresses I would need to take out a small loan if I wanted to purchase. They also had a couple of bathing suits in odd sizes. I looked at the price on a pair of sunglasses and they were on sale for $78.00, and I knew I would not be purchasing anything in there.

I still had a full day ahead of me with no car. I really, really didn't know why I'd agreed to this.

I had my book from the plane and decided to take it down to the pool, fully clothed, and just lay out and read for a bit. Joan and Frank were there, but I didn't see any of their kids.

I started to ask if their children were here but saying "children or kids" sounded like really young kids; their children were adults. Then, I started to say, "Are any of your sons here?" but didn't want to exclude the daughter. "Are your sons and daughter here?" That was a mouthful.

Finally, I settled on, "Did any of your family join you here?" All the while, I thought, wait, I was the new blood right? Who's the old blood?

"You know, not this time. Tim of course is just back from his honeymoon with Margie, the boys couldn't get the time off work, and Angie is back at school."

Angie, score, one name! End of August, sure, back to school — thought I, who was never "out" of school? "Oh, so it's just us?" Just us, you know, your new family!

"Well, we have some friends that are joining us too. I can't remember, did they come back to the house after the wedding, Frank?"

"After the wedding, yes. After the hospital, no."

"Oh, okay, so you may not have met them. Well, they'll be joining us for dinner. Are you going to come, or are you off with Ruth?"

"It looks like Ruth will be tied up until the wedding so I am free, yes."

There hadn't been another restaurant or any anything for miles when we pulled up here. Was I really stuck in the middle of nowhere without any way to get anything for two days? Hmmmm. Thinking this over, I was driving myself crazy. What had I done?

Dinner was at 7:00 p.m. and we all regrouped at the dining hall. I saw Joan at the table and she motioned me over. There were two others sitting there besides Frank. Joan introduced me as a friend of the bride and I settled in with them.

"So, are you from here, or back east?" I asked the two women seated there.

"We're from New York, actually. We were at Tim's wedding just a few weeks ago."

"I wasn't at that one, just the aftermath," I said, but apparently that was a little too strong a word.

"Aftermath," one replied with alarm. "What else happened?"

"Oh, I'm sorry, I just meant when Margie got sick. Everyone

went to the hospital. I was there to pick Ruth up, but she was at the hospital. Anyway, everything was okay, but I didn't know it at the time."

The waiter brought over menus and said the swordfish was the special tonight.

We looked over the menu and I nearly dropped when I caught the prices on it. I would be having the house salad and that would be all. Working too long at the diner I thought! Sticker shock. Too long in a mom and pop place. Each item was a family of five's full meal ticket at the diner.

They all ordered various cuts of beef, which somehow seemed appropriate for Texas, and gave me a look when I ordered the salad. Joan leaned over and said quietly, "Please, Lainey, pick out something you wouldn't ordinarily have. This is our treat." Now, I was doubly mortified. It was too generous of them and I was so uncomfortable. Then, I had a sudden terrifying thought of *oh no, I wonder what the rooms go for here.* I am probably staying at a place where the room per night is equal to my monthly rent. This is why I never go on vacation!

Three nights? Make that three month's rent. Holy...yeah, this was a mistake. She said a cabin, a cabin. I was expecting a bunk bed. I should enjoy it, right? Enjoy being in the lap of luxury, but now I was a mess. Something was going to happen: either I was going to break something, or they were going to leave me with the bill at the end or something. It all just didn't seem right.

If I ordered anything else, I wouldn't be able to eat it and I'd be in knots about it, so I said, "Oh, no really, this is just about right for me. All that traveling today, this will be great." Even I knew that made absolutely no sense, the travelling had made me ravenous.

Anyway, I prayed she wouldn't call me on it.

The ladies from New York were sisters, Sherry and Lyla, and had both been in computer programming and had done quite well for themselves early on. They no longer worked and quite enjoyed traveling. I got some stories about India and China, and appeared to be nodding in at the right moments. I would have been listening if I wasn't so freaked out about the cost of everything.

Our dinners arrived and they all looked amazing, even my little salad was quite impressive so I really wasn't missing out too much.

Wine flowed while I had coffee. They went on for what seemed like hours about their travels.

Exhausted from the day, we finally went back to our rooms and as I headed off Joan said, "So did you want to meet up with us in the morning? We'll be going out around ten."

I felt so conflicted. I had absolutely no other plans but no way to get around anyway. I should have planned for the day. I was in Texas and was about to have one full day of "vacation." Yes, Lainey, I thought sarcastically, your dreams are all coming true. All I'd been concerned with was not missing the wedding. I hadn't thought this out too well. I had originally wanted to rent a car, and I should have just stuck to that plan. But still not knowing if I was going to have a job, or was going to be the owner of the restaurant loomed large. I had to be careful and not spend any more.

I could walk around the lodge all day, stay at the pool for a few hours and not eat a thing for the day. Fasting was good, right? Every once in a while, a fast was a good thing for you.

Breakfast was probably reasonable but then what if they just put it on my room tab? No, I could insist on paying for it. That'll be forty-five dollars, plus a tip please. I knew all too well about tipping.

Ten thousand other, "what should I do?" questions popped into my head.

"Oh, ten would be great. That sounds wonderful."

I did not sleep that night.

At 6:00 a.m. I stopped trying to force myself to sleep and got up, showered, and got dressed. I sat at the writing table and opened my book. I couldn't read. I couldn't concentrate. I could give Ginny a call, as it was an hour later there, but she still may not appreciate a call at 7:30 in the morning. She wasn't *that much* of a morning person. I wanted to know if there was any word from Meg about the diner. But I also knew she'd wait till I was back to tell us.

I'd call Jill but she'd just yell at me. *How did you let that happen?* Come to think of it, that's what Ginny would do too, it just wouldn't feel quite like yelling coming from her. It would be *now why again did you say yes to this?* So, that was no help, just a subtler way of pointing out what I'd done wrong. No, no help at all.

What would Harold say? He was my cheerleader. He really was. Go figure. What would he tell me? He'd tell me this was an adventure and I would actually be so happy it had happened because I got to do — well, whatever we were doing, and it would turn out to be something great for some great reason that I couldn't see right now. He would put in that part about just trusting it would be great. I hated that part.

I decided to wander down to the dining hall and see about coffee. I was up, and I was going to be up for the next however many hours. I would now and forever more associate no sleep with Ruth.

The dining hall was empty, but it was open so that was a good sign. I seated myself and, after a moment, a waiter came over.

"Coffee. I really need coffee," I said wishing I could have "slept in."

"Would you like a menu as well?"

"Sure, that would be nice."

He returned with the coffee and a menu and as expected breakfast was going to cost what a nice dinner would cost at something more upscale than the diner. But, I was fairly hungry this morning so I ordered the full whole wheat, apple, cinnamon, walnut pancakes and scrambled eggs with fruit slices on the side. Everything on the menu looked like a meal and a half. And much to my delight this didn't disappoint.

Just as I was finishing, I saw Joan and Frank come in. I waved hi to them, and they came over and sat at my table. The waiter came over, and they both asked for coffee. He looked at me like he was going to get my check when Joan said, "We're all guests here, room 7A." He nodded. I started to protest and she waved her hand dismissing me and said, "I know I'm going to have the steak and eggs omelet how about you, Frank, the same?" Texas appetites.

Frank nodded and the waiter left. I sat there with my benefactors wondering what had just happened in my life. How did they happen upon me? Despite all the protesting going on in my head a wave of acceptance came over me. Give in Lainey, just give in. You might even be grateful.

"So, have you ever been to the Alamo?" Joan was asking me.

"No," I said. "I've never even been to Texas before, so no, everything out here is new to me."

"Oh, that's right. You told me that. Then, we'll have to do the whole downtown tour. Oh, you're going to love it. Frank and I haven't done it in ages! I'll check in with the girls and see if they want to go as well, although they usually have plans when they come to town."

"Do you come here often?" I asked.

"Maybe every two or three years, so yes. We visit with my brother and his wife, that's Ruth's folks. Other years we go elsewhere to see other family or just travel on our own, but we much rather travel to see people we know. We have such a good time with family."

Their meal came and it looked even better than mine. I worked in a diner for heaven's sake, and now I was becoming food obsessed.

We hit the van for our tour of the city. The girls did have other plans and we said we'd meet by the pool later that night. No doubt, I would be begging for sleep by then.

We started with the Alamo first, then moved on to stroll along the famous river walk in the downtown area. We worked our way through shops and restaurants. It was Joan's idea to stop at several of the restaurants since there were so many. She wanted us to get a taste of it all, so we stopped for "mini meals." We got coffee at the first one, and then stopped again for appetizers and Joan and Frank had a drink there. Then, further down, we stopped again for more appetizers and the last one we had a bit of dessert. At this point, I was probably indebted to these people a couple hundred or so for the meals and, what did I figure, three months' rent for the accommodations? But I was starting to concede they invited me here, I would never have stayed at such an elaborate place, when there was a perfectly decent Holiday Inn on the strip we passed, so that was on them. Or her. Frank had never really chimed in on any of this, just took the tab and paid it.

After gorging at the many restaurants, we walked for a while then headed back to the van and took a ride over to the Japanese Tea Garden briefly; just your basic day of being a total tourist. I could tell Frank was wearing and we went back to the lodge to regroup. I said I would get my book and sit by the pool for a bit. I needed down time and the no sleep was getting to me too.

I found my book and realized I was just about done with it and decided to go into the gift shop and see about another one. I would have grabbed one from the room but was afraid to take it to the pool area and never would finish it by the time I left. If nothing else, I could use one for the plane ride back too, and it would cost about the same here as it would at the airport to get one, so it didn't matter. As a matter of fact, the one I was reading was the one I got at the airport while waiting for Ruth. I perused the book selection, and found one I could handle when mine was done and set off to the pool area with both my books.

I settled in and in maybe four minutes, I was sound asleep. I heard voices around me, and I opened my eyes to see the New York ladies sitting next to me chatting. I still had my book propped open to the same page I'd opened it to when, what time was it? I was feeling so groggy. The sky was dark although the pool area had a rather nice outdoor mood lighting. The pool itself however was brighter than the lighting for the seating area. The New Yorkers were drinking Margaritas and laughing.

"Lainey, hi," one of them said. She must have seen me stir. "Joan and Frank have gone off to dinner up north, would you like to join us in just a bit?"

"What time is it?"

"It's 8:30."

"You know what? I'm just going to head off to bed. My nap did not revive me! But thank you."

I got out of the lounge chair without too much commotion, ready to head back to my room. I was so disoriented and wobbly. Did I have a margarita? I was feeling it!

I no sooner stood up than I heard the crack of lightning. The thunder was nearly immediately following.

"Oh, a storm? A close storm too," I said.

"Damn," Sherry said, gathering up everything, as the next second the rain started with no regard for our belongings. I tried to shelter my books under my shirt and Sherry and Lyla started throwing things in a large tote bag. We ran back inside and stood looking out on the sloshing pool.

"Why don't we go into the dining room and have us a drink?" Sherry was asking, she also asked if I wanted to come along.

I declined again and headed off to my room. I got there and not ten minutes later was in bed. Even with the flashes of lightning and super loud thunder, I couldn't stay awake.

• Chapter 28 •

In the morning, I had a charming bout of confusion. It was 7:00 am, the wedding was at one, but I needed to get there early. I didn't have any idea how long it would take to get there or what time we would be leaving and I couldn't decide if I should just get into my dress now or wait. I hadn't talked to Joan the night before about when we would be leaving, so now I would feel seriously foolish wearing my purple dress with the big side bow to breakfast, but should I suffer through that, or then have to go back and change five minutes later or...

I took my chances and put the dress on. It had made it from the suitcase fairly well, but they also had a steamer in the bathroom to fluff it up if I wanted. I could get used to being pampered I thought, and then I took one look at the steamer and wasn't sure exactly how to use it. I might figure it out, but if I didn't, I'd have me a dripping wet dress to contend with and that I wasn't about to deal with. The dress was fine. It was not a *morning dress* however, and I felt like I was doing the walk of shame going down to breakfast.

The New Yorkers were there, and waved to me. They were not wearing wedding attire.

"Lainey, we have to go get Frank and Joan," Sherry said, somewhat sleepily.

"Go get them?"

"Yes, they called around midnight, they'd stayed at the restaurant too long and the storm caused all kinds of flooding in their area. They couldn't get out — trees are down and they said they were at a motel nearby and asked if we could come and get them this morning."

Sherry looked at me. "Do you want to wait here or come with us?"

I wish I had looked up all the locations of where I was. At least printed out a map of the area. Without knowing if I was going north or south, east or west, or how far anything was in relation to anything else, I felt so unsure of myself. Next time, (like there would be a next time like this!) I would be more prepared, or I would at least have a smart phone on me to figure things out!

"Oh, sure, I'll go." And then it hit me. "But, wait a minute, how are we going to be able to get them, if they can't get out?"

Sherry already nodding her head yes, to say *of course*, and pulled out her phone. There must have been drinking last night.

A moment later, as she was hanging up, she said, "They thought of the same thing this morning. Looks like they'll have to stay put for now. I guess they're going to miss the wedding. Joan said they're pretty quick about getting to the trees, but knew it might be at least a day."

They had already ordered breakfast and the waiter came by with their plates of the apple, cinnamon, walnut pancakes. "Coffee for me," I said, but then changed my mind. "You know what? I'll have the same."

After a now very leisurely breakfast, the New Yorkers said they were going to get changed for the wedding and then we would be on our way.

"How long to get there?" I finally asked. "I should be there a little early."

"Oh, it shouldn't take us an hour." Shouldn't take us an hour… how had they planned to get Frank and Joan and still make it? Well maybe that was on the way. Not knowing where I was in this whole scenario was a little disconcerting.

"Why don't we meet back here at 11:30?" Sherry said.

"Sounds good to me." Half an hour should be enough time to ask someone at the church where I was supposed to be standing and all. They walked off and as I turned, I happened to look down at my dress and noticed what was probably pancake syrup in a small line running down the side. The non-bow side, nooooooo!

I ran back to my room passing the ladies on my way. I rushed in and looked around for some soap. I blotted it with a washcloth then blotted again, and watched the wet part grow larger and larger. The sticky syrup was dissolving, so some progress was happening, but the water was making the lavender seem one shade darker. Just feeling I was making more of a mess I took the dress off so I could look at what was happening better.

I put it on the bathroom counter top and put a towel underneath it. My next step was to get all the soap out and I rinsed the washcloth a few dozen times and then blotted the dress over and over again. This was my dry clean only dress, wasn't it?

The area got darker again from the water and then I started blotting it again with a dry towel. I took out my hair dryer and gave that a whirl on the lower setting fearing I'd probably seize up the material on high.

Now, the spot was definitely lighter. As in, one shade lighter than the material had been. What had just happened? It may not be noticeable to all, but it certainly was to me.

It was just sugar. Did the soap do this? I looked over at the soap again. Spa quality soap of course, a wonderful lemon and neroli essential oil. The oil might have been a bit strong for the delicate material. Or it was the hair dryer? No telling now.

Okay, so my dress was semi-ruined. Maybe no one would notice. Yeah, right! Maybe I could hide it in a fold. Yes, that might actually work. I found a safety pin in my overnight bag and decided it was worth a try. From underneath, I put the pin lengthwise to form a fold in the material. I held it up and gave it the once over. Okay, a little skewed, but it was passable. Definitely passable.

I put the dress on once again and looked in the mirror. Well, it is what it is. The semi-skewed, slightly-stained, once-worn, brides-maids' dress. Awesome.

At 11:30, I met the ladies in the lobby to leave. Now dressed in wedding appropriate outfits, they waved me over. Hats, no kidding, they both had on hats, fit for the Kentucky Derby. Sherry gave me a look and pointing to my dress said, "What's going on there?"

"You noticed..."

I explained as we headed into their rental car. I could hear her chuckle but she didn't look at me when she did it. Once inside, I said, "Oh, and thank you for taking me. I would have been stranded without Joan and Frank."

"Oh, absolutely."

I settled in the back of their rental and couldn't see a thing through the two large hats front and center.

We got to the church thirty minutes early as I figured, but people were already arriving, I wasn't that early. I went to the back room to try and find the rest of the bridal party. I was wishing I knew what I was doing. Ruth's mother grabbed me and started telling me where I would be, and who the groomsman or usher, or "whatever they called the guys nowadays" as she said, would be, and that I would be standing opposite them. Well at least I got my instructions.

"How's Ruth doing?" I asked.

"Cool as a cucumber. I don't know how!" Clearly, Ruth's mom was not cool as a cucumber! Although interesting that Ruth was, I started to think, hmmm, that's Ruth's demeanor so I shouldn't read much into it. I told her mom that Joan and Frank were stranded by the storm last night and they wished they could be there. Then I thought, what if I'd gotten stranded with them? All this way to not be able to go! Wow. Wait a minute...that could have been a good thing!

"Oh, doesn't it figure?" she said. I didn't know them well enough to answer. "We didn't get anything here, just a light rain, it's amazing how those storms come in and can do so much damage in just a small spot." This time I just nodded. Was she upset? I couldn't tell.

Ruth looked stunning in her dress. Simple, yet elegant. A shorter, off the shoulder, satin dress to the knee, with seed pearls along the top of a lace outer layer that went from her collar to extend just a bit below the hem of the satin dress. No one would care what I looked like up there. It was time to forget about my own dress.

Tyler was my groomsman or usher, depending on who you asked. We got to walk down the aisle side by side. He was tall, blonde and really quite handsome. I was feeling okay about the whole thing until he spoke.

"They've been living together for what ten years now? What changed?"

"Excuse me? They finally decided to get married, I guess that's what changed," I started, but I felt he wanted some other kind of explanation. I could have easily gone along with him but it felt so wrong in the moment.

"No, seriously, what happened?"

Losing your 'single' buddy, are you? I decided just to smile and shake my head like, *Oh, I just don't know.* Seriously this was not the time or place.

"You think she's pregnant? I mean I guess she's not *too* old to have kids. But, she'd be one tough mom. Have you met her?" He continued, "Ruth, are you a friend of hers? You know she can be seriously witchy sometimes, that Ruth."

"I'm a *bridesmaid*. Yes, I've met her." I tried to contain my growing disbelief. Was he kidding? But, then, I was even more curious, he knew the other side of Ruth. The side I knew.

"How do you know the groom?" I asked, needing to change the direction of the conversation here. I could feel my face stiffen into a smile.

"He's my cousin. Kind of surprised he asked me to be in the wedding though, we don't see each other hardly ever."

"I see." The music started and I felt a little relief as we were all starting to walk down the aisle. He started to say something else and I gave him a *shhhhh* finger to my mouth with a smile. Do not forget the smile. This could go badly. There was only one other bridesmaid and then the maid of honor. The other bridesmaid was ahead of us and she looked back, probably to shush us, only to see my still straining smile. "Yeah, I know," my eyes told her.

When we got to the front of the church, I was relieved not to have to be looking straight at Tyler, although once in a while I did catch him rolling his eyes. The rest of the service went without incident, which gave it the impression, however skewed, of everything going perfectly.

I caught up with the New Yorkers again after the service to get a ride to the reception.

"Lyla's not feeling so hot," Sherry was saying. "Do you mind if we drop you off and then I'll come back later to pick you up?" Lyla was looking a little ashen and didn't say anything.

"Oh, of course, okay, thank you. I'm so sorry, Lyla, I hope you're feeling better soon," I said, and she nodded.

So, there would be no getting out early if need be. I hoped I was seated with the other bridesmaid and not Tyler. I didn't think I could handle a couple hours with him.

The reception was a really small group of people. It seemed like so many more at the church. They were using a small function room at one of the nearby hotels. I ended up talking to Mark through most of it. He apologized under his breath for Tyler. He said Bren's mother had insisted Bren ask him to be an usher.

Mark was just as curious why they suddenly decided to get married. No job changes or anything. And as far as he knew clearly neither one of them was in any hurry to get married. But then again, Ruth was Ruth. Why was he so surprised? When she decided she wanted something, for whatever reason, she got it when she wanted it. Okay, Mark knew the bossy and unappreciative Ruth I knew. Perhaps it was her parents, a generational thing, respect for elders and no one else, I decided to leave it at that.

I danced with Mark for a bit, until Tyler cut in. (He actually cut in.) "Oh, okay," I said, knowing it wasn't. I'm just gonna say way too much alcohol was present at this point.

"That Ruth, who does she think she is? Telling me I need to chill out," he said as he twirled me around. Clearly, I missed some incident there, but didn't want to provoke anything more. I looked over and Mark was keeping a steady eye on me ready to jump back in if need be.

"Tyler." I smiled, trying to divert his attention. "Do you have any other cousins here? Any other relatives?"

"Say Ruth…" he called out not even listening to me. "What's the deal? Why'd you get married so fast, are you pregnant? Some mother you'll be!"

Excellent, a scene, and he's dancing with me. How lucky can I get? As I tried to step aside Mark stepped over to take my hand and pull me away.

Ruth had already come over. "Tyler." She looked shocked. "What is with you tonight?"

"So, what's the deal? Why'd you get married so fast?"

"So fast? Bren and I have been together for years. The time was just right for us. No big deal."

Mark then walked over and patted Tyler on the back with a firm hand, whispered something in his ear, and escorted him out of the room.

Ruth and I stood there looking at each other.

"Does he think I'd be some kind of a monster as a mother?" she asked me a little horrified.

"I don't know what he thinks Ruth, I wouldn't even begin to

guess."

"Do *you* think I'd be a terrible mother?" Oh no. I wasn't prepared to answer that one. As much as I knew she wanted me say *no*, I hesitated. Figure it out Lainey. But remember, this is *her wedding*.

Her wedding. I couldn't do it. I couldn't tell her what a controlling mother she'd be. How she wouldn't even consider what her child wanted, and how she would be demanding, and if she treated that child anything like me or... hey, not me, what about her folks...

"When I see how you act with your folks—" Okay, that was the perspective. "—I know you have the potential to be a great mother." Sure, I totally wimped out. But someday, someday I would be strong and tell her how she treated me. But not today, today was her wedding. She smiled at me like I'd just given her the best gift ever.

* * *

As I was saying goodbye to the bride and groom, I was getting concerned that Sherry wouldn't be back for me. The crowd had already started leaving, and I had that sinking feeling.

I wandered out of the reception room and back into the lobby of the hotel. I decided to wait it out there and not look as obvious as I would all alone in the room.

Once everyone had left, I wondered why I hadn't thought to get Sherry's phone number. Or even to ask Mark to stick around in case she didn't show up.

I had Joan and Frank's number. Wait, I had Joan and Frank's *home* number not their cell phone. Okay, that wouldn't do me any good.

I sat watching some folks come in and meander around for a while, and then I had the brilliant idea to check at the desk. Maybe Sherry had come in and was looking for me or something.

"Did anyone leave a message for Lainey Evans?" I asked. "I was at a reception here and my ride hasn't shown up yet."

"Let me check," the girl said, and then upon finding the message said, "Oh, yes, a Sherry called and said she was very sorry to leave you stranded, but her sister was sick, and they were at the urgent care. Oh, sorry."

"What? What? Oh no, oh no! Did she leave her number by any chance?"

"No."

I had to regroup, and somehow get a ride back to the lodge now. I thought about Uber, but I'd never used them, and then I had no apps on my phone so that wasn't going to fly anyway. I *had* to upgrade my phone, I was never going to let this happen to me again. "Okay, I guess I need the number of a cab."

Where was I going? The lodge, and where was that?

One hour, and half a paycheck later, I was back at the lodge. I cannot be spending money like this, I could be out of a job soon! My flight was in the morning and I didn't have anyone's phone number. I called Joan and Frank's home number and left a message to call me with their cell phone number. Maybe one of their kids would call me back.

I asked if there was a shuttle or anything to the airport and they said the lodge didn't have one, but they could put in a call to a shuttle service if I liked. I said that would be great, and gave them my flight info. I'd eaten at the reception so I skipped dinner and just went back to my room to change and relax. I was done with the dress and that felt like a blessing.

I changed into my pajamas thinking I would still knock on Sherry's door before I went to bed and see how the sister was doing, but I woke up in the middle of the night still sitting in the reading chair with my book in my lap. I made my way to the bed. I guess, I wouldn't be hearing how it went with Lyla. How could I be leaving in the morning and both Joan and Frank were still missing and I had no clue about Sherry and Lyla as well? None of this felt right. I needed to leave word with each of them, ah, better yet, write out a note for each of them. I wrote to the New Yorkers saying I hoped everything turned out fine for Lyla, and then I wrote a thank you note to Joan and Frank for all they had done for me.

I got up around 4:00 a.m. to make my 5:00 a.m. shuttle. I went to check out at the desk, and gave the woman the two notes. The woman put them under the counter and then said, "That will be $2592.00." Wow, I had estimated pretty well.

I casually said, "Oh, that's actually on the LaMorton's tab. They had insisted I be their guest here."

"There's no note of that here, I'm afraid," she said, looking at me like if I so much as moved the wrong way she was calling to restrain me.

"Didn't they, when they reserved my room, I mean didn't they put it down that they were taking care of this?" I said in my most positive, oh, what a silly mistake voice.

Still, that hideous, horrible, this is where it all goes wrong feeling emerged, and I knew there was no mistake.

"No, your name is listed here. Lainey Evans. It isn't listed under any other name... No, I don't see any mention of that." I could tell she was getting really agitated and this was all about to go south. She proceeded to hand me the bill.

I looked it over and said, "Did they put my meals on their bill then?" Not seeing anything mentioned about that. I had at least been aware of the price of my meals.

"Meals are included for guests."

"Oh, complimentary breakfast?" The pancakes were really good.

"No, all meals."

No wonder she insisted I have what I wanted! Wow. I had totally missed out there.

I couldn't call them, as I had no number. Maybe I should have the woman call Sherry to get their number. At quarter of five in the morning when she's worried about her sick sister. No, that wasn't going to be an option either. I pulled out my wallet and looked in at the credit cards. Two cards stared back at me and I couldn't remember what the limit was on either one of them. I'd done that whole cab thing on one.

"Okay," I said. "Here's what I need to do. I need to put half on this card and the other half on this one here. Is that something we can do?"

"Oh, certainly." The relief was showing on her face. No, we wouldn't have a "situation" on our hands here, now would we? How many times had we gotten stiffed at the diner I thought? And even if that was only pennies compared to this bill. This bill. How on earth was I actually going to pay for this? Would the LaMorton's take care of this or was I really out the $2592.00? Closer to *three thousand dollars*, to be their guest? Oh no. I felt so sick. And I could be losing my job, no! How had this all turned so wrong so fast?

Harold would probably give me some lip service about a silver lining here. No, this was bad. Sorry, Harold, you lose.

My shuttle showed up and as she took my bag and put it in the back of the van, I looked back at the lodge. Well, that was once in a lifetime. Don't forget to tip her I thought, not her fault I won't be using my credit cards ever again.

CHAPTER 29

I staggered out of the plane at my final destination: home. I had worked myself into a tizzy over the whole bill thing at least a dozen times on the flight, and then I decided to just let go for the moment. I would be back to tizzy again soon enough but I was tired from all the travel. I got my bag and went to find my car.

My beautiful blue car sat there waiting for me. How I hadn't really appreciated my car with all that silly license plate nonsense. Boy, I sure could have used it in Texas. Then I saw a couple of pieces of paper tucked under my windshield wiper. I was surprised they allowed solicitations in the lot and wondered how that worked here. No, I looked around. It was just my car. The first one said, "We need to meet, call me" and gave me a phone number. That one would be hitting the trash. The second note said, "Love the plate, give me a call" and the same number. So, ultra-creepy.

I felt a little weird getting in my car, like I had been violated somehow, and maybe I was being watched. But, then wasn't that the problem with the car all the time? It just felt so clear now that it had been on display here for some time! I hadn't thought about my plate in almost four days. I thought about what Sam had said about if I owned the diner he'd use the plate to help advertise, but I wasn't totally sure I was okay with that. Fine at the diner, but here? I threw the notes on the passenger seat and proceeded to head home.

* * *

I called my mother and Jill to let them know I was back from the wedding and it went very nicely. I decided to let all the finer details go unmentioned. Fortunately, I got answering machines both times, so I didn't have to provide the nitty gritty. They would just blame me for being me, if I did. Tell me what I should have done. Yes, I would have to mention it to the LaMortons, blah, blah, blah.

Finally, I was home. As I was unpacking my suitcase, I knocked over the notebook with the page written about Harold's event. Oh, wow, that hadn't worked out either. And, that was supposed to be an easy one! What a mistake. It was all such a mistake. I was glad I hadn't done one for the wedding. What a disaster. I kept meaning to ask Ginny if she had that pamphlet on rewriting your story since I had clearly lost mine, but I was also sure she would have thrown it out by now.

I hadn't done any rewriting about the wedding trip and it still went so off kilter, so maybe the rewriting wasn't affecting things at all. Maybe it was a general thing going on. It just seemed every-thing worked out backwards for me. If I wanted it to go well, it would not. Each time I wrote about an event, it still all went back-wards, or horrible, when it happened. But then it always used to anyway. I hadn't *made* it worse, I just improved nothing.

Maybe being backwards or reversed or upside down or

something was the very thing to rewrite. Not the events themselves, the way events in general worked out. I just wasn't going in the right direction.

My birthday was in a month. Time for new goals, anyway. I'd had a pseudo vacation, I actually had worked some things out with my mother... nothing was black and white, but... at least *that* was going in the right direction. I even liked Sam.

I shredded the story about Harold's event. Put that one behind me. So, I needed to feel I was going in the right direction. I would really give this one a try, and then give it up completely if it went sour once again.

I know that I'm going in the right direction. Despite what I sometimes see, I'm heading in the right direction, things work out for me, sometimes in unexpected ways, but I'm always going in the right direction.

Perhaps, that would cover all bases. I didn't feel all over the moon good, but I felt somewhat more confident. This time I put the notebook in a drawer in my desk. Tuck it away, let it simmer there.

* * *

"Oddly, the wedding itself was fine," I told Ginny, "really nice and all that. Except that every other bit of the trip was not fine." I went on to explain that I had no idea how the sister was, if she really was sick, sick. That Joan and Frank were still stranded as far as I knew, although I had called their house when I got home to make sure they got out okay, and that Lyla was okay, but again it was their home back here, and I just left a message. So, I was left not knowing what happened with anyone. And I ended up having to pay the outrageous bill. Yeah, it was not fine.

"You have to call them and let them know about the bill! Lainey, you can't just let that go! This is a million times worse than not getting the car plate changed. You have to speak up!"

"I know, I know," I said, not having the slightest idea how I would broach it with the LaMortons. I did leave a note thanking them for their hospitality. Maybe, they'd realize they hadn't been quite so hospitable as they thought. And even having spent a day or so with them, I still didn't feel like I really knew these people. Had I been an idiot to say yes in the first place?

"Anyway, that lodge, tell me more about that!"

Good, something I could talk about without feeling at fault! "Well, it was just amazing, and had I known all the meals were included I would have had some killer dinners, but as for the breakfasts I had... we have to start adding stuff to the pancakes here. Apple, cinnamon, walnut is really, really good!"

After I enlightened her on the fine accommodations, I told her about the weirdo notes on my car. Having spouted my rage at being such a target there, I seemed to calm down a little bit.

It was strange: the worse I felt about it, the more I kept thinking of that plate I saw at the vet's. I felt so drawn to go back and check that one out again.

* * *

Meg signaled me into her office and then Ginny. I knew she was supposed to answer Walt while I had been at the wedding but she hadn't said anything to us yet. I felt a little sick.

"It's never easy when you want to do the right thing for everyone," she began, "but I did tell Walt no, I wouldn't be selling if he was going to close the diner." A wave of relief swept over me.

"And then I thought about your offer. And while I know you two would make wonderful owners, I had this sense that you might be overwhelmed at first."

Ginny and I half nodded to each other, knowing there was certainly truth to that. But even still, this was a bit of a disappointment, unless she kept it.

"And *then* I had a long talk with Harold."

"Harold?" we said in unison.

"Yes, our dear friend, Harold. Ladies, Harold would like to go in as a 'somewhat' silent partner with you. We'll go over all the details later, but I think it really is a win-win for all of us. He has a few ideas of things he'd like to update. He wants to bring more of the community to the diner with social events. Your plate inspired him, Lainey. It seems he just can't get enough of the attention it generates.

Oh, wow! Harold…

* * *

When Harold came in later in my shift, we were able to talk to him about the diner, we'd been so careful not to even mention it in his presence or any other regulars for that matter. He was pretty excited to be able to talk to us about it. And I knew Meg had made a wise choice with him.

Then I told him all about my trip without the whole *having to pay for it* part. He said maybe he'd do a show tonight about being left hanging… the unknown things that we never find out about or get back to. Unfinished business or unfinished events/tales. Harold was delighted now having some good material for tonight's show.

I wished I could listen to his show more often. But, it was just too late. I got snippets when I got home sometimes. But my whole needing to sleep thing cut it short. I knew it was a show I would enjoy if I could. Harold needed to do podcasts of his show! I'd have to mention that to him. The thought itself gave me a chuckle. A podcast of a rambling nostalgic show. Quite the oxymoron.

Harold asked what I thought the notes on the car were all about and if I was going to call them, although he immediately vetoed that idea, just as I did. But, there was still a curiosity factor going on. I decided there was no way on the planet I was going to call, but then I thought, I should have Seth give them a call!

• Chapter 30 •

Thursday night was the last of the cooking classes. But this time it felt different. Now that Ginny and I (and Harold) were going to be the diner's owners I felt a whole different sense of purpose in the class. The same with our cooking club. Now it wasn't just for us, now it was a way to try out more recipes for all of our customers too.

In class we were making a French chicken casserole with peas and bacon, along with a hot chocolate soufflé. I would have been all about the dessert this week, but now I was making mental notes about the dinner too. Ginny and Anna also looked so intent on getting every detail just right on both items. Anna seemed a little more enthusiastic this week too. For as much as I liked chocolate, she was busy swooning over the chocolate sauce involved and I felt a little strange witnessing it. Something was up with her. At least Ginny and I had a reason to be so absorbed in the class, but Anna?

"Have you heard our news?" I asked Anna.

"The diner, is there news on the diner?" she asked knowing we were ready to explode waiting.

"You bet! You are now looking at the new soon to be owners!"

"Congratulations! Oh, this is so exciting!"

"Meg told me she wanted to wait until your birthday to tell us, but decided another couple weeks would set us all over the edge! I'm glad she didn't!" Ginny said more to me than Anna.

"Wow, now that would have been a present!" I said, but all of my birthday goals rushed in front of me again. Mom, check. Direction, amazing, check. And vacation, well it was what it was, I'd seen the Alamo! Check!

Maybe I'd work on that whole thing with Ruth for next year.

"What are we making on Saturday?" I asked the two of them.

"Oh, we're doing a zucchini casserole, remember? It was your idea," Ginny reminded me.

"So you didn't meet without me?" I was touched, but also feeling a little guilty for having left them. "You didn't have to do that."

"I think we've figured out the quantity with three, now it's too much math to just do two," Ginny laughed.

"I think we're going to have to do a lot more math with the diner Ginny! But thanks!"

On Saturday, Anna once again seemed just a little too giggly. This time Ginny outright asked her, "Anna what is up? What's going on?" Caught, she suddenly took account of her behavior and looked at both of us with some apprehension.

"Okay, okay, okay. I didn't want to tell you, because, well I know Lainey you're going to be mad, and I hope you don't hate me, but..." She couldn't say it.

"But...?" I felt a sense of dread.

"But, well, I had a date with Gerry the other night."

"And?"

"No *and*, I had a *DATE* with him. He just got that new job, he was so excited, and I invited him to dinner. I made dinner for him and we just had the best time. I didn't mean to swoop in like that. I just... it was jus..., it just fell into place, I guess," she said, looking flushed at the full weight of her confession.

"Is that it?" I asked. "Anna that's great! I'm so glad you had a great time!" I was now feeling totally freed of the whole grape thing.

"But, I thought you, well, you know..."

"No. Me? No. This is wonderful news."

"Lainey's got another plate guy lined up Anna," Ginny interjected with a smile. "She wouldn't want to be two-timing Gerry?!"

"You what?"

"Oh, Ginny. Seriously. Some crank left a note on my car about my plate but that's the extent of that. So dumb."

I hadn't mentioned the whole vet thing to Ginny. But her words were ringing true. I think I did have a whole other plate thing lined up. Part of me hadn't been able to stop thinking about the vet.

"You know he still feels bad about letting that PNT-BTR plate get away. He said he even tried to track him down for you. He went back to work to see if he could get any information about the guy but no one seemed to remember who it was."

"What? He what?" I was totally floored by this information. And, sadly, I wasn't sure if this was good information or bad. What happens when he finds him? I just...

"Oh, what a nice gesture," Ginny said. "I think once you find out who this guy is, Lainey, something will click for you."

"Seriously, that plate! It's like, enough already!" I said shaking my head. "I think Gerry totally misunderstood me. *Yes*, I was curious who owned it, but really I just wanted to let the person know my plate was nothing but a big mistake! It's like everyone is trying to turn it into something else." I felt totally exasperated. I looked at them both. "Sorry." I thought about Sam, the diner, and then the vet. I was a mess.

Anna looked at me, then Ginny, and then me again. "Ooooh. You *hate* your plate!" She looked away and then at me once again. "I never got that before. I know you said it was a mistake but I thought you thought it was funny. Ooooh, you really hate it. Oh, okay, now I understand you even thought, with Gerry... you had no interest in him *because* of his plate!"

Now I was feeling stupid. And shallow. And really, really, horrible all over. Because she was right. I didn't like him because of his plate. Gerry himself never factored into it. Yeah, shallow and stupid and oh, just awful. He never stood a chance, and it had nothing to— do with him.

Ginny gave me a look, and Anna wide eyed just kind of nodded in a new understanding. Not so much a good understanding, but an understanding.

"Okay, maybe I was a little prejudiced at first, but I don't *hate* Gerry because of his plate. There was just no chemistry there that's all." I was trying to worm my way back to decency. It looked like the gals were willing to drop it, but I was still quite mortified by my own realization. Now, if he had been the vet...

* * *

I now couldn't get the idea of the ROL-LLL plate out of my mind. What had happened to me? The whole idea of Jelly-Roll — there was some kind of oddball humor there that I liked, or make that, I only liked it *because* I liked the vet! Because at the same time it was humor I hated in the whole PNT BTR or GR8 PE scenario.

I summed up all of my courage and before work, went back to the vet's office to see if the car was there, hoping it was and that it wasn't just a customers'. When I got there and saw it sitting there, my second thought was, it may not be the vet's, but someone else who worked there. So, I didn't quite know what I was going to say, what I was going to do, but I had to go in there and announce myself. I made it to the reception desk and the woman looked up from her computer screen.

"Can I help you?"

"Umm, I have a very strange question."

"Oh, don't worry dear, we've heard them all! You won't believe the things that happen with our pets!"

"No, this isn't about an animal." Now I felt reluctant to finish!

"Oh?"

"I was wondering if you knew who owned the car with the license plate ROL-LLL?

"What?" She looked at me like I'd hit the car and was reporting the damage to her. I must have looked as nervous as I felt.

"I wouldn't ask," I managed to continue, "but I was just so curious and figured it had to be someone who worked here, in the vet's office."

She looked a little relieved, then said, "Yes, it is Dr. Hawkins' car." Hawkins. Hawk as in bird. He had one of those names! I hadn't caught the name before.

"Yes, Patty?" Dr. Hawkins said opening the door.

"No, this woman was just asking about your license plate. I was telling her it was yours."

"I get that a lot," he said, looking up from his tablet. "The cat! The cat that wasn't yours. You come back to ask about my plate?"

I could feel myself start to blush. This was by far the dumbest thing I'd ever done. Okay, after the whole Texas thing, definitely the dumbest thing.

"I know, ridiculous huh? I just, I'm sorry, it was just that, I just found it very funny...because..."

"Yeah, I get that a lot. It's a little more complicated, but..."

"No, that's not it. It's because of *my* plate." I got the words out. Admitting it was my plate, the first step Lainey, the first step.

"Yours?"

"Mine says JEL-EEE." There, I'd said it, also wanting to hide the second I did.

"JEL-EEE! *You're* JEL-EEE? Did you get my note?"

"Note? What note? The number on my car at the airport last week? Was that you?" I asked a little startled. The creepy one? I hoped not!

"No, not at the airport, it was a while ago, at the grocery store. I left a note telling you my plate said ROL-LLL and I thought it was such a funny coincidence. That was all. And after that I even heard about your plate late one night on the radio."

"The rain soaked note! I thought that was a crank, but I couldn't read it because of the downpour. It was all a big purple blur on my windshield."

"Oh! I'm so sorry about that, I only had a marker on me — I didn't realize... But I'll be... you're JEL-EEE. So, what's the connection? Is that the secret sauce you've been feeding the cat?"

"Uh, no." I chuckled at the thought. "There is no connection, although I do work in a diner—actually will be part owner of one." I felt a surge of pride. "It was just a fluke at the DMV. I tried to give it back but the scowl I got told me no such luck, it was mine now. Several scowls in fact."

"How hilarious." He laughed. "I mean, I'm sorry, but that is hilarious."

"But yours is intentional," I said.

"Well...well, yes. Originally, my intention was to get ROL-OVR, for all our amazing dogs, but it sounded too much like an accident waiting to happen. I had a feeling that one would be turned down, so then I thought of ROL-LLL and figured that was okay. If I'd thought about it longer I wouldn't have bothered getting a vanity plate at all, since now it feels like it's missing something! ROL-LLL who does that? A baker?"

"Well, I was mortified when I first got mine. Okay, I've been mortified with it every single day since I got it! But I'm starting to see the humor in there." Owning the diner, these pieces were coming together, wow. "Okay, well, I'll let you get back to work," I said, not knowing what to really say next. "I just knew I needed to meet the person with that car!"

"Oh, we'll have to get a picture, that radio host is always asking for pictures! Tell you what, can you meet me back here on Sunday say 11:00? The office is closed and we can get a good picture and then maybe a cup of coffee. Besides I think I owe you for the splotch on your windshield. What do you say?" he said with a big smile.

"Oh, that sounds good." My voice just a smidge too high and I could feel myself starting to blush again. I waved goodbye to the both of them and somehow got out the door without walking into it first. Harold, oh, Harold, how did you know?

CHAPTER 31

Ginny loved, loved, loved my story, and couldn't wait to see Harold to tell him all about it. Best it came from Ginny; I'd stumble all over it with Harold. I was a little nervous about the Sunday date to see the vet again, although I also thought I could suggest the Café of Coffee. Something fun. Owned by doctors, yeah, I bet he'd love that. As for the picture, I'd probably hit the car wash first.

I got home about midnight that night and there was a message on my machine from Joan LaMorton. She said Lyla was doing much better, it had been an infection and they treated her with antibiotics and she was doing just fine. The sisters had gone back to New York, and, obviously, she and Frank had found their way back from the flood! She said to give her a call and she would give me the rest of the details.

Hmmm. No word on the room. I tossed and turned all night on that one. Well, so much had happened that day. I liked the vet. How twisted was that I thought, I really liked the vet. Maybe it was time to pay attention to the signs after all. If I hadn't been so resistant to them... well who knew. I wasn't going to try and figure that one out. But, it seemed things worked out with more than a random coincidence. I'd give Harold that one.

In the morning, Calico, a.k.a. Jasper, was sitting on my window sill. I still didn't see how it had room but there he was. "Who let you out today?" I asked. Shocking, but the cat didn't answer. "Well, be that way," I said to it. "I have to call someone this morning, so if you'll excuse me."

I went to pick up the phone to make the dreaded phone call when it rang. I answered without waiting for the machine to get it, somehow thinking it was Joan on the line, but it was Meg. Could I come into the diner right now, Paula had a sick child again.

"Oh, sure." I said. I knew I'd miss chatting with Ginny tonight, although wait, was I now pulling a double shift? "Did you want me tonight too?"

"Would you mind? I don't have anyone to cover you tonight either."

"Okay, let me get ready and I'll be right in." As I said the words I realized this would soon be my new role. It would now all fall to me and Ginny. Wow. What a shift.

Jasper disappeared by the time I was ready for work. I decided to wait and call Joan later. I knew at this point it would be the following day.

Three hundred cups of coffee later (customers — not me), and I was exhausted. When Ginny came on, she was full of advice about my upcoming meeting with the vet. I had said "meeting" and Ginny then said *date,* about a dozen or so times after that. I was really looking forward to the meeting/date with the vet.

During a lull in the back, I thought about all the rewriting I had been doing and how this would never have been something

I could "prewrite," or dream up or anything. That my little plate fiasco could turn into something good. That I resisted anything good ever coming out of it.

"Ginny, did you ever read that pamphlet on rewriting your life from the psychic class or did you throw it out?"

"I glanced at it and then I threw it out, because it didn't say what you were supposed to do. It was about a course they were giving, so they don't really give you any information except to tease you. Why, did you want to take the class?"

Oh, that was rich. "No, just curious."

* * *

The next morning, I looked at the clock then the phone. I should call Joan back, I'm sure by now...well, I didn't know what the deal was.

I could feel my shoulders slouching, knowing I still wasn't ready to make the call. But, I was distracted from my slump when I heard the knock at the door.

It could only be Roger. I opened the door to see Shawna standing there. "Have you seen Roger?"

"No, I just got up," I said to her.

"Oh, sorry! We're going away this week and I wanted to leave some of my stuff here before we go, but he's not up there."

"You called him and...?"

"Right to voice mail, but I figured he was home, okay, then, well, thanks. Oh, wait, is it okay if I leave it here with you, it's just some camping stuff?"

"Uh, sure I guess," I said a little uneasy.

"I'll get my backpack ready tonight," she said as she ran back to the car and then deposited an outdoor stove, and a sleeping bag onto my porch, then another trip with a tent, then once again with a lantern, and a cooler all from the trunk of her car. I got a "thanks," and as she was leaving she handed me a few more pamphlets from one of her many pockets. "I don't know why but I thought you'd like these too." I looked down at them and saw *Rewrite Your Life* on the top and smiled.

I pulled all the gear inside and tacked a note on the other door to let Roger know I had Shawna's camping gear.

Then having been distracted enough, and now irritated enough, I picked up the phone and called Joan. No sense putting it off any longer, but when I got their answering machine I pretty much froze. I got out, "Hi this is Lainey..." and what seemed like an hour later I said, "So, I'll talk to you later." And hung up. I dearly wished there was an "oops, idiot reply" button on my end.

Roger came knocking on my door ten minutes later saw all the gear and said, "Hmmm."

"What's hmmm?" I asked suspiciously.

"I only suggested some day we should go camping, I didn't think it was going to be today."

"You have got some real communication issues there Roger! But you're still going to have to take all this stuff!" I said smiling at him.

"Yeah, yeah," he said, both grabbing the tent and pulling out his phone to give Shawna a call.

My phone rang as soon as I'd ushered him and all Shawna's stuff out of my apartment. It was Joan.

"Lainey, hi, I just wanted to let you know once again how sorry we were to leave you stranded for the wedding. I hope it wasn't too much trouble."

"No, *that* part was okay."

"There was something else?" she asked, also hearing the change of tone in my voice. "What part was bad?"

I had to go through with it, although I was cringing inside. "I, well, I thought I was going to a cabin as your *guest*, I really wouldn't have said yes otherwise, the lodge was much too fancy for me."

"You didn't like your room?"

"No, it was fabulous; I just don't usually stay in accommodations like that!"

"I'm sorry, Lainey, I don't understand. You didn't like it?"

"No, I loved it, it just turns out I really couldn't *afford* that kind of room. I wish I'd known ahead of time." I was both proud of myself and horrified I couldn't actually say the words.

"But you...wait what? Are you saying *YOU* paid for it?"

"Well, yes, I thought you knew."

"FRANK, Frank, come here. Oh, my goodness. FRANK. He must be out of range, Lainey I'm so sorry, let me call you back," she said quickly and then I heard, "FRANK," one more time and she hung up.

So, it was a mistake. Again, proud and horrified. It almost felt like I was gaining courage. She hadn't realized I had to pay my own way there. But had Frank known? Hopefully no. At any rate, it was a relief in a really big way.

* * *

Paula waved me over when I got to work. "Lainey. Lainey."

"What?" She seemed so excited.

"Well, I found him. You're never going to believe this, but I found him."

"Who?"

"Peanut butter."

"What?"

"Yes. I know!"

"How? Where? Who is he?" I couldn't believe it.

"Well, Amy had this nasty rash happening yet again, and I took her in to see the doctor, and this time they suggested I go see an allergy specialist.

"Of course, I had to find the place. Took me forever, that's why I had to call in yesterday to take Amy there. I could have come back but I also needed to run some errands so I took the day off, hope Meg wasn't too upset."

"I filled in." Meaning, get to the point.

"Thanks. Anyway, in the parking lot I saw it. The silver BMW that read 'PNT-BTR.' I went inside the building, and when I was admitting Amy I asked the receptionist if she knew who the plate belonged to.

"'Of course,' she said, 'that's Dr. Cabot. He's an allergy specialist.' Allergies, peanuts, unbelievable! Anyway, it was Amy's doctor. So, when we got in there I asked him about it! He's an older doctor, and he said his family convinced him that this was a great way to advertise." She didn't even stop to take a breath. "I told him about your plate and he laughed. He said he had seen that one once, when he had popped in to see an old friend of his, for lunch one day. He was going to leave a note but then thought that just made no sense, he'd come off as some kind of weirdo!"

"He's an allergy doctor!" I finally responded. "Wow. How

funny. Well I guess this will be perfect for Harold's show. He can interview the good doctor and tell all his listeners to watch what they eat and all kinds of good stuff like that. I think I'll be off the hook here. He can spin it whatever way he wants to!"

"What do you mean 'you'll be off the hook'? There's no way, you know he'll want to do an interview with the both of you!"

"I think he can do a 'one on one' with the doctor and leave me out of it."

"You were mentioned on the show before. Lainey, no one listens to it, remember?"

"No one listens to it, but then the *other* good doctor, did hear of my plate."

"Now, what are *you* talking about?"

"Didn't Ginny tell you? I thought everyone knew at this point. The vet, you know, his plate says ROL-LLL?"

"What? ROL-LLL?" then after a brief pause, "Jelly-roll? You're kidding, right?"

* * *

We met at the parking lot and with my shiny just-washed car next to the vet's and we both took pictures of the plates side by side.

"Quite a picture, even if you don't like the connection to it!" he teased me.

"Well, here's the thing. It turns out I do now have a more invested connection. Somehow, someway, through many twists and turns, I'm about to be part owner of the diner. I'm still not so happy having it on my car like that, but there certainly is a connection."

We went off to the coffee shop, the Café of Coffee, which he loved, and I told him all about my newfound ownership. We talked, and talked, and coffee ended up being followed up with a dinner.

"You know if you don't want to keep your plate you can return it…" he started and I flinched a little bit, "…but I have an even better idea."

I looked at him feeling intrigued.

"You could get your own vanity plate. With random numbers. Just ordinary numbers. I'll look into it for you, but I think you can do that."

Just a random ordinary plate, like everyone else, but it's a vanity plate! I loved the irony.

"The other good thing is they usually let you keep your old plate, so Lainey, you could put JEL-EEE up on the wall in your diner." *Your diner.* The words hit home so deeply.

"What a fabulous idea!" I gushed. Yup, I gushed.

Acknowledgements

Many thanks to my editor Cara Lockwood, who truly helped me
bring the book together.
**I want to thank my family and friends
for all their amazing support.**
A special thank you to my aunt Trudy Gately
for her generous support.
Thanks to:
Jackie (Gately) Volk, Ruediger Volk,
John Gately, Faith V. Gately,
Susan Gately, and the Tagliani family.

Thank you to my early readers and dear friends,
Laura Taylor, Kathy Rohrman, and Tami Harris,
along with
Justin Ortiz,
Kathy McGrath, Laurie Engler,
and all my friends from TM.

And thank you to my folks, forever with me in spirit.